I0771788

ARPress
45 Dan Road Suite 5
Canton MA 02021
Hotline: 1(888) 821-0229
Fax: 1(508) 545-7580

Ordering Information:
Quantity sales. Special discounts are available on quantity purchases by corporations, associations, and others.For details, contact the publisher at the address above.

Printed in the United States of America.

ISBN-13:	Paperback	979-8-89389-159-1
	Hardback	979-8-89676-119-8
	eBook	979-8-89389-158-4

Library of Congress Control Number:

EMP Causality

Michael Kravitz

Dedication

To Ricky and Laurie Waters, whom I have both known for a long time. Also, to my brother Barry Kravitz, Jane Moshy, and Nick—all of whom encouraged me to write this novel."

Introduction

The snow and freezing rain was coming down at a pretty good clip. I was on a plane at the Moscow international airport. Out on the tarmac, there was a single operator with a handheld hose. It took him several minutes to defrost the one wing. The knot is my stomach began to churn. Is this surreal or what? The freezing rain seemed to be falling as fast as he was defrosting it. Next, he moved his cart to the other wing. At this point I could have used a stiff drink. You know, my last rights. Instead of "Sully landing in the Hudson," I imagined Michael ending his journey in a fiery crash while departing from Russia.

Sitting next to me was a Swedish businessman. I asked him if this is normal.

He said, "Once the jet is in the air, the ice will dissipate. Things could be worse; we could be flying an aeroflot airplane. Kidding."

I looked at him. "Do you like playing Russian roulette?" He smiled. We talked at length. It was his impression that many Americans like to know what a person does for a living. They judge people by their wealth. He prefers to know the person, the places they travel, their hobbies, languages, education, type of family, etc.

I traveled to Russia in the winter. Being saddened after being let down by people I trusted, and deeply in debt, I needed to get away for a new prospective. Yes, a nice Caribbean trip, drinking a pina colada would be relaxing. The old saying "Misery likes its own company."

Traveling alone, I saw a lot. Taking a train ride from Saint Petersburg to Moscow, I met an old lady who spoke broken English. I hired her to be my translator.

For over ten days, I met a lot of normal Russian people. Their dress code was usually gray and a little depressing. At train stops, I saw military veterans looking for handouts, many of them with missing limbs due to the Afghan war.

The government had very little funds to take care of them the right way.

I have also traveled throughout Europe, Scandinavia, and Africa— never as a tourist but alone or with friends. Traveling as a tourist can be educational and safe. Still, you lose the real flavor of the people and their culture.

My third book, *An EMP Casualty*, is a sequel to my other two books,

Boston Darkens and *Boston Flickers*. I have met a lot of ordinary people both here and abroad. Using characteristics from these people, I decided to throw them in a large bin. Slowly, like a Christmas grab bag, I found a place for each different character.

Using a cookie-cutter approach, I cut a little section in a Boston metro west town. Actually, it could be any town in the USA. The story involves a major catastrophe: an EMP blast that sets our way of life back to the 1800s. With a few twists, I could have chosen an upper class, lower class, or maybe just people without any kind of class (we all know them). I chose mostly the lower-middle class, the forgotten Americans.

Do we really know our neighbors? Ever wonder who are these people who live near you? Do they have the same problems and desires as you? Hmmm, enquiring minds want to know. I feel you will enjoy the mixture of people that come together in this neighborhood Collaborative. Their sole purpose is survival.

The union man, who feels the government is the be all and end all for the masses. The divorcee, with her daughter. After a bad marriage, she needs a better environment for her daughter. The construction man with his two strapping sons, salt of the earth. They do a hard day's work and have a few beers at night. A "drunk" who lives like a hermit in a broken-down house. Yet no one knows why he drinks so much. The neighbors assume he is destitute. Their assumptions are wrong. A neurotic man. He eats like a bird and takes care of a challenged man. The challenged man. We all see them in our lives, but we don't understand them. In this book, I have taken this challenge man, and showed you the reader how he might react to an EMP blast. I have also taken a mother and daughter, who have lived in the projects. They are ordinary Americans, of African descent, who are trying to better themselves. They are close friends with main characters in the books, the Randal family.

As in the first two books, the Randal family are transplants from Nebraska, living the classic dream. Ben works as a microbiologist and his wife is a schoolteacher. Their son is a talented auto mechanic. The love of his life is his classic red Buick. Without a new electronic ignition system, it is one of only a few running vehicles.

Trouble in paradise. Their daughter, Jessica, becomes involved with an older and refined man. The EMP blast has given this insecure teenager a feeling of being cheated. She wants to live the life of an independent woman. Without rhyme or reason, she sees an illusion of happiness and fulfillment with this man. The Randal family has been torn apart. Ben has enough on his plate. Ben founded the collaborative. It needs him for their survival.

Besides the needs of the insecure teenager girl, there are also the needs of the challenged man. the needs of Camille, a close friend to the Randal's. She is of African descent, a collaborative member whose sister lost her only son due to violence. There are road trips and encounters with thugs and biker gangs. The journey they take will not only be filled with emotion and drama, it will also captivate you to the end.

I have used a little dry humor and a few times I have gone off the reservation. I do this to give you the reader a little break. Like in a Greek tragedy, humor is needed to keep us sane. Without further ado, let the story continue.

Another EMP Casualty:
An Uneasy Homecoming

Jessica unleashed her backpack. The weight of it seemed to grow as she put the thing down to catch her breath. She and Joshua had been on a long roller coaster ride of emotions. All this was more of a wearing exercise than she was accustomed to. Gym class used to be just an hour of strenuous effort followed by a refreshing shower. But, since the EMP blast, everything slowed down to a strenuous standstill without the shower. Looking for food and surviving the various gangs were now the priority exercises. There was a lot weighing on Jessica's mind. She missed her parents, school friends, and simple things that only electricity can provide. Without the distraction of light, it was difficult to hide from the void that went deep inside her soul.

"Can I help you?" interrupted a tall and burly border guard. His fatigue uniform was cleaned and pressed. He hadn't shaved in several days. With a rifle smartly strung over his shoulder, he had the look of a seasoned soldier. When he approached, the effect was a little intimidating.

"We are on a journey home, and we just arrived this morning from Tent City," quipped Joshua as he watched Jessica undo her long hair. Putting his bag down, he had to be prepared both emotionally and physically for the next leg of his journey.

The border guard held a clipboard in his hands. It outlined the bounds of the next portion of their journey. The small area that they were about to leave was like a green zone. It was a secured area extending from Boston's government center (near the waterfront) to several miles outward. Here, within this "green zone," one could get food, water, and current information.

The outer wall was a demarcation of civility. Beyond the walls lay danger.

It was the Wild West. Roving gangs, fires, and a littered landscape sent a strong signal, a feeling of dread for all who entered. The EMP strike caught everyone off guard. A huge reset button had taken a large part of the country into darkness. The grid no longer functioned. The government was unprepared to handle a disaster of this magnitude.

Waiting for relief, minutes became hours. Hours became days. Soon, the good and bad of human nature bubbled up. A new reality had surfaced.

Government became a skeleton of its original self. The logistics of feeding, providing medical services and security support for millions without a robust information update mechanism, was unrealistic. The nanny state had become unglued. You might say the circuits of government shorted out into a huge pile of poo.

Ah Joshua, dear Joshua. He was a young and strapping man. In his early twenties, he had the gift of gab, the personality, and the looks to match. His self-confidence was false to the extent that it had not yet been tempered down by the test of fire. Speaking several languages led to an unfair advantage over other competing salespeople. Like his father, he was a people person. Selling came natural to him. Seeing the success of his father tainted him. College bored him.

Joshua wanted to dive into deeper waters. That is what he yearned for. Paying close attention to his attire, he became a skilled hunter in pursuit of its prey. His customers were more enamored by him than his product.

Jessica was more than he bargained for. Who was hunting whom? Joshua was her every dream in life. Romance, a provider, adventure, her sexual fantasies.

Like a moth to a flame, she was drawn into his web of influence. The EMP strike made a wasteland, not only to a functioning society but to her hopes and dreams. Being an insecure teenager, Jessica knew she had to have Joshua. Her logic gave way to her impulses and desires.

In her mind, the EMP strike was robbing all that was promised her. Like a thief in the middle of the night, she felt betrayed. The stage was set for the play to begin.

Joshua looked at the guard, trying to focus on his next and final leg of the journey home. It was time to man up. Easier said than done. Jessica's father was enraged that Joshua plucked his beautiful daughter from her nest. Before the rose could bloom, Joshua took the rose from the bouquet. She was the seed he had planted, nourished, and coddled since she entered this world. His emotions clouded all rational parental thought.

Crossing the barrier would be a dangerous journey into a lawless land full of gangs and desperate survivors. Both Joshua and Jessica had traveled through these lands to come to this green zone. Now Joshua is gathering his wits and composure to traverse it again. He carefully checked his gun, making sure it was loaded. Ah, to walk through this hell, he thought, only to enter another hell. Once he got to their homes, he must face Jessica's father (Ben Randal). On his last meeting with Ben, he was warned to stay away from his daughter, Jessica. If that was not bad enough, he still has to face his own father.

"Sir! Sir!" shouted the burly guard as he looked at Joshua. "I need to record your names before you can pass through the barrier."

"W-what did you say?" Joshua exclaimed. He was really deep in his thoughts while trying to muster his courage for the journey ahead.

"I have orders to record the names and time for all that pass through these barriers," the guard continued in a slow and commanding voice.

"Oh! I am Joshua and this is Jessica Randal. We just came from Tent City and we are now returning home. Jessica needed some medical attention," Joshua replied with nervous hesitation. At this point, he pinched himself hard. Inside, his nerves now were exploding. How much stress can one man endure? What if the guard asks their ages. Maybe Jessica's dad got the word out. Too many what-ifs,

The guard started flipping through his clipboard. It must have held at least twenty pages. Jessica twirled her hair. Joshua knew that she too was nervous. After a few tense seconds, a smile appeared on the guard's face.

"I have it. Joshua and Jessica Randal. Do you know Officer Ryan?" the guard asked in a deliberate voice.

"Of course we do," Jessica said to bolster their position. "He is in our collaborative and a friend to my dad." Jessica sensed Joshua needed a little help to hold off a full-scale inquiry.

"I have orders to call Officer Ryan and give you a safe escort. He is within range of our CB communications. It is dangerous, especially for a young woman like you. Your dad will be happy to know you are all right," the guard said with a smile.

F——! thought Joshua. *A police escort.* He pinched himself harder. That's good! Going through the "Bad Lands" will be easier. But now there is no way for Joshua to escape his personal "Stalag 13." And that's bad! Jessica's dad had already given Joshua due notice about his daughter. *Screw it,* Joshua thought. It might be better to get it over with sooner than later.

"Why don't you two just sit over there?" the guard said as he pointed to a makeshift bench. "I'll make the call and you are welcome to some sandwiches and real brewed coffee."

"Please don't worry Joshua," Jessica said as she grabbed his hand. "My dad needs to learn a lesson. I love him very much, but in a few months I will be of legal age. It is in his court. He must sense he will lose me forever with his stubborn attitude. I need to be a woman now and face up to him."

As they sat on the bench, Jessica saw the tension in Joshua's forehead. She grabbed Joshua's hand and held it with her two feminine hands.

"Joshua, this is my doing, not yours. I came onto you. This EMP strike has changed all our lives. You have bought me a joy that I thought I would never experience. I thought I was cheated, and you came into my life. I have no regrets.

You have protected me and now I will stand up for you. I will confront both my father and yours. They will listen," she said with a gathering confidence.

At this point, Joshua put his arms around Jessica's shoulder to coddle her.

"Funny!" Jessica commented with a smile.

"What's funny, Jessica?" he asked in bewilderment.

"Your mother! I really hit it off with your mother. She really liked me,"

Jessica commented as her smile grew even bigger.

"That is strange," Joshua replied as he shrugged his shoulders. "She doesn't get along with anyone, especially my father. She definitely has a warm spot for you."

"Good news!" shouted out the burly guard. "I got a hold of Officer Ryan. He should be here in three to four hours."

"Yay! Great news," Joshua said in a slightly sarcastic tone. At this point, Jessica just put her hands on Joshua's thigh. It was a gesture of solidarity that she was with him all the way. It was time to face the music.

As they sat there, one could see many others trying to enter this little green zone. It was a safe area to roam about. There was food, water, and medical supplies. One could pursue these supplies without the danger of encountering the various gangs. Most of the gang members are afraid to enter this zone. The border guards have the option to search and confiscate any and all arms. Martial law is in effect.

"Joshua, I need to pee," Jessica said in a soft voice as she got up and walked toward the porta potty.

"Be care—!" Joshua exclaimed as he caught himself. With the burly guard and his rifle nearby, they were in an extremely safe place.

Most who came into the area were on foot with an occasional few on bicycle. Coming in was easy enough; it was leaving that presented a danger. Many of the elderly or frail were advised to wait for a state trooper or army personnel to escort them home.

As Jessica closed the door to the toilet, Joshua walked over to a table that had coffee. They had skim milk and a bowl of sugar. *Gads!* Joshua thought. *Not your Starbuck's drive through.* Both Joshua and his dad were used to the finer things in life. His dad has taught Joshua well. "When you are a salesman, there are certain rules to follow to be successful. Dress well and treat your clients to the better upgrades."

Like his dad, Joshua always treated people with some class. Taking notes on their conversations, he would recall names and habits for each client. This way, they all thought they got special attention from him. Joshua's dad was born in Egypt. Being Jewish, he was always being bullied. It was no way to live. So Joshua's dad became a survivalist by nature. He learned many languages, a gift for sizing up whether a person was going to be a threat. Eventually, his dad immigrated to Israel, and then to the United States. In the mold of his dad, Joshua also became very streetwise.

Now Joshua had a different kind of streetwise challenge. He had to confront both his dad and Jessica's dad. With his stomach tied up in knots, he searched for courage. Two very strong men, physically and emotionally; he knew they both were disappointed in him. In Joshua's mind, the best thing to do is to let them both vent. Just be a man and let the chips fall where they may.

Ah! The aroma of freshly brewed coffee pulled him out of the dread simmering in his brain. Joshua was never a smoker, but caffeine kept him alert and helped pass the time when waiting for clients. It was a small crutch. Not much flavor; one cup will do for him. It was just a nervous habit; something to sip on that's a little tastier than water. His self-imposed one-cup limit kept him from having to excuse himself while speaking with a client.

"I feel better!" Jessica exclaimed as she returned. "When I am a little nervous, I pee a lot." She sat down next to Joshua and put her warm feminine hand on Joshua's thigh.

They sat there for a couple of hours, occasionally distracted by the appearance of a state trooper or army vehicle. It was a little nerve-racking. In Jessica's mind, she felt naked while waiting for the judge to scold her. Both Joshua and Jessica were ready for this to be over with.

Finally, as another state trooper approached, the driver looked familiar. As the vehicle drove closer, both Jessica and Joshua recognized him as Officer Ryan. Jessica squeezed Joshua's thigh a little tighter. For Joshua this was fine, but he was also a little nervous. Officer Ryan pulled up to the burly guard. The guard raised his clipboard in a gesture of greeting. They exchanged pleasantries before the guard pointed to where Jessica and Joshua were sitting.

Joshua smiled. It was like being in a courtroom. The prosecuting attorney asks the defendant, "Can you point out the guilty party?" The defendant would point directly at them. "There! Over there, your honor!"

Damn, thought Joshua. This would be the first leg of his inquisition. He watched as Officer Ryan thanked the burly guard. He started his jeep as the guard lifted the makeshift gate. Officer Ryan drove to a parking spot within fifty feet of Joshua and Jessica. As he exited his vehicle, he leaned in and grabbed his hat. With all the chaos, Officer Ryan was still spit and polish, a duck out of water. While most people were just trying to survive, he is still trying to impress the masses.

"How are you doing, Jessica? A lot of people are going to be happy to see you," Officer Ryan commented when he was within ten feet of them.

"We are both doing okay, considering what we have been through," Jessica lamented. She was really angry that Officer Ryan did not include Joshua in his salutations. The look on her face showed a slight disgust at his demeanor.

"I see," Officer Ryan said as he now felt a little uncomfortable with his failed approach. He is a trained professional. His mind raced very quickly. He knew that if he spooked or just pissed off Jessica and Joshua, they would run again.

If that happened, he would be blamed for his conduct.

"Nice to see you, Joshua," Officer Ryan commented with a fake smile.

"We are both doing fine," Joshua said as he lifted his eyes to meet Officer Ryan.

Ah, thought Officer Ryan. *They both used the word* we. *We, as in a couple—as one.* The mood and tone were definitely set. Officer Ryan from this point on did not want to use any offensive or antagonizing language. Even though he got off on the wrong foot, he knew better than to apologize. That would definitely send a sign of weakness. He still had to control the situation.

"How long have the two of you been here?" Officer Ryan asked as to change the tenor of their interaction.

"Over three hours," Jessica said in a more receptive tone.

Joshua did not want to speak. As a successful salesman, he can usually size up people pretty accurately. But he was on the fence on whether to be nervous or angry at Officer Ryan. He knew enough just to bite his tongue. Joshua did not want to burn any more bridges. There has been enough damage. He did not want to cause any more grief between Jessica and her family and within his own family. He needed to find his way now. Jessica was not a conquest for him. She was a wounded bird that needed to be protected.

As Officer Ryan was trying to make small talk, Joshua was in a daze. This whole episode had knocked down his ego, from Mt. Everest to Death Valley. Instead of acting on instinct, he found himself thinking things through. Perhaps for the first time in his life, he was unsure of himself. There were a lot of people who were definitely going to be affected by his actions. He stared at Jessica, not wanting to hear the conversation. It would disturb the zone he was in. He thought, *How could I make lemonade out of lemons? Her age is just shy of legal.* Damn, if the EMP strike did not happen, he could be brought up on charges. God knows he did not want or imagine this outcome.

Officer Ryan spoke up breaking into Joshua's zone. "I'll be back in less than an hour; I have to escort a young boy to his mom's house. His mother has a large frame and is a diabetic. The boy is bringing back food and medicines. I need to see him to their apartment. God, I even had to give the boy a gun and show him how to use it. Otherwise, the gangs would confiscate everything. A young boy doing a man's deed," Officer Ryan said in a slow, deliberate pace.

Sensing that he had allowed his frustration overflow into his professionalism, Officer Ryan did a quick pivot. "Cheer up, both of you. It will all work out," he said, trying to instill some confidence in both of them.

As Officer Ryan left, the burly guard came over with some food: baked potatoes, string beans, and a little meatloaf. Napoleon learned, you can't keep the morale of your troops up on an empty stomach. Fortunately, the remaining skeleton government understood that it was important to keep the guards fed.

"We will get through this," Jessica said to Joshua as she clasped his hands.

Damn! thought Joshua, who's the grown-up now? His feelings were in a confused state. From a protector to maybe a soul mate. No. Maybe. What of his family? What of her family? *This is going way too fast.* He felt like the police and their hound dogs were chasing him. He could see the boundary line where he would be safe—the time when Jessica would be of legal age. That is what Jessica wants and now he is starting to feel the same way. *Ah, yoga. Take deep breaths and inhale slowly, breathe out slowly, clear my mind, take control.*

As Officer Ryan left in his jeep, he indicated he would be right back. It was just a short dive to the government center. Joshua and Jessica sat there without looking at each other. After several minutes, Joshua excused himself to go to the porta potty. The coffee did not seem to agree with him. Jessica just nodded as Joshua was about to enter the portable facility.

Jessica then noticed a young man approach the burly guard. He seemed rather young and frail. Wearing wrinkled tan pants, he almost looked defenseless. With several bags of food and medicine, the guard pointed him toward where Jessica was sitting. His manner seemed a little downtrodden as he slowly came over toward her.

Joshua was washing his hands as he noticed the young man walk over and say hi to Jessica. He put his bags down and just sat on the ground. Joshua now was a little distracted from his own miseries. He came up to the young man and introduced himself. It turns out he was also waiting for Officer Ryan. It seems last time he procured supplies, he was attacked by a gang of thugs. It was a harrowing experience. Not only did he lose all his supplies; for the first time he felt his life was in danger. When he came back the second time, the burly guard told him what day and time to come. It was better for him to have an escort. His mother was disabled and really needed her heart medicine.

As they were siting, Joshua half-smiled. *The three amigos. What a hapless crew. Each with their own sad story.* Joshua mumbled as he sat down, "You can't make this stuff up."

"Make what stuff up?" Jessica asked in an insecure but sarcastic tone.

"What?" Joshua stated. "Oh, nothing to do with you honey," he said quickly, to diffuse any tensions. "Here we are, with what seems to be insurmountable problems, and now we meet others who are a lot worse off than us," Joshua said with a definitive voice.

Inside Joshua's mind, he thought, *Boy, that was close.* Being a seasoned salesman, he had learned to think quickly on his feet. Jessica just put her hands back on Joshua's thigh. His words seemed to hit the right cord with her.

All three sat there for a good forty minutes. As the minutes ticked by, each of them wanted to get going. The old army saying "Hurry up and Wait" sure was accurate here. After they get to their destination, *What's next?* Joshua thought. Would the young man just sit in a confined apartment with his mom, fearing to go out when his mom really needed him to go?

What of Joshua and Jessica? First, they need to face their terrible tribunal.

After facing the two daunting dads, what's next? Actually, both Joshua and Jessica's mind were on the same wavelength. Time was short. Officer Ryan was due any moment. Who would speak first? It is bad enough not to have cell phones; but to have two dads, who were going to put up barrier walls? Man, how many obstacles could they overcome?

In the distance, they both heard and saw Officer Ryan's jeep. Joshua felt nervous. He wanted to speak, yet he feared this tug of war inside him. Was it love or lust? But why was he at peace when Jessica was near him? What was best for Jessica? He did not want to hurt her or her family anymore.

"Jessica, I-I . . ." Joshua stuttered.

"Listen, Joshua, I love you very much, but I need for you to be a man," she continued intently. "If you love me, we need a plan. If not, cut me free."

Damn, thought Joshua, *Is Jessica growing up fast or what?* She said the right words. His path was clear. It was like a plane landing at night. Someone just turned on the runway lights. Now it was time to touch down.

"Jessica, I do wan—love you," Joshua stated as he caught himself. Words matter. He did not want Jessica to feel as though he lusted her.

He knew she was still in a fragile state of mind. "No matter what, Jessica, they will let you go to William's house. There is a maple tree a hundred feet north of the house. We can put letters under the rock near that tree. No one will know. I will bike over there in one week. By then, we will both know our status."

Ben has made it clear that Joshua was not welcome inside the boundaries of his collaborative. William's house is on the outer part of the collaborative, The rock is just hundred feet past his house. Joshua will be with his dad's collaborative.it is a half hour drive by car or a two hour bike ride. The rock is as close as he dares to come under Ben's constant watchful eye.

Jessica smiled. A plan with hope. It gave her a lifeline, a line of hope for her mounting insecurities. Perhaps her womanhood was just a fake facade.

Inside she was a tangled web of nerves. Now Jessica feels there is direction in her life. She started to relax and composed herself while the three of them waited for Officer Ryan. It wasn't long. Afternoon was bearing down. It was better to go through the badlands before dusk.

As Officer Ryan pulled his jeep near the three of them, the burly guard approached with his clipboard. He made everyone sign their names. With military precision, he looked at his watch.

"All aboard," Officer Ryan stated with assurance. "Let's blow this pop stand," he bellowed as he tried to ease the tensions.

"You can ride shotgun," Joshua stated to the young man. He wanted to be with Jessica in the back seat. Who knows when he will be allowed to be with her again?

As the young man entered the front seat, Officer Ryan just shook his head.

Deep inside, he knew this was a bad idea. *Well,* thought Officer Ryan,

I will give them their "last rights," so to speak. Before he reaches the Randal residence, he will ask them to switch seats. He knows Joshua will understand.

As the guard lifted the gate, it was like turning off the lights.

They now entered hostile territory. The young man was nervous. He already had emotional scars from his last encounter. He knew that his mother's life depended on him. As they drove slowly, Officer Ryan put his shotgun next to him, his gun on his lap. He had driven this route several times. By now, most of the thugs understood, this route has been marked. Sometimes following protocol doesn't always work.

Officer Ryan considers martial law to have a different venue. There is no press core, nightly news, or others judging his every action.

The brutal fact is both government, police, and military are running with extreme skeleton crews. Most of the gangs and thugs also know this. It is a dangerous game of cat and mouse, each trying to maintain their own safety.

As they were driving, the scenery took a drastic nosedive. There were very few windows on lower levels that were not broken. Debris, smoke, and a fowl stench seem to be everywhere. Officer Ryan turned to the young man. He could tell that this young man really needed a bath. His blue jeans were dirty and his undershirt ripped. It was probably from his last altercation. The most startling observation was sadness. It was like the man was broken. He knew his mother's life was now totally dependent on him. What is really sad is that Joshua and Jessica were in the back seat. They did not interact with Officer Ryan or the young man. If only they knew that Joshua and Jessica came back from Tent City. They saw the repairs to the power lines. It would surely give the young man a little hope in his miserable situation despite the many tragedies during this trying time.

In less than fifteen minutes, the jeep neared where the young man lives. The thugs started to show themselves. The sound of the jeep means many things to different people. As he stopped the jeep, Officer Ryan let the young man get out with his bags. His trained eye quickly homed in on the thugs, surveying their every mood. With his shotgun in his right hand, he turned slowly as he escorted the young man to the door. *Damn,* he thought, *this young man and his mom were easy targets.* He knew they would not last the night.

"Stay right here." Don't go inside. I will be right back. Officer Ryan went back to the jeep. He took out a 9mm gun that he confiscated from a previous firefight. He slowly looked out of the corner of his right eye. He knew the thugs were watching him. As he approached the young man, he came between him and the thugs. He made sure they were seeing everything. "Here, take this. Be careful, it is loaded," Officer Ryan said slowly. "Always take a deep breath and exhale slowly if you use it. Use both hands." But the young man hesitated. Guns always frightened him. As he looked into Officer Ryan's eyes, he looked shocked and a tear ran down his cheek.

"Listen, son, just look at me. They are watching you now. Don't look. They can see me giving you a gun, just take it. I really think they will leave you alone. Just trust yourself and the Almighty. Do this for your mom. You cannot show fear to your mom. She needs you to be strong. If I were a betting man, I'd say that you will never have to use this. Do you understand what I am saying?"

The young man nodded his head. He looked down at the gun and then up to Officer Ryan's face. The veteran officer just nodded his head, signaling time to go. He knew the young man was on edge. To show fear to these thugs is akin to drawing blood in the presence of a hungry shark. The young man took the 9 mm, put it in his bag, and turned around to enter the large apartment complex. The thugs lost sight of him. They did not know which apartment the young man lived.

Officer Ryan turned around and walked toward the jeep cradling his shotgun across his arms. He stared at the thugs. They knew Officer Ryan was not afraid of them. He started his jeep and drove slowly for a good two hundred feet before stopping. With the windows lowered, Officer Ryan pointed his shotgun in the general direction of the thugs. It was a deadly cat-and-mouse game. Thugs are generally selfish cowards. As Officer Ryan drove ahead, the thugs retreated into their shadowy environment. They probably left to find easier prey. So today was a standoff; no mistakes were allowed.

It was now off to the Randal residence. Like a last meal request, Officer Ryan allowed the two to sit in the back seat. Just a couple more miles of the danger zone. Most of the gangs stay in the inner city. In the suburbs, the odds drop for these lowlifes and they know it. The terrain is now familiar. They were within five miles of the Randal's' residence. Doing the prudent thing, Officer Ryan pulled his jeep over.

"I think it is better if Jessica sat in the front seat." As Officer Ryan adjusted his rearview mirror, they all knew this moment had arrived. No need for any more words. Reality has reared its ugly head. With a little sigh, Jessica just slid over and opened the back door. Joshua just bowed his head. It was an extremely painful moment.

In Venice, there is a bridge called the Bridge of Sigh; it was the last bridge that the convicted walk over before their incarceration. For both Joshua and Jessica, this was an uncharted moment, their personal Bridge of Sigh. Would there be another bridge, one going in a different direction? Both hoped so, but best-laid plans could always go awry.

As soon as Jessica sat down, the raindrops hit the front windshield. What an omen! To Joshua, even the kitchen sink was thrown at him. *Remember only rank and serial number,* he thought as he smiled, to ease the tension. The real odd thing is that no one talks of their experience in Tent City. What was it like?

Was there any news from the government? Was there any hope of the grid being up and running? Officer Ryan did not seem interested in the big picture. Instead, he was all consumed in the moment—the moment of acting both as a state trooper and the ambassador of his collaborative.

As each moment went by, the tension increased. Both Jessica and Joshua were doubting their own wisdom. It would have been easier just to keep running. With the EMP blast, no charges would have been filed. They could have written a letter and sent it on the next bus to the state police. They could have started a new life, perhaps in Canada. Then reality sets in; there would always be a void, an emptiness of friends and family never to be seen again. Even for Joshua, how could he ever face his father or mother again? How does that saying go? *Oh yeah,*

"No pain, no gain!" Trouble is, this is way too much pain.

With his stoic demeanor, Officer Ryan drove the jeep into the Randal residence. Ben was outside by the fire pit. Many of the neighbors were just sitting on makeshift chairs. Hearing the sound of the engine, Alice ran out of the house. Her hair was stringy and unkempt. Her pants and sweatshirt seemed to be too large for her. It looked like Alice had not been eating much. She had lost some serious weight. Her face has become gaunt and shown signs of real stress. Alice had not coped with this misadventure very well. Ben had a shot glass of whiskey. Obviously, the drunk has given him some liquid comfort. It is really unbecoming of Ben. The test of a man (or woman's) character never had a rule for the possible loss of one's child.

Alice's immediate reaction was to clasp her mouth with both hands. As Jessica slowly stepped out of the jeep, Ben put the shot glass down. Perhaps for the first time in his adult life, he was unsure how to act. Alice knew how immediately. Her motherly instincts went into high gear. She cried uncontrollably and ran for her daughter. As she reached Jessica, she flung both arms around her and kept crying.

It was a touching moment.

"I am all right, Ma! I am all right! I miss you, Ma," Jessica said in a stern but soft voice.

"Everything will be all right, everything will be fine, my precious baby," Alice responded, as she could no longer control her words or actions.

They were both at the center stage. Everyone took a back seat. Ben just observed. He glanced at the back seat of the jeep. Seeing Joshua, Ben's face and hands tightened. Joshua noticed the threatening stare; he immediately bowed his head.

"Let's go get you something to eat," Alice said as she put her arms around Jessica and led her toward the house.

"This calls for a drink. Let's celebrate," said the neighborhood drunk, except no one responded. "Damn, it's like telling a joke at a funeral home."

He didn't get why everyone wasn't happy.

"Welcome home, Jessica," Ben said in an unassured voice.

"Thanks, dad," Jessica retorted without even looking at her dad.

Alice just stopped. I guess her instincts were right on. She turned and looked at Officer Ryan.

"Thank you very much for everything you did for us. Bless you," Alice commented as she wiped away her tears. She then gave him a hand gesture; that he should really get going. She was now the commander and chief. The moment was extremely fragile. There were many open wounds. Alice was not going to allow Joshua and Ben to try to resolve anything at this time.

You could see a crack in Officer Ryan's professional conduct. *Could it be?*

Nah! Why, yes! There it was, an actual tear from his eye. *He is human after all.* He turned around and wiped it with the knuckle of his second digit finger. He then turned again and gave a half-hearted salute with two fingers. Both Alice and Officer Ryan knew that he had to get Joshua out of there.

As Officer Ryan climbed back into the driver's seat, the occasional drop was now turning into a more steady rain. Ben wanted to take another sip, but couldn't.

Camille's Quest

It was a painful night for most of the collaborative. Only Alice seemed joyful for her daughter's arrival. Her precious daughter was safe and under their roof. Alice bought in a plate of food and a drink for Jessica. They both had lost some serious weight over the ordeal. Stress takes on many different coping mechanisms. Alice and Jessica, for the most part, eliminated many meals. Ben, not an alcoholic, had more drinks than normal. Alice just wanted her daughter back at all cost. Ben was carrying many burdens. He really loved Jessica but felt betrayed. He had a wife and the collaborative that relied on his leadership. But he had no mentor or therapist to turn to. For his whole marriage, he felt like the provider, role model, and protector of his domain. He knew enough to let Alice keep this fragile reunion together. Funny, no family dog, just the neighborhood drunk to commiserate with.

Using her female instincts, Alice just tried to make small talk. Her mind was running feverishly. She had many questions. What was her real relationship with Joshua? What happened on her two journeys? Was she in the midst of some physical or emotional damage? Perhaps as a mother, Alice is not the right person to pry into these sensitive areas. Perhaps her close friend Vivian could reach her. Alice understood well that her sole mission was to make sure that Jessica felt at home and that she knew that she was missed and loved. It was a daunting task. Instinctively, Alice knew that the solution must include Alice's father, her husband Ben.

Somehow, Alice needed to hear Jessica's side of the story to begin to help her daughter. Timing is everything. Jessica was worn down physically and emotionally. Her face, hair, even her mannerisms suggest a beaten-down person. Very seldom did Jessica lift her head to look at her mom. Alice was doing everything herself not to break down. She knew she had to be strong. She had to be the monolith that kept the family unit together.

As Alice sat in silence watching her daughter eat, her emotions started to turn to anger. *Damn Ben!* she thought. *All this should have been prevented.* His damn alpha-male ego. If he could only see how vulnerable his daughter looked.

Seeking a key, she realized that any parent should know how one offspring is in tune with their siblings. Keeping her cool, she called to Randy who was also outside. He too was overjoyed to see his sister come home safely. Randy is a very sensitive and caring person, caught in the middle of this fray. Being handy as a mechanic, he really had more in common with his dad. But he loved his sister, even though they were five years apart. Perhaps he could bridge the distance between Jessica and her father.

"Hello, Jessica, glad to see you," Randy commented as he entered the house. "Good to see you, Randy," Jessica said as she raised her face.

Immediately, Randy saw how much weight Jessica lost. He knew enough not to say anything.

"I'm really happy to see you, sis," Randy commented as he put his hand on her shoulder. Inside he really wanted to hug her. Even though they were not close, Randy realized his sister was becoming a woman. He knows that the time had arrived for them to have a different relationship. This adventure that his sister went on gave Randy a wake-up call. Randy did not take sides with his father against his sister. In all fairness, Ben never asked nor expected him to take sides. I guess it goes with his alpha-male ego.

"Randy, can you fetch and heat up some water so your sister can wash herself?" Alice asked in a polite manner.

"Sure Mom!" Randy replied as he exited the door.

"Ma, you don't have—" Jessica commented as Alice interrupted.

"I know, honey! I am just so glad to see you! We all are glad to see you!" Alice replied with a little crackling in her voice.

Jessica looked up and made real eye contact with her mother. She saw a tear and how distraught her mother was.

Normally, she wanted to just hug her mom. It was the cold war, what she had with her dad. Her dad was still the husband of her mother. She knew her place.

This adventure has turned her into a woman. To be with Joshua seemed so natural and nourishing. It is the end game. The EMP strike with all its bad affects had a silver lining. It fast forwarded Jessica into womanhood. She would not interfere in the relationship of her mother and father. Truth is, her appetite to leave the nest was whetted.

Sometimes the good lord has a way of lifting your burdens. She knew detente had to come from her dad. Ben did not allow anyone to try and reason with him. It is weird, though, that the only one who affected Ben was the neighborhood drunk. I guess he doesn't give a crap. The drunk just told Ben it's good to see your daughter back. That did affect Ben; the drunk had nothing left.

When he lost his wife, he lost his will to go on. Ben felt his innocent wisdom piercing him. No one else seemed to reach his. His Christian dream was shattered by that playboy Joshua. The drunk actually made Ben get off his horse and take reality in.

Now what? Good question! No real easy answers. Before a battle gets underway, a good officer sends a probing party to assess his opponent. Ben had the good sense to stay out in the rain. He saw his son Randy fetching water for his daughter. *Ah crap,* he thought, *is this going to be a three on one?* He was too tired to build himself a dog house to sleep in for the night. Ah, but if he did, maybe his family would have pity on him. Nah! Just his opening intake of the prevailing moment. With the drunk leaving and the rain coming down harder, perhaps all of this is his own doing.

Silence is truly golden. The rain was a real omen. Not just for Jessica, Alice, the collaborative, but also for Ben. Randy walked into the house with the warm water. Ben decided to stay outside for another hour. Usually Alice would yell for Ben to come inside, but tonight is different. The fire was still burning, but the cold rain and his emotions put a damper on the moment. Ben did come in after an hour. By then everyone was in bed. Ben just took off his wet clothes and put on some dry ones on. He knew enough not to talk to Alice. The air was gloomy for everyone. Before he slept, Ben grabbed the Bible to hold onto. Yes, there was tension in the Randal residence, but the drunk is right. His whole family was safe under one roof. Before he fell asleep, he gave himself a little smile. Still, it was a smile the Lord had blessed him with. Now in the morning, he will collect himself.

Surely this rain will stop.

It was a restless night. Ben felt his grip on the family slipping away. He needed to take a step back. He slept on his side facing away from Alice. He did not want her, to smell what little alcohol he had on his breadth. Outside of a few bathroom runs, the night went uneventful. In the morning, Alice was up early. She was hopeful that her daughter would not escape again. As each one arose, Randy was getting his Buick ready. Today was his run to the armory. The collaborative was getting low on supplies. Randy also wanted to pay a visit to the lady down the street. Her husband was shot by a gang of thugs. It would be nice if she would go for a ride.

Alice, Randy, and the divorce woman next store started to organize a morning breakfast. Randy was getting pretty efficient on building the fire. Besides, Randy really enjoyed being around his neighbor's daughter. Seems like Mr. Henderson's son also enjoys her company. Without the social media and the internet around, one's choices became very limited. It was a strange morning. Ben is usually the first one up, yet there was no sign of him. With little else going on, many of the collaborative members started to show up. It was really eerie. As the members sat down around the fire, one could see smoke in most directions. It was a constant reminder that their collaborative was like an army outpost in hostile territory.

Late morning and the atmosphere seemed to be a mix bag. Everyone was glad that Jessica has returned, yet she had not come out of her bedroom. Even stranger was Ben. He is their rock, their leader. Still in bed by mid-morning, it seemed like two combatants who had yet to enter the arena. Finally, Jessica opened the front door. She had on her jeans, sneakers, and a loose sweater. Even with a baggy sweater, everyone noticed she definitely lost weight. With her drawn face, unkempt hair, she looked like a beaten puppy.

"Morning, honey! Isn't it a beautiful morning?" Alice commented with a glee in her voice.

"Good to see you, sis," Randy said, trying to support his mother.

"Happy to see you," the drunk said with a big smile.

Seems like the alcohol had brought out his uninhibited self. Perhaps it was the right medicine that was needed?

"Coffee and eggs this morning, dear?" Alice asked in an upbeat tone.

"That will be great, Ma," Jessica said as she looked like a condemned prisoner.

Many of the other members were afraid to speak. It seemed to be like one's first dance. What if I am shot down? Wouldn't I look like a fool?

After several minutes, Alice bought the eggs, coffee, and a piece of toast to Jessica. She thanked her mom and started to take small bites. As she sipped her coffee, Jessica noticed everyone looking at her. She immediately put her head down as if in shame. Alice, being very much in tune with her daughter's feelings, decided to talk to the divorcee. Soon even Randy started to talk to Mr. Henderson's son. It was an attempt to make Jessica feel less conspicuous.

The plan seemed to be working, except now Ben came out of the house. It was unlike him not to shave before making his entrance. Alice was still making conversations with her friend when she noticed Ben's appearance. Almost always, Alice would comment if she felt Ben, Randy, or Jessica's dress code was awry. Today was a mulligan however. Alice did not want to upset the delicate detente that existed. At this moment in Alice's life, her daughter's fragile state of mind was front and center.

"Morning everyone," Ben stated as he went to the fire pit for coffee.

Crack! Crack! Crack! was the greeting sound of a 9mm gun that went off in the distance. "Looks like there's a new fire to the south of us," Ben said as to redirect any more unsettling anguish.

"I think there is a new gang to the south of us," Mr. Henderson said. "I sure will be glad when Officer Ryan comes back. He should be able to give us an update."

"So, Jessica, I heard you went to Tent City," the drunk said as he walked over to Jessica. He had his shot glass and took a sip before sitting down near her.

"Yes! I thought . . . yes, I did," Jessica said as to catch herself. She wanted to mention to the drunk that it wasn't noon yet, and he is already drinking. Yet Jessica no longer felt worthy to make such comments.

"We all really missed you—I missed you," the drunk said with a tear in his eye. With the shot glass in his right hand, he wiped the tear away without spilling a drop. *Ah! Practice makes perfect.*

Jessica raised her bowed head as if the governor was giving her a reprieve.

"I missed you too. I missed all of you," Jessica said in a stoic tone.

Alice was trying very hard not to break down. This EMP strike has affected everyone's life. It was like a master test that all human life on the East Coast was going under.

"Thank God for the drunk," Alice mumbled quietly.

"It will all work out. Wounds take time to heal," the divorced woman said to Alice as she put her hand on Alice's shoulder.

Poor Ben. He was like the unwanted guest at a black-tie event. It was as if he came in his farmer's attire. He just didn't fit in. Like Humpty Dumpty, Alice knew she had to be neutral. Her motherly instincts were to rush over and hug her daughter. In the end, it would only escalate the tensions between Ben and Jessica. The thaw had to come naturally if at all. Jessica was very stoic; perhaps before she could be in tune with others, she had to be happy in her own skin. They say "Time is a great healer."

The wisdom of the drunk perhaps was more reaching than one knows. He had no more family for him to console with. He does give pause to others who dwell in their own misery. Dysfunctional as it was, the Randal family was still intact.

That is a feat, considering the devastation of the EMP attack. Jessica, as miserable as she was, did not show or feel any hostilities toward her family and friends.

When a wild horse is broken, it becomes passive. It is the state of mind that fills Jessica's head. Family is important, but to her, Joshua is her future. The EMP strike and her dad have her pinned down. Like a short-timer in the service, all she can do is await her window of opportunity for release.

For Ben it is a time of anxiety and tepid moves. He is fully aware of the minefield that he must traverse. Slowly, as the day unravels, more of the neighbors start filtering in. Ben's son, Randy, has brought the survival radio over. Maybe they can get info that will give the collaborative hope. Many of the podcasts are simple repeats or government BS statements. As they were all listening, the president of the US made a statement. "We are making progress in repairing the grid. Teams are moving from northeastern Maine, south, and from the Mississippi east."

"What a bunch of bullsh—" yelled the disgruntled union man.

"No, it's true," Jessica said in a soft voice. "Joshua and I saw a few teams in northern Maine. We saw them as we were headed to Tent City. It's a big job, but they were out there. Even at night the crews are working."

The drunk raised his glass and bowed his head. It was like a commercial. "Drink wisely my friends." The divorcee put her hands on her mouth. Most were in awe of a glimmer of hope, a light at the end of the tunnel.

"What we saw, it's going to take a long time before they reach us," Jessica commented as if she was the new spokesperson. Still, she did not have a smile on her face nor did she make eye contact with her dad.

As Alice and her son Randy hugged. Ben's reaction was very different. His head was filled with many conflicting emotions. To be sure, the thought of the grid coming here is what they all were praying about. In Jessica's choice of words: "Like an arrow through his heart." She used the words "Joshua and I" and "What we saw." Ben's hands trembled as he glanced at Jessica. Her head was bowed again. Perhaps it was in sadness, or maybe it was in defiance. Either way, it struck fear and pain into Ben. He has lost. He is losing his daughter, his dreams. His seeds were planted but were now uprooting, not to be nurtured and used in a traditional Christian format. As Ben looked again, he recognized something was different about her. Besides her sadness, something was amiss. His son Randy was predictable; the apple that did not fall far. Jessica was his pearl, the glow that surrounded his soul, the fulfillment of his life's journey.

As everyone was in a joyous moment, Ben's head seemed like a circuit board that was overloaded. His blank stare now turned into a reality check. What's different about his daughter? It hit him hard! He finally understood. Her face was really drawn. The clothes on her frail structure were loose-fitting. She really lost weight. Ben's stomach turned into knots. Was it her misadventure? Or was it him? Who can he turn to? What of his wife, Alice? Can he confide in her? In his mind, he knows, Alice feels, he has caused the family rift.

With a deep breath, it now becomes a time of reflection. Ah, when the dreaded Yankees lost four in a row to Red Sox. Especially when they were ahead by three games for the American League pennant. Everyone thought it was a lock. As the Sox won in that final moment, how awful it was for the Yankee players. That is now how Ben feels: his confidence broken, his bravado taken.

How misery likes company. What to do? Ben took his eyes off Jessica. His eyes acted like a mobile TV cameraman. Slowly, he glanced the whole collaborative area. Many had smiles, but William did not. William was sitting next to Fred, his challenged client, and his wife. Being very polite, William just sat quietly, chewing on a few cashew nuts. Fred, on the other hand, was always on the hunt for food. Seems like his stomach would never be satisfied. In this needed moment, Ben was drawn to join them. Being around happy people would just make his emotional wounds worse.

As he slowly walked toward William, he noticed that the drunk was taking his shot of whiskey then staggered over to join Jessica. *Damn,* thought Ben. The drunk now has a better relationship with his daughter than he does. *How low can he go? Better cowboy up.* Ben walked over to William, his wife, and Fred.

"You mind if I join you for while?" asked Ben.

"Delighted to have you. You must be happy?" William said in a monotone voice. William was tall, slender, and real neurotic. He was always clean but could care less if his clothes were matched or pressed. William's father was a famous chemist. Before his death, he left William with a house and some funds. His only sister estranged herself from William. A combination of William's behavior and a little bit of jealousy, she always thought their dad pampered and favored William. There was also a deep and dark secret in William's soul—a real evil act committed on him by a family member. Even the therapist could not penetrate William's innermost sanctum. Life always has its sadness. After all, none of us are perfect.

When a perfect storm or event unfolds, it alters the path that we travel. For William, it was a constant battle of *Why?* Why is human nature so cruel, and was this a test on William's soul? William's perfect event happened at a therapy session. He met his wife-to-be. She was on the same wavelength, a very sensitive person. William loved it. She was a good listener and was attuned to his needs. Another person at the session was a caretaker for Fred. There was a complication, though. Parkinson's was taking its deadly course on the caretaker. He had to find another home for Fred. The caretaker was trying to put off relinquishing Fred. He knew Fred inside and out; it would be hard to let go.

In his darkest and most vulnerable state, William met two souls who needed him. He felt a calling. It was a calling that told him, "The time is now." This is his purpose: two souls who would not betray or hurt him. William had a dark and empty spot in his heart. With a slow but deliberate courting ritual, William invited both his wife-to-be and Fred over to his house. When they left, William began to miss them. Soon the caretaker informed William that the state wanted to put Fred in a group home. The caretaker was physically unable to take care of him.

It was at that moment that his wife-to-be offered to help William if he took Fred in. It was a big step, but William went through with it. As the days rolled by, the three of them spent most of their time at William's house.

"Where is this going? What is it that you want, William?" his wife-to-be asked.

Instinctively, she let William be the man. "I do not want to be used or hurt anymore," she said in a cautious but deliberate tone. On that note, she excused herself and decided to stay away from William for a while. It was the trigger that sent William into making a commitment. They went to a justice of the peace. To this day, although not perfect, it is a marriage that has lasted.

Ben sat down next to William. It was an ominous sign not only to William but to the others in the collaborative. Ben's options had run their course. William, being very sensitive and analytical, said nothing to Ben about the family rift.

"Seems strange that there is no mention of the electrical crews on the survival radio," William's wife stated in a frustrated tone.

"I know, big government, they probably do not know themselves."

Ben stated with a little bit of cheer. "I have heard on the survival radio they are having real problems with Biker gangs. Most of them coming in from California and the southwest, especially the illegals that have crossed the border."

"Never let a good crisis go to waste," said Mr. Henderson, who chimed in.

"I think you're right, dad," Mr. Henderson son stated.

Now, it seems that Ben is accepted by the other members of the collaborative. *Damn!* He worked so hard for his family and the welfare of the collaborative. It was good to see the others not picking sides in his family feud.

"Ben, since you are here, I did want to talk to you about Fred," William asked in a worried tone.

"What's wrong?" asked Ben as he now has his thoughts redirected from his own grief.

"I understand that the recovery is underway. Being realistic, that is going to be many months," William said with sadness. "Fred cannot wait that long. He is a bad diabetic, plus he needs his psychiatric medications soon."

"I am sorry, William. What would you like me to do?" Ben asked with some hesitation.

"I would like to see if you can find a way that I can get him to Tent

City. They would have more access to the right medical help," William asked in a pleading manner.

Now Ben was caught in a real quandary. He knew his daughter went to the Maine tent city. This is real stress. For a few moments, there was dead silence.

Every action that Ben makes has to be measured. He has made enough mistakes. Ben bowed his head; William sensed not to say anything more. Like being in the eye of the storm, neither Ben nor William spoke. After a few seconds that seemed like an eternity, Ben lifted his head. His thoughts were misdirected. He slowly glanced at his daughter. There she was talking to the drunk. His first reaction was still jealousy, but that soon faded. He knew the drunk lost everything when he lost his wife. But Ben had his family physically there.

Still, there were serious emotional wounds.

When you're under massive stress, exercising logic is hard to do. The drunk's loss was God's work. It was time for his wife to go to heaven. Neither man nor beast could have prevented this. In Ben's case, it was human miscommunication—an extremely costly miscommunication. Could it be repaired? Some wounds can be repaired, but there are always scars. Sometimes emotional scars are deep, like an albatross that is always circling around you. In the pit of Ben's stomach, he stilled deeply loved his daughter. He knew she was now blossoming. In his head, he has played out this movie hundreds of times. Trouble is, this scene was not in the movie.

Each time when we watch a concert or see our favorite sports team, we appreciate and some even envy them. Few make it, many try. Ben bowed his head one more time. He put both his hands on the top of his head. It had been a good thirty seconds, but to Ben and William, it seemed like an eternity. Truth is, our thoughts race in a warp drive. When we speak, it is always slower. Many people have expressed when they are in a near-death experience, one can see their whole life play out in a moment. Ben removed his hands from his head.

Slowly, he raised his head.

"William, I truly empathize with your situation. I will try and help you.

I am having a difficult time with my daughter," Ben exclaimed as he stared out to the heavens.

William just bowed his head. He felt as if he was denied a stay of execution.

"Still, it is not my daughter who I should be speaking to but Officer Ryan.

It is the authorities that are issuing special passes to Tent City. I will get on it tomorrow," Ben said as he slowly turned and looked at William.

William started to look up and speak. He could not. Being sensitive yet being a brave man, he was coming unglued. He put his right hand over his eyes and started to cry. An emotional roller coaster had taken its toll on William.

"The Lord has plans for all of us; we just have to play it out," Ben said as he put his arm around William.

William gave thanks, but inside he knew Ben was overwhelmed with his own problems. Fred, being a little clueless, just enjoyed all the company. William's wife was just beside herself. She did care a lot for Fred, but she was mainly concerned about her husband state of mind. The rest of the afternoon became a little awkward. Where to go? What to do? Ben was at the end of his ropes, and William, being eccentric, was also at a dead-end. Ben got up and tried to put on the survival radio. Everyone missed their electronic gadgets. It was an escape from human interaction. Somehow, there are legitimate times when an escape route is called for. The best Ben could do was go to the survival radio. Problem is, much of the info is rehashed, kind of like watching old reruns of *I Love Lucy*.

Making the best of a bad situation, Ben's son came over.

"Hey Dad, should I start to get the fire pit and some food ready?" Randy said expressing some empathy.

"Just what the doctor ordered," Ben exclaimed with a sigh of relief.

As Randy started to move things along, the rest of the collaborative also lent a helping hand. Yes, there was tension in the air, but it was a mixed bag. Without Ben there would be no collaborative; now many of the members are repaying him. They are trying to make the atmosphere a little lighter.

As the afternoon went by, it became a time of reflection. All families have their spats. What happens when one reaches a point of no reconciliation? It becomes a path of hardships for all.

Ben, being a microbiologist, is wired to be analytical. Reality and acceptance really need to take its time. As Ben was slowly headed to the fire pit, the drunk left Jessica's company. If he had to take a sobriety test, he certainly would fail. Put your finger on your nose and walk a straight line. At this point, the drunk would fail at putting his finger on his nose. Ah! What's poison to one is a lifeline to another.

"I thought you could use a little drink," the drunk commented in a slurred voice. It looked like he drooled on his unwashed sweatshirt. *Hmmm,* thought Ben, as he looked at the drunk. He was acting like the court jester roaming around, trying to instill a smile on everyone.

"Perhaps just a small nip," Ben said as he wanted to find a glass or mug to put the whiskey into.

Deep inside him, he really needed relief from all this stress. The only thing is, he knew his wife and daughter would be watching. What else are they going to watch? Not much on their TV; in fact, not much on anyone's TV without electricity. You know the term "I double dare you"—well, Ben was in a "double doghouse" state of mind. His wife and daughter were sending out bad vibes in his direction.

What the f——? thought Ben. *It's time to think of me.* He found a coffee mug.

The drunk poured in some whiskey until Ben said, "When?"

"Thank you," Ben said with a smile.

"You're welcome," said the drunk, raising his glass to salute Ben.

Ben decided to just nod. If he saluted the drunk in a reciprocal manner, it would put a nail on the door to his double doghouses. With his wife and daughter glancing at him, it would become a life sentence, without a chance for parole. Being analytical at times really sucks. It's kind of like being a nerd at a singles' dance.

Ben just took the mug and tried graciously to make a little small talk with the drunk. As a few more of the collaborative members came over, Ben found himself making the best out of it. The little bit of whiskey that Ben consumed took the edge off his stressful state of mind.

The afternoon and evening went without a hitch. Ben felt a little sorry for the drunk. On the outside, he looked rough; on the inside, he was a beautiful person.

Maybe fighting his own demons, the drunk has to obliterate all his senses.

It was a cat-and-mouse game. Every once in a while, Jessica would eye her dad. Alice would also do the same. Once a tight-knit Christian family, they now acted like strangers. Who—or what—would put all the pieces back together on Humpty Dumpty? It seemed insurmountable. Sometimes the best course of action is no action. At least, until the waters are no longer murky.

I am sure this will be one day that will live on in the minds of the Randal family.

As evening came, the departures slowly started. First, Jessica excused herself.

Then it was the divorcee, Henderson, William, his wife, and Fred. Randy has really made his father proud. He diplomatically waited for his mom (Alice) to turn in. He knew he had to stay and at least give his dad a little company. He did not want to take sides, and he hoped his dad would not bring up the issue.

Ben, being happy that his son at least remained neutral, knew better than to rock the boat.

Darkness finally came and, like a curtain at half-time, gave pause to this sorry state of affairs. Ben waited until everyone was tucked in. He grabbed his Bible and looked skyward. "Thank you, Lord, I am really trying. Please show me the path." With that said, Ben entered the house. As he crawled into Bed with his wife, he noticed she was on her side facing the outside of the bed. *Ah,* Ben thought, *at least it's better than sleeping in the doghouse.* Who is kidding whom? It's not better. It's like sleeping with the Ice Queen. "Sorry, Lord, I was out of line," Ben muttered under his breath. It was a long day, this first day of an uneasy homecoming. With a new dawn coming, hopefully there will be hope.

Another EMP Causality: Part II
An Unsettling Time

"Good morning, Vietnam!" the enlisted man spurted out on the PA system. It was a wake-up call. Everyone was under stress. His attempt to inject some dry humor was a welcome break from the reality of war. Problem was, the enlisted man had a nemeses: his immediate officer. The man was an uptight, overbearing army officer, who made life miserable, for the announcer. The part of the enlisted man was played by Robin Williams. Bless his soul. He had come a long way from his *Mork and Mindy* days.

In this Hollywood classic, the announcer was forced out of his job. His immediate officer thought his comments were not proper for army decor. They rubbed him the wrong way. After he got him railroaded out, the officer got his proper dosage of karma. The uptight, smug officer was reassigned to a new duty station in a distant and cold climate. Top officers at the army base understood morale. They knew these young soldiers were at their limit. Sometimes, the army way is not always the right way. In combat, discretion can be warranted.

After the EMP strike, reality reared its ugly head. For some, it was visible in a matter of minutes. For some, it was hours, and for others, days. For those with an already damaged inner being, self-preservation opened the door into denial. Will there be school again? Work? Movie theaters? TVs? Will we get protection for our friends and family? The list of how each person can react to stress goes on and on.

Before the strike, our stress was with everyday life—getting to work on time, paying bills, passing exams, dealing with family and spouse problems, etc. We all deal with it in different ways: after-work activities, running, walking, biking, and playing sports. These help by providing a healthy escape mechanism. Others are drawn to less healthy approaches: drinking, smoking, binge- and comfort eating. For some, a more passive approach suits their personality: immersing themselves in social media, electronic devices, or watching sports.

Within the collaborative, there is a different stress. It is the one of responsibility in an uncertain world. Most understood Ben's role. He has helped organize a means to provide food, water, and safety for the collaborative during an uncomfortable time. Even if Ben was at fault, within his family feud, how can they ostracize him? His fire pit was the collaborative safe place.

In this quiet suburban town, the insects and animals start stirring before dawn. Usually these noises has gone unnoticed by most. The only exception is Randy. He has taken a different path in life. Randy like his dad was blessed with a high IQ. Living in rural Nebraska, school became boring. He was way ahead of his classmates. Perhaps, he should have been advanced and skipped a few grades. Perhaps it was a combination of Alice and Ben being too busy, or the complacency of not "rocking the boat."

Randy's mind was always in warp drive. His father was a hands-on dad. Randy would watch and help out as his fascination with putting mechanical projects together developed. He picked up auto magazines and was given a free pass by his parents to pursue his natural interests. When he worked outside, he observed the natural cycle of seasons and how animals, insects, and plants intertwined their existences.

When the family moved from Nebraska to Metro West Boston, Randy kept up with his habits. The rest of the family was engulfed in their everyday fast-paced life. But Randy was one in his surroundings. Working as an automotive mechanic was stress-free. He could have time and funds to work on his real love: his classic vintage Buick.

More precious than gold, his classic Buick was the lifeline for all in the collaborative. Still, Randy remained humble; him and his classic machine. It would be kind of like Tom Brady, arguably the greatest quarter back of all time, but humble as a part of a well-oiled team.

Sometimes it is strange how events unfold. As morning approached, it was Ben who awoke first. Maybe God is playing a master chess game, understanding how and when each piece should move. Truth be told, Ben did not sleep well, tossing and turning all night. His mind was acting more like a massive traffic jam in New York City. No matter which route or bridge he took, there was blockage. Alice, Jessica, the collaborative, William's cry for help, the dead woman in Providence, Rhode Island—all of it represented a major clusterf———. If this were a Hollywood script, he would be portrayed as a troubled man. He would be tossing and turning in a cold sweat. Finally the camera would zoom in on his face. Presto! His buggy red eyes would open—a classic movie shoot.

Why did Ben arise this one time before Randy? Maybe it's God's doing. Randy sensed the tension in the air. He had to let his father and sister do their own peace dance. Randy decided to let his dad get up first so he could play out his own hand. Randy did not want to degrade his father. A student should not outshine or humiliate his teacher. But he also was aware of each of his family member's perspective in this stressful and complex feud. He knew that any more interference would only delay the possibility of a happy solution.

Ben sat up in bed, his feet touching the floor, away from his wife. It was not a happy day for him. *Damn!* So much weight on his shoulders. Doesn't his wife understand how much is on him—the collaborative, food, water, protection, just giving hope to everyone—so they will endure this nightmare? In Ben's heart, he knew he had to be a solid rock. His inner emotions had to be bundled within. Moses opened the seas so his followers could have safe passage. Ben had to be the monolith that gave the appearance of a protective shroud. This conflict with his daughter, Jessica, was wearing on him.

What to do? My own father would say, "If nothing else works, try two aspirins and two shots of whiskey. If that doesn't work, forget the aspirins and double the shots. But in reality, it will only make matters worse."

How about Alice's take on this? She has been a faithful wife and mother. She has supported Ben financially so he could pursue his master's degree. Her motherly instincts say, keep the family together.

In her heart, she gets upset with Ben for being so stubborn. Quietly, she would say, "Damn you, Ben! Why won't you at least let them talk? Jessica is in a fragile state of mind. You are so pigheaded. Now everyone is suffering."

Imagine, if Ben and Alice were two aliens from another planet. Since they are not talking to one another, they still can read each other's minds. It would be a telepathic communications. Their war would only escalate. Maybe that's why aliens are often drawn with big heads. Pressure just keeps expanding inside, always pushing outward. *Back to earth, Ben! Time to motivate.* With all these thoughts running through him, he shut them down and clasped his Bible with two hands. Breathe in, breathe out.

He sensed his wife was awake. She was waiting for him to leave. The feeling inside of him was strong. He just knew it was time to boogie. What to wear? Shorts or cargo pants? Coming into the summer days in the Boston area can be tricky. Even though it was a little cool, within a few hours, it could be hot and muggy. Just then, he heard a little annoying buzzing sound. A familiar sound just the same. *Slap!* He just killed a mosquito. *All right then, cargo pants it is!* A little more protection from those critters.

Off to the bathroom to use the john and wash his hands. The town water was only trickling in. He filled the back of the toilet with a bucket of water. After putting the Bible on the bookshelf, Ben wrote and left a note. As he was writing, he just shook his head. Pretty sad. Communication with his own family was at an all-time low. Karma, something good has to happen. He wrote, *Taking a walk to Officer Ryan's house. Need to do a favor for William.* He signed it *Ben.* He could have wrote on the top of the note. *To whom it concerns . . .* That would be like pouring salt on an open wound, and there would be no hope of reconciliation.

Peace, serenity was found as he closed the front door of his house. It was like the Genie went *Poof!* Inside the house was his family. They didn't care if or when he left. Back to being single, a new reality, that no one cares about you. *Ah! Got to have hope.* Just surviving the EMP blast was enough of a challenge. Coffee, need that fix? A coping mechanism.

Like smoking, a daily shot of alcohol. Actually, a morning run or walk would be better. Today, Ben is going to do both. Officer Ryan's house was on the outer limits of the collaborative. There were several houses in between that were not in the collaborative. Allowing a police officer in was a no-brainer to all the collective members. Officer Ryan offered protection and communication for the collaborative.

Ben washed his cup out and started to walk. He cleared his mind of stress and negative thoughts. As he was walking, he took notice of his surroundings. He saw the neighborhood with more clarity than ever before. Before the EMP blast, everyday stress was intense. Driving to work on the mass pike was a challenge. His work also was an intense mental workload. He has his master's degree, but in this Boston area, many had their masters and PhD degrees. He was working with some of the most talented people on the planet. He had to be on the top of his game. Driving to and from the Boston metro west suburbs was different than driving in Nebraska. In winter, there were snowstorms; summers, the hot and sweltering heat. Those damn tolls. Traffic would back up forever. Finally an upgrade was made. An electronic "Easy Pass" was installed. The toll takers lost their jobs, but driving was made easier.

After months of hard work, he finally bought a new Honda Accord. Sweet, such a nice ride, air-conditioning, the all-around speakers for his radio. The Honda became his safe space, a break from work and family. As he drove into his driveway, he never really looked at his neighbors or their homes. It was the castle or perhaps prison for the typical middle-class life, as each grind out their daily lives.

The Honda Accord wasn't even broken in when the EMP blast went off. In a split-second, his car went from a luxury ride to a pile of metal. What a sorry state of affairs: no job, no Honda Accord, no electricity. It's gone. What's even worse, his own family has put the hex on him. But on the bright side, all his bills are in limbo. Mortgage payments, electric, cable, taxes, even his food, clothing, and educational bills were gone. Wait! All he has to see now is the US postal service delivering his income tax bill on horseback. Wouldn't that be a bummer? No one can get to a job to earn money. You wouldn't have to worry about the gangs because there would be no money for them to steal. There would be massive suicides, and the postal man on horseback would say, "Don't blame me, I'm only the messenger."

Ben started his journey on foot to Officer Ryan's house. His view of the neighborhood is different. Like *The Twilight Zone,* a different dimension. He sees things that he never noticed before. The divorcee's house looks so inviting—the plants, shrubs, and even her front door. She seems to have an eye for beauty. Mr. Henderson, a contractor, has a well-built dwelling.

The garage, shed, tractors, heavy equipment, and tools give it a masculine touch—inviting to a hands-on person but not to many others. The union man's house was well maintained but lacks the charm of the divorcee. I guess one knows who the boss in that house is.

Now, Ben looks at the drunk's house. *Ah, how misery likes its own company. Whew! What a mess.* Broken shutters, moss on the roof and stairs. Shrubs that seem to be swallowing the whole house. It looked like the house on *Wuthering Heights.* Most of all, the drunk has nothing to look forward to. Dust to dust, he was waiting for his calling—his calling to exit the vessel he was living in. He so wanted to be in the afterlife. The loneliness and pain were unbearable to him.

Ben's sadness now enabled him to see it. He never looked at it his way before. It was a cry. The real sad thing is it was not a cry for help— instead, a cry for an ending. Most of us fear death, but to the drunk, it was a welcoming journey. A journey that he pinned for, every single day, as he got lost in his bottle of whiskey.

As a microbiologist Ben had an inquisitive mind, always trying to put a new puzzle together. The lab where he worked needed talent— talent that would keep them viable and up-front in a competitive field. Ben knew he was in the big leagues. Coming to work in Boston afforded him that opportunity, and he was humble about it.

Scientists deal with facts, theories, and building blocks. Even music has a series of steps, octaves, harmony, beginning, ending—a certain beat, a sequence that would entice an audience. Looking at an abstract painting? If Ben walked into a museum and saw a patron with his hands on their chin, first thing Ben would think: *What's up? What are you looking at?* Looking at an abstract painting and understanding the soul of the painter is beyond Ben. I guess that's what makes the world go around.

In a practical sense, the last house in the immediate collaborative belonged to William. He was neurotic but rich, and it showed. His house was always well-maintained. The grounds were laid out by a professional and maintained by a lawn service company. The grass is now overgrown. One has to strain to see hints that William once employed professional landscapers. Officer Ryan's place was the outlier for the collaborative. There are many other houses between William's house and Officer Ryan's place. He was a real asset, a real score for the group, but unlike the other members, Officer Ryan did not need to live within the protective bounds of "fortress collaborative."

Coming to William's house, something looked amiss. It was still early morning. No watches, but looking at the sun, Ben knew it was not even 7 a.m. William's client Fred was outside the gate. He had a bag that looked like he had his lunch in it.

"Morning Fred" Ben said in a curious tone.

"Morning, Mr. Randal. I'm waiting for my ride. That damn William, he is lazy, that's all."

Fred proclaimed in a louder voice, "I don't know what the matter with him is. I told him he had to pack my lunch! Lazy, he's just damn lazy."

Fred, William's client, usually goes to a state program three times a week. It's a structured itinerary. He is there with like-minded clients. They have social workers, nurses, a program director, and various staff members. Usually Fred is picked up by 8:30 a.m. and home by 3:30 p.m. It is perfect for everyone. They also schedule dances, luncheons, ball games, etc. It is funded both by the state and private contributions. The odd thing is, most of them are happier than us. With no bills, driving, making meals, washing clothes, their lives are simpler. Yes, once in a while they get angry or have something to stress about. The staff is generally very professional. They place them in a "time-out spot," a safe place where they can unwind.

Fred is generally happy, but the EMP strike has left him bewildered. He blames William. He wants to see his girlfriend, LuAnn. Once a month, Fred goes to the flea market. There he buys a ring for his girlfriend. Like clockwork he asks LuAnn to Marry him. Liking the attention she gets, she always says yes. Ever watch Bill Murray in *Ground hog Day?* He keeps repeating the same day, over and over. Fred wants to be a fireman, buy a motorcycle, and ride off in the sunset with his new bride. He has a fireman's badge. In his mind, this lets him be an important person, since at some level, he knows he can't get a job and have kids.

William is a great caregiver. He listens to Fred's stories and his desire to be like everyone else. Why spoil a dream? You never see someone jump off a bridge with a lottery ticket in their hand. When there is hope, there is a kindred spirit to push ahead down that windy road. Fred likes to sleep on the sofa. His mother always flies down from heaven to visit him at night. In the morning, Fred describes his dreams to William. He misses his mother badly. Every once in a while, he would look up in the sky and say, "Mom, someday I will be buried near you, and I will go up to heaven to visit you. He would cry for a minute, then William would try and redirect him. It is an ongoing battle. Most psychiatrists and therapists recommend that you pick your battles. Making any kind of change is slow and tedious.

William tried to explain to Fred what has happened. It is of no use. Fred is a creature of habit, like most clients. When a nor'easter snowstorm hits, homes are often left without electricity for hours or a few days. But this is now turning into months. Many clients feel they have done something wrong. Most challenged adults have a hard time without their TV. William would like to take Fred on a road trip. Getting to a tent city would serve many purposes—primarily, satisfy Fred loves of being in a car or jeep. Second and most importantly, Fred should see a doctor. The insulin he is getting is old and not the right type. A high sugar count is destructive to any human being.

"Fred, I really don't think the bus is coming today," Ben said in a low, sensitive tone.

"*G——!*" Fred yelled out as he threw his lunch on the ground. He then kicks the dirt up. He raised his right hand up with the palm facing inward. "This isn't right! How am I going to see my girlfriend? It's not right!" he yelled out as he kicked some more sand.

Caught off guard, Ben just kept quiet. After Fred calmed down a bit, Ben responded, "Listen, Fred, William loves and cares for you. He is doing the best he can," Ben continued in a soft yet commanding voice.

"I know, I know. It isn't his fault. I have to see my girlfriend." Fred went on in a sad voice.

"It will all work out, Fred. I have to go, catch you later," Ben explained as he continued his journey. Ben got back to his walking. Why didn't William come out to greet him? he wondered. Maybe he was superstitious. Perhaps he did not want to jinx the mission. William checked his 9mm, making sure there was a round in the chamber. He felt confident there would be no problem. Although there was one gang killing nearby, he felt safe. Most thugs are cowards, and with transportation almost nonexistent, it would be hard for them to get here. Besides, Ben was a good shot in the army.

Going by the homes seemed eerie. Grass was overgrown everywhere, hardly a dog around anywhere. If someone was inside, they would not know who Ben was. There is one constant that almost the whole street knew. Officer Ryan and his wife were just a ten- or fifteen-minute walk away. Talking to Fred provided a needed distraction for Ben. It got his mind off his own family problems. It was a needed pause in Ben's ever-mounting stress. The smell of distant fires, and the occasional crack of a 9 mm pistol was a constant reality check. Dangers lurked everywhere.

Approaching Officer Ryan's home, Ben decided to walk to his side door. An old-fashioned pull cord lawn mower stood nearby. Officer Ryan and his wife liked to keep the outside tidy. It was a good omen for the neighborhood. It was as good as reading a sign that said: THUGS BEWARE! THIS PLACE IS OCCUPIED. The two family cars were neatly positioned on the driveway, but in reality, they were now just a pile of metal slowly rusting away. If things ever got back on track, the price of junk cars would plummet.

Fortunately, Officer Ryan does have access to an old relic of a motorcycle. Officer Ryan is clever enough to maintain it himself. He opens the sliding door in the back of his house to wheel it into his living room. Now that's what is called "under lock and key."

Ben came by the side door. As he knocked, he yelled, "Officer Ryan? Hello, this is Ben Randal." After a few minutes, Officer Ryan's wife, Annett, came to the door. Everyone calls her Ann. For most middle-class people, Ann is easier to say, especially up in the northeast.

"Hello, Ben, I didn't hear the Buick. Did you walk?" Ann said with curiosity.

"I did; it is a long story," Ben replied in a timid voice.

"I hope there is nothing wrong with the Buick? Everyone is dependent on your son's car," Ann replied with a little hesitation.

"The car is fine, really. I was hoping to speak with your husband," Ben replied, looking past Ann to see if Officer Ryan might be home.

"I am sorry, but he is doing a shift at the prison. Strange, many of the prisoners are now happy to be in prison. Many were offered an early release after the EMP bomb went off. Can you believe more than half refused? They are aware that they have food, water, and a secured place to live," Ann said with a smile.

"That is weird." Ben stated as he shook his head.

Ann Randal is also a police officer. She met her husband at the state police academy. She is of Italian descent and grew up in the north end of Boston, the well-known Italian section of the city. It is now a tourist area near the seaport. Many gift shops and noted Italian restaurants are located there.

Her father was an abusive man, always yelling and sometimes beating his wife. It was a real dysfunctional family. Life was hard for Ann and her three brothers. Two of her brothers were near her age. The third, Dean, was a lot older. They lived in a large multifamily building; it was built before rent control and better city codes. Her father went off to work with a lunchbox every morning. When he came home, the yelling and the hitting would start. Her father would often complain about his meals and put everyone down.

His behavior kept going until Dean put a stop to it when he was in junior high school. By then, he was almost as tall as his father. He told his father that if he hit his mother one more time, he would kill him.

Dean had reached a breaking point, a point where his rage was greater than his fear. The father did stop, but each time her brother came home from school, he could feel the tension in the house. This dysfunctional family left emotional scars. A few years later, her father developed dementia and was no longer able to work. It was a difficult decision to leave high school, but Dean had to. Someone had to pay the bills.

Whenever Dean left for work, Ann was left with the responsibility for her other two brothers. When they came back home from school, they often tried to pick on her the way they saw their father mistreat their mother. Bad habits have to start somewhere. Finally, one day, Dean saw a bad bruise on his sister. With tears in her eye, she explained what happened. He spoke with his two brothers, but his instincts realized that it would not be enough. He took Ann to a karate studio on Saturday mornings. She had to learn to defend herself, and defend herself she did. By the time she obtained her brown belt, she was able to stand up to her other two brothers. Finally, a fragile peace arrangement arrived in their home.

A few years later, everything changed. Her mother died and her father was in a nursing home. It was time for each to be on their own. A sad upbringing, but not all families can live the perfect dream. Ann did get a job and an apartment. Although she kept in touch with her brothers, she had a special love and admiration for her older brother. One day, when Dean came to visit, he told Ann he had met the dream of his life. This was it. He was going to get married and move to California. Ann was both happy and sad at the same time. Yes, there were aunts and uncles, but no one else gave her unconditional love.

Dean's dream match was a pretty woman, but Ann felt something very wrong. His fiancée often wore a very short skirt. Her whole manner of dress was rather provocative. The three of them were at a local restaurant when "the truth" appeared. As the three of them left the restaurant, warning bells went off in Ann's mind. Her brother was happy to a have a show model as a girlfriend. However, other men were looking at her. It was his brother's fiancée who looked back at some of the men. That bothered Ann. She always regretted not warning her brother.

After Dean moved to LA, he became a police officer at the LAPD. He would call her from time to time. She was proud of her older brother. Ann had just turned twenty. She was working during the day and going to school at night. It didn't leave much time for a social life. Besides, the way her two other brothers treated females had an effect on her. Instead of talking about what they were about, her brothers were often making references to girl's body parts. To Ann, it was a turn off. She thought all men can't be this shallow.

A few years later, Ann received a call. It was her brother's friend at the LA police department. He had been shot while off duty, at a restaurant with his wife. When they were outside, they were confronted by a gangbanger. The guy drew his gun for a robbery. Her brother stepped in front of his wife to protect her. A shot rang out. Dean fell to the ground. He couldn't move his legs. He was paralyzed from the waist down.

It was a long time before Dean would let anyone visit him in his wheelchair. When Ann finally arrived at his apartment, she rang the doorbell. It took a long time before her brother came to the door in his wheelchair. Ann reflexively put her hand on her mouth. The apartment was a mess. Her brother wreaked of his own urine. She asked him where his wife was.

"She's out," that's all Dean would say. Ann helped clean up the place. When the wife came home, Ann could see she was up to no good. Ann tried to talk to her, but she told Ann to mind her own business. Her brother did not want a fight. In order to keep peace, Ann decided to go home. Before she left, she hugged Dean and said, "I love you very much; you are my only real family"

He replied, "Don't worry about me, little sis, I have this." But Ann knew better. She flew back to Boston. It was less than six months before she got the dreaded call. Her brother's friend told Ann that he just gave up. He lost way too much weight. When all hope is gone, a tormented soul can sometimes only see relief by giving up the effort to their struggle. Although suicide is never the right answer, it is their only solution. They stop expending energy to keep themselves afloat. Sad, but it happens too many times.

At the funeral, Ann was there with her two other brothers. Dean's friend gave Ann his police badge. The flight home was long and lonely. Ann's life was profoundly changed. As she tightly gripped her brother's badge, she made a vow to become a state trooper. She knew if accepted, she could excel in law enforcement.

Ann qualified, passing the requisite physical evaluations, and scored high on the written exam. She was accepted to the Massachusetts State Police Academy. It was there that she met her future husband. Like herself, her future husband (now Officer Ryan) was striking out without any family support. Although Officer Ryan's father and grandfather were police officers, he was different from them.

His grandfather had moved to Boston from New York City. As an Irishman, they were dealt with unkindly. When coming from Ireland, brutality and getting a job was a constant challenge. Many people of Irish decent relocated to Boston—South Boston, to be exact.

Their friends, and the Irish Catholic Church, became a social network for housing and jobs. Soon many of the Irish had populated South Boston. It was a "safe place"—all outsiders beware. The Irish took to their own.

Soon they became a dominant factor in the unions, workforce, and politics. It was an unwritten truth. If you were Irish, a registered Democrat, living in South Boston, life was your oyster. Getting a good-paying job or entering into the political field, being Irish gave you a real bargaining chip. Today things have vastly changed. It was the prejudice and bigotry that drove Officer Ryan from his father and grandfather. He decided a long time ago not to get into family arguments. It is hard to change the spots on an animal. Maybe it was a blessing to Officer Ryan. He lived with bigotry his whole life and he wanted to break the chain.

At the state police academy, Ann and Officer Ryan became close friends. They both came from dysfunctional families. She saw in him the qualities of her older brother. At the shooting range, fitness tests, and classroom, they both excelled. Ann, with her emotional scars (caused by her two other brothers), had a hard time committing to any man. Ann informed Officer Ryan that she only wanted him as a friend or confidant. After graduation, they still remained close friends.

One day Officer Ryan came to Ann and informed her that he joined a dating service. She told him that was great. He also told her that he met someone special. Her heart sank as he was talking; she was filled with countless emotions.

Why does life throw these firebombs? She was finally getting into a serene state of mind without therapy; Ann was becoming emotionally normal. Why can't Officer Ryan just go at the slow pace Ann was traveling? To her this made no sense. Several minutes into the conversation, Officer Ryan, being sensitive, saw a frown on Ann's face. He was puzzled. *Why?* he thought. *Why she is not overjoyed? Please, why?* He kept quiet for a moment. Ann gathered all her emotions in one tight bundle and grasped at her next sentence. Officer Ryan was always attracted to Ann emotionally and physically. Ann could sense it. Being stoic and a gentleman, Officer Ryan accepted his role with Ann. Now he was puzzled.

Ann clasped her hands and touched her nose. It was like she wanted to pray. Ah! She was unsure of herself. Did she care what's best for Officer Ryan or what's best for Ann? Her mind clashed with her inner emotions. She was in shock and stunned at how fast he wanted to move on. Officer Ryan was ready to settle down. You know, family, kids, white picket fence, and a dog. He wanted to drive his car with the family sticks on his rear car window. He was ready. Ann looked up at Officer Ryan. With all the courage she could muster, she stated, "Why are you going so fast?"

Huh? was Officer Ryan's response. They both looked at each other. It was not the look of brother and sister. It was a look of a courting ritual—a ritual that can't be taught, only undertaken. It is hidden in our deepest inner sanatorium and is brought to surface in rare occasions. After a few stunned seconds, Officer Ryan looks at Ann and says, "Do you like fairs?"

"No," Ann said with her eyes fixated on him.

"Neither do I. How about we both go this weekend? I really think it's what we both need," he said confidently.

To Ann, it was as if Officer Ryan mounted a white horse. He stopped in front of Ann. She put out her arm. He grabbed her arm and swung her on top of his horse as they galloped off into the sunset. Ann was mesmerized; Officer Ryan took over the courting ritual. He was in complete control. She was now putty at his feet. He started to understand, and confidence just took over.

That Friday night, they went out. Neither admitted that it was a real date. Both knew the stakes were high. For the first time in both their lives, they were on the same road. Somehow without regrets, they both had to take this journey on this Friday night. Being at the fair was incidental; it just filled in the blanks.

Both wanted to put their best foot forward. Officer Ryan put on his designer jeans and cowboy boots. Ann had a more difficult time. She wanted to entice him. Then she had flashbacks of her two brothers and her late brother's wife. *No,* she thought, *I will not show cleavage, but I will put a nice fitting pants. After all,* she mused, *I do have a nice figure, don't I? Perfume? Jewelry?* After many tormented moments, she said to herself, *Only a watch, with a hidden dab of perfume, just a hidden dab.* She had to be herself. This was not a one-night stand.

As Officer Ryan picked her up, he saw not a coworker but a beautiful angel, an angel that he wanted for himself. From Boston, they drove south to the fair. Neither one smokes. Both were only social drinkers and they both enjoyed their coffee. Coffee without the doughnuts keeps one up, not round. (Hmmm. I've always wanted to know if they left their pistols at home that night. You know, maybe instead of jewelry, they had his-and-her pistols.)

At the fair, it started out like all the other times they got together. The conversation flowed naturally. Both were in sync with each other. *Gads,* Ann thought, he was here all the time; like her brother, it was everything she wanted in a man. Tall, sensitive, and physically fit. *Damn, what was I thinking before?* Ann asked herself. *How can I let him go?* As they tried the shooting range (Please! You know, they both were attracted to the shooting range), the smiles and feelings overcame them both. Both laughed; they went by the food concession stands and various rides. Officer Ryan stopped at one special ride. It was the one that you sit in a large teacup. It went in a circular motion. The teacup itself also did circles. You know, circles inside of circles. If you don't understand, go back to sixth grade. It was the best three years of my life.

"Let's Go!" Officer Ryan announced as he extended his hand.

"All right, Ann said as if she were a little girl again. As the ride was about to start, Officer Ryan made his move. (I know, I know, you were all waiting for the moment.) He put one hand on the bar rail and the other around Ann. She was succumbed by a feeling of being protected and loved. It was what has been missing in her life. First, she wanted to put her hands on the bar rail. Instead, she made a counter-gesture; she put her right hand on his thigh. Officer Ryan played his poker hand. He did not look at her but smiled. Now they were both traveling on a road that took them into the clouds. Most of us who were alive when JFK was shot knew where we were at that moment. Likewise, both Ann and Officer Ryan will never forget this moment. When the ride was over, Officer Ryan asked Ann what she would like to do.

"One more time!" was her answer. It was sort of like asking her *Will you marry me?* And she said yes.

* * *

Ben noticed that Ann was wearing her pistol. He had his tucked in his belt. The difference is that Ben does not wear a pistol at home. Ben does not need to wear his gun in his collaborative. He has several neighbors and three Dogs, all whom would sound an alarm of any unwanted quests.

"Is there something I can help you with?" Ann asked.

"I am not sure if you can, but maybe," Ben commented in an unsure way. He had to collect himself. He did not want to insult Ann, but at the same time, she might be insulted if he did not confide in her. After all, she went on a road trip with his wife. Ben was losing confidence in himself. Everything he has done lately has gone wrong. His ego was so low, he needed a shovel to find it.

"It's about William and Fred," Ben just spurted it out.

"Did something happen?" Ann said with alarm in her voice.

"Nothing like that, they are still okay," Ben said without much confidence.

"That's good," Ann quipped.

"William is getting really concerned about Fred's welfare. He should be seeing a doctor on a regular basis. The insulin is old and not the right type. He also needs to be tested for sugar levels. And a much-needed full blood test should be performed. William really wants to take Fred on a road trip to Tent City."

"Oh, I see, I see," Ann said as she pondered a response.

Instead of immediately replying to Ben, Ann walked side to side. Ben stepped back, somewhat doubting himself. *Damn,* he thought, *did I just blow it again?* Man, if he were in Vegas, he would be a sure winner. If he put his money on red, everyone else should bet black. The ball would land on black. You know, when Charlie Brown would walk around on a sunny day, there would be rain clouds over his head. This is how Ben felt.

Finally Ann stopped. Without looking at Ben, she raised her right hand up. With her index finger pointed at her temple, she made a gesture pointing down several times with her finger. Like hitting the C note on a piano.

"There is something coming up. We are trying to put all the pieces together,"

Ann said as she shook her head side to side. She was in a trance, as if she were watching a Jumanji board. Seeing how the pieces move. "Ben, my husband, has the highest regard for you. In this nightmare quagmire, you arose to the test. He feels—no, we feel you are one of the reasons that all of us will survive," Ann said in a heartwarming response.

Ben was in complete shock. His confidence and ego were spiraling downward, faster than a speeding train, faster than a speeding bullet. "It's a bird, it's a plane. Nope, just Ben's ego dropping like a giant corkscrew drilling through the earth's crust. First through the outer bedrock layers, then downward, into molten lava." As Ann spoke, Ben's ego started to rise.

"Captain Kirk here! Reverse all engines. Turn this corkscrew around," screamed the captain of the corkscrew vessel, carrying Ben's ego. "What's going on, Scotty? Why can't you turn this vessel around?"

"It's the GPS system, captain. It's melted in the molten lava," an alarmed Scotty replied.

"Captain, please! Let me be so bold and take it from here," Spock said stoically. And with his Vulcan instincts, he righted the corkscrew vessel toward the earth's surface.

As the vessel neared the earth's surface, Capt. Kirk yelled out, "We will attach a booster jet to our vessel so we can carry Ben's ego into the clouds."

"Booster jet, attach, not logical," a stymied Spock retorted.

"Yes, I ordered one from Priceline.com," Captain Kirk said proudly.

Indeed, as the corkscrew vessel was safely on the Earth's surface, the crew then attached booster jets and continued upward toward the clouds. Ben's ego was not only returning to normal, but maybe inflating a little. As the vessel penetrated the cumulonimbus cloud, it started to stall dramatically. It seems they miscalculated the weight by several pounds.

Right at that moment, Bones came up to Capt. Kirk. With his arms crossed in front of his chest, he looked at the captain.

"Put on a few pounds lately?" Bones said with his own touch of sarcasm.

"What? Can't a man enjoy the fruits of his success?" Capt. Kirk interjected, with his arm out, his palms facing upward, and his head shrugged. "On the ship *Enterprise,* all I got was this small size. Nutrisystem meals. Really? I wanted to call the ship 'The Empty Prize.'"

"Fruits, you mean cheeseburgers," a disgruntled Bones quipped.

Slapping his forehead, Spock commented, "Wasn't he making enough money doing those infomercials?"

Before the corkscrew vessel dropped, Ben's ego softly exited the vessel. Doing a graceful pirouette, Ben's ego tiptoed on the clouds. Below the clouds, there were thunderstorms and a falling corkscrew vessel. The last noise from the corkscrew vessel was Lieutenant Uhura. She was screaming, almost wetting her pants, as the vessel disappeared from sight.

At that moment, Ben's ego only saw sunshine. His first impulse was to step in toward Ann. He wanted to hug her and kiss her on the cheek. On second thought, maybe she might pull out her gun and shoot Ben. As he lay on the ground in pain, she could shoot him twice more just like the Mafia would.

Reining in his imagination, Ben composed himself and thanked Ann. He said, "William's spirits will have a glimmer of hope. With all of his thoughts and emotions squeezed tightly inside of him, Ben exited. He did not want to turn around. Maybe she would change her mind? Or maybe . . . just shoot Ben? For doubting her (only kidding). Leaving her driveway, his aura was glowing. It felt like he was gliding on a pair of Expensive Air Jordan sneakers.

The trip was successful. Now the gates of his tormented mind opened. The pressure oozed out, the wrinkles on his face relaxed. It's good to feel like a human being. There was a bounce in Ben's step. Not too much though. He still had a loaded pistol in his pants. All he needed now is another incident. If it went off, it could take out his pride and joy. Not been in use much since his family's cold war, he thought.

On the return trip, some of the neighbors—not yet part of the collaborative—came out of their homes. They have not yet met Ben. Like a new puppy, these neighbors were unsure of Ben's intentions. They saw him walking to Officer Ryan's house with a pistol in his pants. Now as he walked backed, they figured out he belong in the neighborhood. Most thugs were young and in packs. Ben was a middle-aged man and so did not come across as a threat.

Even though Ben engaged them in a conversation, he did not extend an offer for them to join the collaborative. First of all, he already had too much on his plate. Secondly, it would be tense to bring them into the fold during his family's cold war. Thirdly, and more pragmatically, they were protected on both ends: the collaborative on one end, and Officer Ryan's house on the other; thus forming a "safe place" where they resided.

Ben was in a cheerful mood as he came into view of William's house. In the background, Fred was feeding his birds but still yelling at the squirrels. Those pesky squirrels always seem to steal the bird's food.

Fred did not like that. But at least it took Fred's mind off his girlfriend. William was sitting on the front steps with his long frame and a pair of clean but wrinkled khaki pants.

It was till early in the morning, but one could feel that it would be a warm day. But somehow William always seems cold even though he had two layers of shirts on. Maybe because of his being too thin, he was more adaptable to warmer temps.

From the manner of Ben's walk, William sensed Ben had some positive news. William would make a good poker player. He kept his emotions in check. Ben always had an admiration for William. He saw not only a kindred spirit but a human being of an above-average intelligence. Just like Ben, William had a high-pressure job, but in the insurance business. Something dramatic must have happened to William for him to leave his profession. To work as an executive in downtown Boston requires a high-level skill set. But that mental aptitude often gets tossed into a grinding, pressured job environment.

When William talks, his words are usually measured. He listens carefully, taking in everything like a giant mulching machine. No need to repeat oneself. Like a detective, lawyer, or diplomat, William's approach is very calculated. He senses body motions, inflections, and word uses. Ben feels William has shortchanged himself. There are certain people who possess a high IQ—surgeons, scientists, even many types of artists. Unlike most people, William was set for life, financially. Although his domestic needs were simple, he still had an above-average house, clothes, and car. Well-organized, he only owns items he actually uses.

It is odd that William lived with Fred and his wife. They were a polar opposite to him. Perhaps opposites do attract. Fred was a pack rat constantly collecting anything he can: magazines, pens, used clothes, souvenirs—any item he could claim as his own.

Confrontations, yelling, and always being at odds with someone, accomplishes nothing. Even William's wife is not very neat. In William's mind, he accepts Fred for what he is. Although his room looks like a scene *Sanford and Son*. William keeps the rest of the house clean and tidy.

In the sitcom of *The Odd Couple,* one scene has Felix (a neat freak) going into Oscar's room (a total slob). Oscar was under his covers. A pile of clothes and debris was on his bed. Felix was trying to wake him. Thinking that he was shaking his head to wake him, Felix was shocked to realize that he was touching his feet. So he left the room just to breathe. Oscar got up in his baggy shorts and went to the bathroom. Oscar then brushed his teeth and gargled with a can of beer. Although it was funny as heck, it showed how opposites can coexist. William knew enough not to be a controlling person. In William's heart, he knew Fred and his wife were not evil. William had enough evil in his life. Now he was very concerned with Fred's health. As Ben approached William, he knew there would be answers. Hopefully, answers that would help solve William's concerns.

"Morning, William," Ben remarked

"Morning, Ben," William replied with an air of caution.

"I see Fred is still yelling at the squirrels," Ben said with an air of amusement.

"It's the never-ending story," William said as he smiled.

"You're doing a great job with him," Ben responded.

"Thanks," William kept it short, hoping to get rid of the opening salutations.

"Well, William, I did not see Officer Ryan. But I did talk at length with his wife."

At this point, William decided not to ask questions. Ben was going to tell him the important info without asking.

"It seems that Officer Ryan is pulling duty at the prison. They lack staff there and use a few state troopers to fill in. I decided to talk with Ann. Being both his wife and a state trooper would give me a good start. The two of them really work well with each other," Ben stated as William just listened. "It seems a road trip is in the works. She commented that she would talk to her husband about Fred. I do want to warn you, William, this next road trip is not going to Maine," Ben replied with a little trepidation.

"Maine is the only tent city I know of . . . north of here?" William asked with curiosity.

"Yes, north of here. There is one in upper Michigan, but the one she is talking about, is Southwest near the Mississippi River." Ben said, as to just put it out there.

"Southwest? William asked. "Besides, having to go on a long trip, I heard it was dangerous."

"Yes, William, I heard the same report on the survival radio as you," Ben replied in a serious tenor.

"Fred really needs to see a doctor. I will await Officer Ryan's visit. Hopefully, it will be soon," William commented. "Thank you, Ben."

"No problem, you have a tough decision to make," Ben said with sadness.

At this point, any further discussion with Ben was useless. Ben understood William perfectly. With his mission accomplished, he continued his journey home. Arriving at his house, he found several of the neighbors near the fire pit. He approached the area with caution. Hopefully, he would not be tarred and feathered. Salutations were given to Ben from many of his neighbors. To his shock, he received a "Good morning" from his wife, Alice. She said it without looking at Ben. She also continued to prepare the morning chores. The war is not over, but at least there is a truce, a step in the right direction.

Over the next several days, there was an uneasy peace. As long as no one bought up the family feud, there was coexistence. Instead of following the yellow brick path, everyone needed to avoid the land mines. That said, it still remained a step up from no communications. Like any storm, being in the eye provides only a brief calm. Soon a few leaves fluttered with a new and gentle breeze. One could feel the change.

While William and Ben awaited Officer Ryan, Jessica was hoping to receive some word from Joshua. Alice's point of view was dramatically different. She saw Humpty Dumpty completely shattered (her family's structure). She wanted to cement the pieces back together very carefully. Even though she sided with her daughter Jessica, Alice knew there would be no family without Ben. Hence, the cool salutation when Ben returned from Officer Ryan's house.

The only smart one was Randy. He took the right attitude: "I know nothing." He made no deep conversations with any of his family.

"If I were Randy, I would walk to the house that look like in *Wuthering Heights.* Then I asked the drunk if I could visit him for a while. Say about, I don't know, maybe three weeks." The drunk would hand him his own bottle of whiskey. Next he would tell Randy where the bathroom is. You know, where he can crawl to so he won't fall. As they say in Canada, "pretty dismal, eh?"

The second half of the storm had begun. It was more bark than a bite. First, Jessica was getting restless. Several days without Joshua was like going through withdrawal. She needed Joshua to be whole again. Family is family, but to her, Joshua was the future. She wondered countless times how Joshua was feeling "right now." As the lyrics in the Meatloaf song go: "What is it going to be boy, yes or no?"

And he better not say, "Let me sleep on it." Without cell phones, it is really torture.

Jessica was pacing in her bedroom. She had to go to the rock that was just past William's house. How can she walk there by herself? It would start another flare-up with her family. Who can she walk with? Hmmm . . . her mother? Corny.

How about her brother Randy? Awkward. She could walk with Mr. Henderson's son. After all, he really liked her. But no, that would be using him. She had been down that road before. How about the drunk? It would have to be before noon. After noon, he would be crawling. Maybe she could put a leash on him. She could be practicing walking a dog. There has to be an answer.

Sometimes the Lord answers in mysterious ways. She went to the fire pit to get some coffee and eggs. Seeing her dad gave her the chills. She was not in an accepting state of mind toward her dad, at least not yet. She sat some fifty feet away. Poor Ben, he must feel like a man with a contagious disease. When she sat down, she found herself next to the union man and the divorcee's daughter. Jessica was now emotionally attached to Joshua. It seems the divorcee's daughter is in her own predicament.

Mr. Henderson's son, Steven, being turned down by Jessica, has turned his hopes toward the divorcee's daughter. But she, due to her own mother's social steering, was interested in Randy. Randy is

Jessica's brother. Gads, I know what you're thinking. You think this is complicated and turning into a daytime soap opera. Trust me, it's not.

Feeling a little awkward at first, the divorcee's daughter started to talk to Jessica. At first, Jessica seemed annoyed with her. She let Jessica know that Steven was sending out vibes to her. She has feelings for someone else. *Hmmm,* Jessica thought, *there is no else in this concentration camp* (at least that's how she now views her living conditions).

"Someone else?" Jessica said. (She thought it better that it not be her dad. She would definitely leave this concentration camp.)

"Yes, Randy," the divorcee's daughter said.

"Randy, my brother," Jessica spurted out as she gagged on her coffee.

"Yes, he is polite, caring, and highly intelligent. I think about him a lot.

Jessica was now totally distracted from her own sorrows. She wanted to tell her that Randy was in love with his Buick. After they get married, Randy better sleep on top. If he slept on the bottom, his new bride (the Buick) would crush him. Like her dad, Jessica composed herself. *Crap!* she thought. Her dad is messing up her life; she does not want to mess up her brother's life. After all, her brother has always been kind to everyone.

Poof! A light went off. No, strike that. A whole gaggle of lights went off—enough lights to light up a ball field.

"Let's go for a walk," Jessica said to the divorcee's daughter. "I don't want to talk in front of other people. Just one minute. I will tell my mom, so no one will be nervous."

"Okay," the divorcee's daughter explained.

Damn, Jessica thought as she pinched herself while they walked toward William's house. It's a triple play. She can help the divorcee's daughter, her brother Randy, and herself all at the same time.

Meantime at Joshua's collaborative, it was a different situation. The only one who had an issue with Joshua was his father, Daniel. He feels Joshua did not use common sense, going on a road trip with an underage girl. Now Daniel feels his son has caused a real problem. Not only is there tension between Daniel and Ben, but this is a reflection on Daniel himself. Being a father of both a girl and a boy, Daniel understands how Ben felt. Still, Ben had no right to confront Daniel.

Fact is, Joshua being twenty-two, is of legal age. The bottom line: Joshua did secure a gas generator for their collaborative. And the whole collaborative is grateful to Joshua.

What is really strange is Joshua's mom likes Jessica, and she is a hard lady to please. She has her PhD in psychology. Most of her friends live in Cambridge, Massachusetts. She did attend a university in Cambridge and set up a practice nearby. There are well-renowned colleges and universities in Cambridge. It is a highly liberal city; perhaps more liberal than San Francisco. Her friends are on the same mind-set as she is. It is the reason she will not make friends in her local community. It is Jessica's beauty and charm that impresses her.

Oftentimes, she is at odds with her husband, Daniel. Both have a strong personality. One might say that two type A personalities do not mix well. Jessica approached her on that day. Jessica took an interest in Joshua's mom's books and her writings. It is something that no one in the community, or one of Daniel's friends, has done. Jessica did try and smooth out a trying time. She hopes that her son and Jessica can have a lasting relationship.

It is tiresome to see her son with so many different woman. She blames her husband, Daniel, for this atrocious habit. Joshua did explain to his mom what happened on their road trip. But Joshua did leave out the encounter in the hot tub. Both Joshua and Jessica will keep that a secret. What would there to be gain by telling anyone? It was a beautiful moment for the both of them. It was the first time that Jessica spent a night with any man. They had encountered danger on the trip. Jessica and Joshua depended on each other. There were no cell phones or police to protect them. Here on the East Coast, the place resembled the early Wild West during the 1800s.

Being in the hot tub with Jessica was different than all the other women in Joshua's life. After all, Joshua was at the top of his game: tall, good-looking, and spoke a number of languages. These qualities made him appealing to women. He really enjoyed his popularity. Even his father was proud of his son.

It was that particular road trip that really affected Joshua. It was to be a quick trip down and back. If they did not engage in those firefights, perhaps it would be just a day trip. When Jessica was sitting next to him, he felt good. The EMP strike really has affected everyone. Staying inside of a home all the time, one can get cabin fever. With cars littering the roads everywhere, Joshua was blessed to be driving a jeep that works.

Like in a Mad Max movie, Joshua and Jessica went on that road trip together. Joshua could see that she really looked up to him. She needed Joshua to protect her. Staying at his friend's house that night will live in both their minds forever. Making love in the hot tub was emotional and special for both of them. Although she did not conceive that night, Joshua cannot stop thinking about her. She is a few months short of legal age. That thought haunts him. He never asked her, but deep in his soul he knew.

The EMP strike is both a curse and a blessing. If the EMP strike did not happen, he would not of meet Jessica. If the EMP strike did not happen, and he did an overnight with Jessica, he would be in a jail cell with some unsavory characters. Joshua has not really interacted with his other collaborative members. They only know Joshua has helped them. Not only did he produce the gas generator, but he takes them to the armory for food and medicines. It is only his father that is giving Joshua a hard time. He has told Joshua to stay away from Jessica. Trying to reason or talk to him would be useless. Joshua is of legal age and his own person. Discretion is the better part of valor.

Both the physical and emotional bonding with Jessica was strong. He does care for her. In his mind, he wants to do the right thing. Joshua has been around making a good living and dating females when it suits him. He understands that Jessica has not had that experience. Would Joshua be robbing her of her youth? How disappointed would her father (Ben) be? He promised Jessica that he would leave a note under the rock near William's house. Not to leave the note would cause even more pain to Jessica, perhaps even death. She has lost some serious weight. If anything happened to her, he would not forgive himself. *I am also sure neither will a lot of other people.*

Stress, too damn young to have all this stress. What a paradox.

Joshua's dad hopes he never sees her again. His mom is already planning for the wedding. As Joshua paces back and forth, indecision is eating at his soul. Too young to have wrinkles (Botox anyone?), time to get off the pot. He will write a note. He has to have some honor, or what kind of a man would he be?

With his father by their fire pit, Joshua headed for the house. Seeing his mom, is always a pleasant encounter. Walking in the front door, he noticed his mother on the sofa reading a novel. As long as his mom was in the living room, his father would stay away. It's kind of like putting garlic and a few crosses to create a safe zone. Not that his father is a vampire, but at least there would be a temporary truce.

Joshua went to the desk. He grabbed a pen and paper. His head was spinning. *Dear . . . Nope, maybe that is too impersonal. My dearest Je—damn! How to start?* Joshua clasped his hands behind his head and rocked back and forth. At that moment, his mother glanced up. She looked at Joshua and uttered.

"Truth dear, just the truth," His mother decried in a soft but deliberate voice.

"Huh?" Joshua said in a puzzled tone.

His mother just looked at Joshua with a half-smile, but a smile just the same. She then went back to reading. Joshua was stunned. How could his mother possibly know what he is doing? *Holy crap!* Joshua thought. *Maybe females are more in touch with their emotions than men.* Maybe it's time for him to grow up. Now Joshua unclasped his hands. With paper and pen in hand, he says to himself. "Truth, I will just write the truth." With emotions running high, Joshua's words started to flow like Niagara Falls:

> *My Dearest Jessica, to say that I don't think about you every waking moment would be a colossal lie. During the trip we took, no matter how much danger we were in, you were my guardian angel. I did not plan to spend the night with you. Perhaps the Gods intervened in my master plan. The time I spent with you was precious. Sometimes it is hard to face reality or the truth. I kept my feelings about*

your age, in a denying state of mind. Your family, your upbringing, it is of a purity that is hard to find. From this point of view, I understand your dad's anger (my dad's also). In my short few years of working, I have experienced a lot. To say that I do not want you for the rest of my life would also be a colossal lie. Yet I do not want to rob you of your youth and future, to experience a world outside of your home and family, mostly of you having a chance to meet other men. The EMP strike has certainly changed our lives. We both saw the power lines being put in the State of Maine. It is a matter of time before they come to us. To be with you always, is really screaming from my heart! I know you are living in a tense and fluid situation. It is only a few months before your magical birthday. Selfishly, I would like to run off with you. Where would we run to? How would we survive? To save your honor, I would like to approach your dad. I am not asking for his forgiveness or blessing, but just explain the dangers we went through. You are the first woman I have ever fallen in love with. I will write once a week. As strongly as I feel for you, I also feel strongly that I must confront your father.

—Love Joshua

With a sigh, Joshua put the letter in an envelope. He went into the kitchen and got a plastic baggy. With the letter sealed, he put it into the plastic bag. Without even looking up, his mother did another half-smile. *Holy crap,* thought Joshua, *it's like he was following his own mother's playbook.* Joshua walked outside, his hands on the plastic bag. He then put it in his back pocket. Looking at the sun, he knew it was getting on to late afternoon.

The army jeep that was on loan is for trips to the armory. The armory is the only place where anyone can get supplies. Since the EMP strike, all pharmacies, stores, even churches have been looted; many of them set on fire. It is a sad state of affairs that those who possess evil in their hearts cause so much pain for the rest. Cargo planes that were equipped with a Faraday shield are flying in supplies. They have also bought in some planes from the unaffected areas, mainly anything west of the Mississippi.

Joshua knew his father was watching. What? Am I under house arrest? There are two cardinal rules for the jeep: one, someone has to ride shotgun; two, there has to be a least one firearm inside the jeep. The jeep was old, long before electronic ignitions. They have tried to bring in a few more jeeps on the cargo planes. Trouble is, it takes so much room and weight. The space and weight is needed for food, water, and medical supplies. When the jeeps do come in, there is a priority list. Military, police, and hospitals usually grab them first.

Joshua's dad (Daniel) has taken the keys. Daniel usually asks another collaborative member to accompany him. Like a forward scout on patrol, Joshua was taking in his options. Being grounded was his father's motive. No sense to show anger; it will accomplish nothing. Not wanting to show his hand, Joshua kept his cool.

Today was not the right time to do anything. After all, he just came back from Tent City. As he was milling around near the fire pit, he grabbed some food and water.

As Joshua was sitting and eating his supper, other neighbors approached him.

Everyone wanted to know about his trip to Tent City. Mostly, they were all hungry for information. As Joshua started to tell his tale, many more of the collaborative neighbors gathered around Joshua. He was in his element.

Like giving a performance, he was the star of the collaborative. First of all, he did procure the gas generator. All the neighbors received some electricity for an hour each other day. It is enough to keep the fridge cool, do some ironing, and use what gadgets that were not fried by the EMP strike.

Joshua was a natural-born salesman; maybe he should have been a performer. Everyone listened as he told his tale of walking through the dangerous parts of outer Boston. He was very careful of what he said about Jessica. He did not want his words to come back and haunt him.

As Joshua was talking, there must have been at least fifteen to twenty people who were there. At one point, one neighbor bought over a few bottles of wine. For a while, the neighbors were happy to get news and to be entertained. What pleased most of the neighbors was valuable information—information of hope and humanity.

There seems to be a smile on most faces. Joshua did not degrade or dishonor Jessica at all. In fact, just the opposite. He told everyone how brave and composed she remained as danger was everywhere. Maybe someday Jessica might be his wife. He wants to have fun memories of all his actions hence forward.

Joshua's dad was a good thirty feet from where he was talking. His father was smiling. But when Joshua looked at him, he had to turn away. Like a cat-and-mouse game, each had to check their demeanor. When Daniel turned away, he would mutter to himself, "That's my boy."

For a couple of hours, Joshua had them eating out of his hands. To be fair, there were no other tickets to be had. It was the only show around. Being fatigued and having a couple of glasses of wine, Joshua excused himself. The whole drama of Jessica, her dad, Joshua's dad, and the trip to Tent City has stripped him of his inner soul. It is strange how when one door closes, another opens. Joshua was at the end of his rope. This impromptu performance had energized him. Joshua had gotten his mojo back. Now he must push forward walking on eggshells. No more missteps. With his confidence building, he headed for his house.

As he opened the door, Joshua wanted to wash up and count sheep. After using the bathroom, he had to fill the back of the John. When the town water did flow, it came in with a light dirty-brown color. It could be used for the John, but not washing clothes or dishes. His mother was still on the sofa.

Joshua usually says "Good night, Mom," but tonight is different.

"Mom, I know it's early, but I am turning in. In the morning, I will be getting up early for a bike ride. I will be back by late morning. I need my exercise," Joshua said as concisely as he could.

"I understand, son, time to be a man," his mother said without looking up.

"Good night, ma," Joshua said cheerfully.

"Good night, Joshua," his mother replied confidently.

Like a sentry dog, his mother will be sleeping on the sofa all night.

Usually Daniel sleeps in the room that Joshua sleeps in—a little dysfunctional, but it makes for coexistence. Most of the time Joshua's mom lives alone in the house. Joshua is only home because of the EMP strike. Daniel loves the Florida heat, tango dancing, beach, and making his business calls. Joshua's mom is more of a homebody: reading, culture events, PBS, concerts, and calling her liberal friends in Cambridge, Massachusetts. She has been a good mom to her son and daughter.

It felt good to sleep next to a soft and beautiful creature like Jessica. At the same time, it came with a price. He had to not only be confident of his own actions, but to make sure Jessica was always protected and cared for. Tonight was for Joshua, a night of good sleep, with just one bathroom break. He slept well with his letter under the pillow. On the floor next to his pants, he kept his 9mm gun. Next to Jessica and his family, they were the two most personal items in his life.

When morning came, the outside weather was a little drizzle. It has been days since he came back from Tent City. He quietly got dressed. Checking his 9mm, he decided to bring a few extra clips with him. Usually his father sleeps at least until 8 a.m. without any clocks. Even though it was cloudy, many of the insects and birds were aroused. It was a precursor to the beginning of the day. Without electricity, Joshua used a Bic lighter to see with. He briefly opened the fridge door. There was a brown bag with his name on it. He opened it up. It was a sandwich made of eggs, veggies, and onions. With a smile on Joshua's face, he mumbled, "Bless you, Mom."

Wearing his blue jeans, boots, and a poncho, Joshua headed for his bicycle.

By car, it is close to a half-hour drive; by bike, at least a good two hours. Checking his water bottle and 9mm, he was set. No turning back. In his mind, it was the opportune time to bike. Most gangs are night owls. With the light drizzle, even they might not venture out.

It was a little weird to bike in the dark. He knew the roads well; his mind filled with thoughts of Jessica. It was his thoughts that kept him company. Ah, the thought of being in the jeep with Jessica. It is his ultimate goal. It is what drives him on this long and dangerous trip. Peddling for several minutes, Joshua could see the dawn of the new day. Perhaps he should be on a wharf at Key West, sipping on a Bloody Mary to welcome the sunrise with his new bride, Jessica. That is where he will suggest. What a daydream. Oh well, back to reality!

The night did fear him a little. Dogs or a wolf could come out plunging for him.

With daylight, Joshua felt safe with his 9mm, tucked in his pants. A bike has little more stealth than a car. He rode on mostly back roads.

After a couple of hours, he approached Officer Ryan's house. Joshua pulled the hood over his face, stopping a couple hundred feet before Officer Ryan's house. He took a sip from his water bottle. With the drizzle coming down, perhaps it gave him some cover. He could walk in the woods to their house, but he decided to go for it. Joshua came to the rock. He carefully looked around. No one in sight. He kissed the plastic bag with the note and placed it under the rock.

On the way back, it became a little more perilous. A dog started to bark. Joshua ran into the woods with his bike. Looking out for poison ivy and wet terrain, Joshua walked a good half hour. A few neighbors did step outside their homes to see what the commotion was about. Behind Officer Ryan's house, Joshua could see the sliding glass door.

As Joshua was walking slowly, quietly, Officer Ryan opened the sliding door. He wheeled out his old relic motorcycle. With helmet in hand, Officer Ryan looked around for a brief moment. Joshua's heart beat fast. He did not move. With the drizzle hitting his face, Officer Ryan put on his helmet. What an omen! Best to bike under the cloak of wet weather. As Officer Ryan kick-started his motorcycle, Joshua walked on another ten minutes.

Bringing his bike back onto the street, Joshua peddled back home. On his way, he could see the fires and heard the occasional crack of a 9mm gun. He smiled, even in this new battle-torn territory, love still conquers all.

An EMP Causality: Part III
Camille

Jessica came out of the house telling her mom, Alice, that she was going for a walk with Sarah, the divorcee's daughter. Her explanation was that she wanted to talk to Sarah about Randy. In reality, it was an attempt to deflect her mom from worrying about her. Jessica did not want to raise any more flags. Sarah is a little older and wiser than Jessica. In her mind, this is a win-win situation.

Jessica never really bonded with her brother Randy. He is five years older than her, and secondly Randy was always a hands-on guy, not much into relationships. During the day, he was an automobile mechanic. As far as Jessica knew, his only real love relationship was working on his own classic Buick. She had always referred to him as a grease monkey. But now, she feels ashamed of her thoughts and words toward her brother. Jessica had been so occupied with Joshua that she never paid attention to Randy. Somewhere in her quiet moments, she knew Randy was a kind and talented person. So if she was going to enter womanhood with Joshua, she knew she has to do a one-eighty with Randy.

Jessica always had a special bond with her dad, Ben. She knew her dad was hardworking and loyal to his wife, Alice. Jessica also knew her dad protected and guided her toward her adult life. After the EMP strike, it was her dad, her best friend Vivian, and her who went on the road trip. It was a journey filled with fear and excitement. They ventured out in search of water and supplies. Randy stayed behind to protect their home and the collaborative. The road trip was a bonding experience that few people will ever encounter. She truly was daddy's little girl.

As with most family feuds, the emotional scars ran deep. Perhaps, she hoped, the trip might benefit the entire family. The EMP attack and the road trip might provide a way to allow a little light into the family dynamic.

Sarah is a good bit taller than Jessica. She dresses modestly, is a good listener, and has many of the better qualities of her mother. She is a good cook, well-read, and her actions show a good upbringing. Her mother took her away from the inner city. As a single parent, the challenges are many. Her mother wanted to be in a good school system. She also wanted to live in the suburbs to give her daughter the best environment to succeed.

Both Jessica and Sarah have one thing in common. That is Mr. Henderson's son, Steven. First, Steven took a fancy to Jessica. It was difficult, but Jessica did not lead him on. Next Steven tried to take up with the Sarah. She thought well of him, but the chemistry was not right. Randy is more to her liking; he also is a hands-on guy. Difference is, Randy is more diversified and well-read. It is his looks, stature, the way he dresses, even his scent that appealed to her.

Sarah was nervous to have this special encounter with Jessica. She had no idea that Jessica and her brother were not that close. Now Jessica has to be on her game. She really wants to go to Williams's house to see if Joshua left her a note. He promised to leave the note under the rock, just past William's house.

Multitasking, Jessica really had to take an interest in this new friendship. She must take it seriously. They both started to walk slowly past the drunk's house.

"I'm a little nervous to be talking with you," Sarah said, trembling.

"Don't be. Just be yourself. Really, my mom thinks you are a classy woman.

When I saw you talking to Steven, I felt a little jealous. Truth is, I knew Steven was not for me. When I looked at you, I see a beautiful woman," Jessica said with a smile.

"Thank you," Sarah said as she touched Jessica's forearm. "I was hoping to understand a little about Randy. To be honest with you, I am attracted to Randy."

"My brother has not been dating since our move from Nebraska. When we were in Nebraska, there was one woman he liked. She was pretty and bright. She hoped Randy would go on to college, maybe to be a premed student or high-tech software type. She got accepted to a California University for nursing. My brother had great potential, but he was drawn to work with his hands. She just gave up on Randy. "Last I heard, she met someone in California," Jessica said while her mind drifted someplace else.

Approaching William's house, Jessica was definitely nervous. She had to know if Joshua left a note, as he promised. Rubbing her hands with a fast-pounding heart, it was obvious that she was extremely anxious. Just then, Fred came out of the house. Fred always likes to greet any newcomers that might visit the household.

"Morning, how are you?" Fred said with Joy.

"We are both fine. And you?" remarked Sarah.

"I am mad today!" Fred said with a tone of anger.

"Oh no! Why are you mad, Fred?" asked Sarah.

"William won't take me to work today. I need to see my girlfriend, LuAnn. I think John is going to start talking to her. I told him to stay away from my girlfriend. She's my girlfriend. He needs to find somebody else," Fred said in anger. "I am going to get you, John, you just wait and see."

"Whew, I think William's car is not working, Fred. I am sure LuAnn misses you too," Sarah commented.

"Excuse me for just two minutes. I just need to check on something. It will only take a couple of minutes," Jessica said with bated breath.

Without even looking for an answer, Jessica left Fred and her together. Like a junky who needs an immediate fix, Jessica walked fast toward the big rock still within eyesight of Sarah and Fred.

At first, she hesitated. What if the note isn't there? How would she act with other people? Frankly, how can she carry on? What does she have to live for? Who can she trust? Her life will be a massive dark hole, moving aimlessly down a dark canyon. Why did Joshua come into her life if he does not come through?

Her soul and body belong to Joshua. Life without him is not life at all.

At this moment in time, Jessica's thoughts were not rational. Yes, Joshua did come on to Jessica. He possessed looks, charm, and some worldly experience. Many a young man might do the same thing. It is an immature act. An act of being selfish and a little bit (may I say) being egotistical. Jessica, on the other hand, could have sought the advice of someone else, an older woman with a more experienced perspective. Even without that insight, her best friend Vivian did warn her that she was over her head.

Vivian is still her best friend. She is a tall, statuesque woman of African American descent. With her mother, Camille, she grew up in the bad sections of Boston. Living in run-down, multi-apartment dwellings. She has been exposed to a lot: drugs, crime, prostitution, and the bad sides of human nature. A constant flow of men came into their apartment complex. Most of them had the same characteristics: false promises, fast talk, and mostly just users. Many became fathers, but most did not stick around to father their child. Her mother, Camille, who always wears a big cross on her necklace, tried to shield Vivian. She did not want her daughter to become the victim of the ghetto life. She swore that she would have her daughter break the chain.

At one point, she and her daughter, moved to Kissimmee, Florida. The surroundings there were better. A warmer weather and a different pace of life seemed to agree with both Camille and her daughter. After some time, however, complications started to arise. The cost of living was less, but finding work was difficult. One had to know someone. Employers were not as understanding as in the north. In addition, the health benefits, food assistance, and housing support were less. But mostly, family support was missing. There were no aunts, uncles, or cousins around. So when her mother needed surgery, they moved back out of necessity, in spite of the wintry weather.

Through persistence, Camille was able to secure living accommodations in the suburbs of Boston. Vivian attended the same high school as Jessica. They were both outsiders: Jessica from Nebraska, and Vivian from the projects and Florida. Vivian was street-smart, statuesque, and just intimidating. Inside she was smart and kind. Vivian was drawn to her, as a good friend. Jessica, on the other hand, had a good family life: mother, father, brother, and a nice house. It is the missing family structure that Vivian yearned for. Yes, her mother gave her everything, but she missed not having a dad around.

When Joshua met Jessica, Vivian was there. Jessica was totally infatuated with him. She was in a trance. Her eyes and body were melting as he was talking. Vivian, on the other hand, saw through him; she has been down that road many times. For Jessica, it was a soothing musical masterpiece. To Vivian, the soothing musical piece was sugar coating, like a belly dancer with the sound clips in her hand. As the soothing music was playing, a tall cobra came out of the basket. The snake was coiling up, higher and higher. Finally the soothing music stopped. The belly dancer faded away and the snake bent its head back just so slightly. Only Jessica was in the snake's path. *Hiss-whap.*

This is how Vivian saw Joshua. She tried to warn Jessica, but Jessica was already over the edge. She was in a trance, in desperate need of an exorcism. Vivian and her mother did still come over. They depended on Randy to pick them up. Coming to the Randals' house was a safe place inside the collaborative. It was a timeout from the dangerous apartment building where they lived.

At the rock, Jessica seemed to be frozen in time. The few brief seconds there seemed like an eternity to her. As Fred and Sarah were talking, Jessica blocked the noise. As her emotions reached a fever pitch, she bent down, her palms sweaty and heart pounding. When she put her hands under the rock, she felt a plastic bag. What? A plastic bag? Is this some kind of cruel trick? If her heart pounded any faster, she would certainly have a coronary. She picked up the bag and saw a note. Damn her emotions! This is too much to take. Now Jessica felt a mix of emotions. She was elated she received the note, but she needed to be alone. She read the first few sentences. Joshua had feelings for her. Time, she needs time for herself. She cannot blow off Sarah.

While Sarah was talking to Fred, she kept looking at Jessica. She was puzzled. What was going on? Jessica looked and saw a bewildered Sarah. *Oh Jesus,* thought Jessica, *I have got to pay attention to her or it will lead to problems.* Jessica put the plastic bag with the letter in her front denim pocket. Hastily, Jessica walked back to Fred and Sarah. Within a few minutes, she arrived; all was calm.

"Sorry, I was in a daze. I have been through a lot," Jessica remarked.

"I know, and I shouldn't just be talking about myself," Sarah said with a tone of empathy.

"It's okay, you're a nice person, and my brother is a good soul," Jessica cried out. "Well, Fred, it's been nice chatting with you; we have to get back," Jessica commented as she grabbed the divorcee's daughter's arm.

As they walked back to their respected houses, Jessica stopped.

"Listen, my brother or most men do not like to be overwhelmed. They have to think it was their idea. I could talk to him; even my mother could talk to him. Trouble is, my brother is very intuitive, and it could push him away." Jessica spoke in a calculated manner. She was starting to grow up fast. She continued, "I feel, I do know him better than most. Go to him, and ask him for a favor. Tell him the next time he goes to the armory, you would like a few baking products. You would like to bake a casserole for the collaborative. Make sure you say it's for the collaborative and not just for him. Hopefully, he will invite you to go for the ride. Two are always required for any rides. It is for the security of his car and that of the collaborative. Too many gangs out there."

"Thank you, Jessica, thank you very much," Sarah commented as she headed toward her own house.

Soon it would be their turn for the generator. She really wanted to help her mom. Each house has access to a generator every other day, for an hour or two.

Even though it is noisy, it makes them feel like human beings: the refrigerator, iron—even vacuuming the house is a joyous time. Imagine before the EMP strike, doing house cleaning was work then. Now it is a welcoming event! The divorcee would be in a daydream while running the vacuum machine. Quickly, she would also turn to use the iron to take care of those delicate clothes—a little bit of humanity, while outside, there was smoke and the occasional sound of a 9mm gun.

Jessica's house was a little bit further on. For her, it was a double whammy. She had a big-ass smile. So big that even an undertaker could not remove it. As she got closer to her house, she saw several people around the open fire. It was a morning ritual in the collaborative. They cook food and listen to the survival radio; some wash their clothes. Others even take a hot bath behind a protective tarp. Was it the sight of her father that caused a mood swing? Jessica kept her cool.

"Morning, Jessica," her mom said.

"Morning, Ma," Jessica replied.

"Morning, Jessica, I made some breakfast for you," Jessica's dad (Ben) said with as much courage as possible. It was an oak leaf, a sign of a truce.

Before Jessica could open her mouth, she noticed several people looking at her. Her mother, brother, the union man, even the drunk were looking at her. For one of the first times in her life, Jessica thought of a proper response. If she wanted to make a life with Joshua, it was time for her to grow up.

"Thanks, I like to wash up a bit. I will be out in a few minutes," Jessica replied in a monotone voice. Jessica felt comfortable and happy with her response.

As she approached the front door, she noticed her mother. The pain on her face said a thousand words. Jessica felt bad. She did not want to cause any more pain for anyone. The fact is, she too was going through an enormous transformation.

Coming back from Tent City, she saw the power companies hard at work. It will be several months before they reach their own collaborative.

Jessica quickly entered her bedroom. Locking her bedroom door, she took the plastic bag with the letter in it out of her front pocket. Pulling the letter out of the plastic bag, she began to read. With deep emotions, she concentrated on the parts of the letter that she put her hopes and dreams in. Parts of the letter said Joshua was thinking of her constantly. Parts of the letter said she was there by his side during their perilous journey.

There is an old saying, "Many people do perceptive listening," which means they extract only what they want to hear. It is a way of denying part of the truth that is unpleasant. What Jessica was doing is "perceptive reading." She only saw what was pertinent to her dreams. Joshua did tell her the truth. It is what Joshua's mother recommend that he do. The Truth is that she is young, and if she hooks up with Joshua, she would forfeit her youth to Joshua. The truth is that they need a plan to live, work, and a means to survive.

Joshua had the same desire for Jessica, but he was also a realist—a realist, because Joshua has been on his own. He knew the hardships of paying bills, buying food, clothing, and car expenses. He has expressed these concerns in his letter. Jessica just ignored them and fast-forwarded to her dream of a never-ending existence based on love alone. To go from high school right into marriage would strip Jessica of a life—a life that helps in the building blocks of fruitful and rewarding memories. Joshua did understand this, but Jessica did not. If Jessica did date other men, how would they compare to Joshua? It would be like playing in the big leagues, and then being sent down to the minors.

Jessica felt she had what she always pined for. She was not going to let it go. Now it is a matter of time, and a few difficult pleasantries with her dad. After a few moments, Jessica put the letter back in her front pocket. Time to grow up and go outside. As she went outside, she saw her mom.

"Hi mom, I have to get my breakfast. I'll come back to talk to you," Jessica said with a smile.

"All right, dear!" Jessica's mom replied.

Painfully, she walked up to her dad and took the plate of food he prepared for her.

"Thanks for the food, and the coffee," she said to her dad without even looking at him.

"You're welcome," he commented in a sad and hurtful tone.

Jessica sensed the pain in her dad's voice, but she too was sad and upset with him. Jessica walked by many others, including her brother Randy. She knew if she talked to Randy, it would cause even more family upheavals. She could talk to the drunk; that would be neutral, friendly. Jessica proceeded to her mom. If there ever is a chance for family peace, Alice would be the power broker.

Alice was happy to see Jessica come to her, at the same time, she was a little nervous. Jessica looked drawn; her weight was seriously down. If electricity is ever restored, Alice would probably take Jessica out to get a few cheeseburgers.

She could use some meat on that frame of hers. Jessica and her mom had a cordial but superficial talk. Jessica did tell her the wishes of Sarah, the divorcee's daughter. Alice was grateful that Jessica took part in the welfare of the family. She wanted to open up with Jessica about her relationship with her dad. Somehow, Alice knew, this was not the time. Progress has been made, but let's not blow it, she thought.

For the next several days, there was a truce within the Randal clan and across the collaborative. Finally, it was time for Randy to do his weekly armory run. What was shocking was that he had asked Sarah, the divorcee's daughter, to accompany him. The two people who were ecstatic were Jessica and her mom, Alice. It was not a real date but a joint adventure. Randy did come over to where Jessica and Alice were. He asked Jessica if he wanted her friend, Vivian, to come back with him. She had to think about it a minute. Jessica did miss her best friend, but she did not want to be lectured. She knew Vivian would give a series of warnings about Joshua. To Jessica, this had to be her decision alone. When and if she needs help or guidance, she will ask for it.

Jessica was maturing, she hesitated, and then she thought of the positives. If she invited Vivian, her mom and others will think Jessica is coming back emotionally. She needed time—time for her to work on her master plan.

"That will be fine, Randy. It will be nice to see her again," Jessica said, putting up a false front.

Jessica felt that if she was up front with Vivian, she would back down and not talk about Joshua. Jessica had to take control of destiny in her own life. What a difference a month makes. Last month she was an insecure teenager who needed her dad to shield her. Now she was a woman on a mission—a mission that will take her into womanhood.

Randy smiled and said, "No problem, sis."

"Sis," he had called me that before. I never knew how precious that was to me. I never had a close relationship with my brother. Now, I really cherish

it. No matter what my future is, my brother and I are destined to be closer. In her mind and prayers, she asked her brother for forgiveness—forgiveness for not seeing the qualities and the kindness her brother processes. Seeing his smile sent a warm glow that penetrated her soul.

Randy started up the Buick; it was a familiar sound, the sound of the heart of the collaborative beating. The Buick was not only humming but glowed like a shiny star that lit up the darkest of nights. With a few gasoline cans, a 9mm gun, and several clips, Randy had enough firepower to fight a small battle. They took off. Most of the collaborative members did not pay heed to what was happening. It was at this most important moment that Alice and her daughter were in sync. They both smiled to see Randy with Sarah, a beautiful woman. They both hoped it wouldn't be the last time.

With a temporary inner peace, Jessica decided to circulate. She calculated that if she was to stay any longer with her mom, it would send the wrong signals out. Her beef was with her dad. She did not want to degrade him in front of the other members of the collaborative. When all else fails, the drunk was the go-to person. She knew that he always enjoys talking to a pretty woman.

The afternoon went as any typical day: the sounds of the generator, and an occasional crack of a 9 mm. News was always hard to come by. Many times, listening to the "survival radio" was like listening to an old rerun of *I Love Lucy*. The government did not want people to panic. Down south, there were many causalities because of the lack of air-conditioning. A little west, past Ohio, Biker gangs were on the prowl. Lastly, near the epicenter, just outside New York City, there was physical damage. That is where the largest loss of life occurred.

As Jessica was circulating, many of the collaborative were curious about her trip to Tent City. How large was it? Most wanted to know what the government was doing. Only the union man had cynical and sarcastic remarks. He was still angry that the government was not better prepared. He was a devoted union man and a registered Democrat. The Hendersons and Ben tried talking to him. They told him that no government preparation could handle the magnitude of this catastrophe. He was not going to listen. Most pitied his wife.

It was getting on late in the afternoon. Today was a warm and humid day. Soon the bugs and mosquitoes will be out. Many have already gone home. Go home to what? Without electricity (except for the generator), it is quite boring. Those who stayed are close to the fire. It keeps the bugs away, and there is always something magical about a fire. Whether it is a camp or a frat party, gathering around a fire gives off a cozy feeling.

By mid-afternoon, those who were still outside were anxiously waiting for Randy and his Buick. Alice, Ben, the divorcee, and even Jessica were waiting for Randy. Finally, a little before dusk, the sound of the Buick could be heard. There was always a sigh of relief when they return home safely. Jessica noticed there was somebody in the back seat. It wasn't Vivian, but who? The Buick finally stopped. Randy and Sarah got out. They started to unpack supplies from the back seat. In the back seat, jammed with all the supplies, was Camille, Vivian's mother.

Hmmm, thought Jessica, *this is a turn of events.* She was a little puzzled and also frightened. She knew Vivian's cousin was shot right outside their apartment complex. They are in a no man's land, an extremely dangerous place. Every time Randy pulls in, he is always on high alert. If Camille hears the Buick at her complex, she runs down the stairs with a loaded gun. Camille has already fired her gun at several thugs. Most of them are cowards; they will go where there is no resistance.

Camille exited the Buick. She looks a bit disheveled. Her pants are wrinkled and her hair is in a mess. It was not like her. She then saw Ben and walked to him.

Randy and the divorcee's daughter, Sarah, continued to unload supplies. Toilet paper—that was what many, especially the women, were looking for. Randy and a few of the collaborative members carefully divided out the haul. Each member got their fair share.

Jessica was getting anxious. She really wanted to know if Vivian was all right. After a good ten minutes, Camille finally went over to grab some cooked food. As she was about to sit down, the drunk came over and offered her a drink. She had a smile on her face—I guess that means yes. Ben was busy working the fire pit and talking to William. Jessica could not wait any longer. She got up and walked over to Camille.

As Jessica reached them, the drunk raised his whiskey glass.

"Today is my lucky day, I have the company of two beautiful females," the drunk commented, taking a sip from his glass.

"Now you know you have to eat" Jessica said, in a caring tone.

"Yes, I know, I will "The drunk replied.

"Why don't you grab a plate of food, and join us" Jessica said, using a little firmness in her voice.

"Okay! Okay! I got the message," the drunk replied as he gulped the last of the whiskey in his glass, he then stumbled over to the fire pit.

Today, both William and Ben were doing the honors. It is really weird to see William cook. He seems like a good cook, but he hardly eats anything. Taking care of Fred requires a lot of cooking. Fred is the opposite of William. He is a compulsive eater. William would like to hide some of the food for Fred's own good. If he did that, it would be against Fred's "human rights." Before the EMP strike, William carefully monitored Fred's sugar level. Now, without any test strips, it is impossible.

"Oh, hi Jessica. How are you? You're looking good." Camille asked in a friendly manner. "I am fine, thanks for asking. I am surprised to see you here. Is Vivian all right? I hope there is nothing wrong. Please tell me there is nothing wrong with Vivian!" Jessica asked, exposing an extremely nervous voice. She now had a strong guilt feeling. Since she had tied up with Joshua, Jessica had all but dropped Vivian.

If anything happened to her, how would she forgive herself?

Camille was famished. As Jessica was talking, she started to eat. She wanted to wash the food down with a drink that the drunk gave her. But Camille saw the anxiety in Vivian's eye, even though she did not understand her alarm.

Camille put the food down. She looked for a towel, then decided to wipe her mouth with her sleeves. It was a little gross, but better than talking with her mouth full.

"My dear, heaven's no! She is fine. She could not come here today. I don't want my sister to be left alone. It is a lot more dangerous there than it is over here. My nephew was shot and died. The thugs are always prowling around. I taught my daughter how to use a gun. We have moved away from the projects to get away from this crap. I was really impressed with your high school, with the caliber of your students. Vivian has really taken an interest in school. Now, we are back to square one." Camille started to weep. "I think the devil works in threes," Camille said as she could no longer talk.

"Please don't cry, everything will be fine," Jessica commented. With a bit of humanity, she put her arms around Camille. She was standing and decided to stoop down. Jessica put her head on Camille's shoulders. It took everything she had not to cry with Camille.

"My nephew was such a good boy. High grades and trained in the martial arts. He was just trying to protect an elderly woman. The thugs shot him. It meant nothing to them. Every time when the elderly come back from the armory, they become easy targets. When I saw those B———, I shot at them; it was not a warning shot." Camille spurted out, not trying to hide a tinge of anger.

At this point in time, the drunk came back with his food. He almost dropped his plate as he stumbled, trying to sit down.

"You're really lucky, Jessica, to have your father. He is such a good protector and provider," Camille said, trying to hide her envy.

"Here! Here!" The drunk said with a salute.

Jessica was feeling a little uneasy with the praises about her dad, Ben.

It was best just to keep quiet. What the love of a man can do to the family clan.

"I really hope that I can see Vivian sometime soon," Jessica said, trying to deflect any more talk about her father.

"We'll see, my dear. She has told me you are taken up with your new boyfriend," Camille said as she put her hand on Jessica's shoulder.

"I . . . have been . . ." Jessica said as she composed herself. "Yes, I have been seeing someone, but Vivian has always been my friend. I don't see any reason why we still can't be friends."

"Hmmm." Camille mumbled out, "Vivian did not want to talk to me about your new friend. She only said you were extremely taken by him. Listen, Jessica, Vivian does not have a lot of good friends.

Boyfriends can come, and boyfriends *can* go, but good friends should stay together a long time."

"You are right. I really do miss her. I am just going through a lot right now.

This EMP strike has really messed up my life," Jessica said with a little confusion.

"I understand, but you are so young, and beautiful. You have your whole life in front of you," Camille said, using a touch of motherly advice.

"Egad! This is so complicated. No one seems to understand what I am up against!" Jessica cried out.

"It always is at your age. You forget, we adults have been there. We weren't born old. It just kind of crept up on us," Camille said.

"Funny, Joshua said some of the same things," Jessica replied with a bewildered smile. "I just did not want to listen."

"So he has a name! Well now, we are making progress," Camille uttered, continuing on with her wisdom." It sounds like he also has some honor."

"Yes, honor, looks, charm, and he is very talented. He speaks many languages. How can I ask for anything more? I know it is going too fast. He even said that we should slow it down. It's just when this EMP blast went off, I didn't know if we would survive it. We didn't plan on it. We were caught up in a serious firefight. Joshua stood by me. He risked his life for me. My father wouldn't even let anyone talk. I am so angry and hurt," Jessica said as she started to cry.

Like the changing of the guards, Camille put her arms around Jessica. It took several minutes for Jessica to stop crying.

Poor Ben, he was a good seventy feet away as he witnessed the whole act play out. Like a poor soul at the Spanish Inquisition, Ben felt he was being tried by a series of judges, each one slamming his gavel down. "Guilty." It was unanimous. Where is the drunk? Ben has a last request. He needs a drink quickly. It might be his last request before the sentencing.

Both Camille and Jessica decided that it was enough crying for one night. Stress—too much damn stress. Camille looked at Jessica.

"Listen, Jessica, can I ask for a big favor" Camille spurted out.

"Anything. What can I do for you?" Jessica said with optimism.

"Can you ask your brother, Randy, if he could set up a hot bath for me?" Camille replied with anticipation.

Jessica smiled and commented, "Yes, I can. I will ask him to boil some hot water. I am sure his friend Sarah can help with your clothes."

"Sarah? Friend?" Camille remarked with a big smile.

"Well, we are working on it," Jessica said proudly.

"We?" Camille said with a little curiosity.

"My mother and I. It's time for Randy to take a break from his Buick."

"My god, this is better than HBO. You have a regular soap opera going on. We will call it *The Daily Events of the Randal Clan.*"

Jessica smiled; she needed a little humor. Immediately she got a hold of her brother. She also told him that Camille needed to borrow some clothes. She insisted that Sarah could handle that department. Her mother, the divorcee, was close to Camille's shape. Randy said fine. Little did Randy know, he was being set up, like a frog on a slow burn. Truth be told, Randy does find Sarah attractive.

He isn't the forty-year-old virgin yet. Without Jessica and her mom, I am sure he would be. It's not divine intervention. More like a family nudge, to steer him in the right direction.

In Ben's eye, this is going from worse to super-super worse. Maybe he should use his gun to end it. How about just burning at the stake. After all, the fire pit was super-hot. No, how about using a knife? He could charge at a gang of thugs. Of course they would fill him with the spent bullets from their 9mm. At least he would go out in glory and get the respect he deserved.

Ben put his hands on his knees. He smiled, like in a good Rocky movie. Ben said to himself, *Heh! Adrienne, I am getting the crap knocked out of me. Time to go to bed. In the morning, I'll climb those stairs in my sweats. Whoops! No stairs. How about just a casual walk to William's house? Yeah, that's it.*

At least William is friendly, neutral. Ben decided to check out early.

He could read a book. Maybe *War and Peace*. Actually, a book with a lot of pictures. This was not Ben's night. Maybe tomorrow would be better?

Will you believe next week will be better?" Realizing it was too much for him, Ben just went inside the house."

Both Alice and Jessica are noticing the toll that this family feud is having on Ben. Then Alice thought, *What about Jessica?* She was an underage woman going into hostile territory. No one knew if Jessica would be seen again alive. At least Joshua did protect her. He also saw to it that she came home fine. How many have already lost their lives because of this EMP blast? Even though things are tense at the Randal clan, they are still alive.

The rest of the afternoon went well. It was strange to see Randy sitting next to Sarah. Jessica helped her mom with clothes and a little house cleaning. Camille was in heaven. She was sitting in a nice hot bathtub. The drunk even offered to bring her a glass of red wine. The divorcee told him she would bring her the wine. Doesn't get much better than this. Alice and Jessica did wash Camille's clothes. Tomorrow was going to be an important day for her.

She was going to meet with Officer Ryan.

Now both William, Fred, and Camille are seeking safe passage to Tent City.

Ben had asked Ann (Officer Ryan's wife) about William and Fred. Ben knew he could not choose between Camille and Fred. He could not have wars on multiple fronts. Let Officer Ryan take the heat for choosing. Neither Camille nor William knew that each were seeking passage to Tent City. Camille did confide in Ben. He basically let her know that Officer Ryan should show up tomorrow. Ben did offer to let her sleep on the sofa.

As the afternoon wore on, Camille just circulated with other collaborative members. Soon even Jessica decided to turn in. It was strange; as dusk started to settle, only a few people were still up. There was smoke and the crackle of a 9mm going off almost every hour. To most of the members of the collaborative, it became tolerable.

Randy and Sarah were still sitting up by the fire. They both will have war stories to tell their young'uns. That is, if Randy doesn't become a forty-year-old virgin. Maybe Sarah needs to start the foreplay. Still, it was a comforting site. It only took an EMP blast to wake Randy up.

It was time, even for Randy and Sarah, to get some shut eye. Everyone to his own castle. The only sad one left was the drunk. He was a welcoming relief for the collaborative. Yet he was alone, and his house was in need of repair. He was left a lot of money when his wife died. He only went to the liquor store. To him, he just wanted to stay in a constant alcoholic stew. In a way, it's like going to the dentist; you get the Novocain to numb the pain. When the drilling is done, the Novocain wears off. The drunk really feels when the alcohol blitz he is on finally subsides; he will be in heaven with his wife. He never cared about his house. But he was always paranoid that he would run out of liquor.

Each time the social worker went to the drunk's house, she (or he) would see more and more liquor added to his personal stock. When they ask him "Don't you think you have enough liquor?" he would always reply, "There's never enough liquor." With canned goods of food piling up, they started to bring him meals on wheels. Thing is, he did like the company. He would always be polite. He just didn't want any lectures about how he should be living his life.

To him, it was like a prolonged type of suicide. He was not hurting anyone. The only person who can make him whole has left this world and has gone to the other side.

Besides the social worker, the only other person who has tried to help him was Jessica. Now Jessica has her own problems, her own path to travel.

She still encourages him to eat, just not as often as before.

Today was a warm day, but nights are now becoming a little uncomfortable. One can open a window as long as there was a screen. Without electricity, there is very little one can do to keep cool. At least Gilligan's island had a constant ocean breeze. Here in Boston west, everyone suffered. But not as much as in Florida.

Ever hear the phrase "Something is in the air"? The Jumanji board was now moving several pieces at the same time. Tomorrow will be a new beginning. Many had a restless night, but dawn started with a slight drizzle. This was a welcome break from the heat.

Today Ben did get up first. He knew Randy would be up soon. Ann (Officer Ryan's wife) said Officer Ryan would be back from prison duty. When he returns from work, he always makes the rounds. There are several elderly who are near his home. He graciously checks on them. He then stops by Ben's collaborative. It is a time for him to unwind. Usually he stops by in the early afternoon. This way, if he had a few drinks, he would not have to worry.

It was early morning. Ben just made himself an egg and ham sandwich. With canned ham, how you can go wrong? He felt in the afternoon that there will be a variety of food. There were lots of cooks in the collaborative. Walking to William's house served a few purposes. He needed to clear his mind, time to focus on William's needs. Fred is a human being. Isn't his life just as valuable as the rest? Both William and Ben feel it is. Fred really should be with a doctor for a needed checkup. It is like a ticking time bomb. It is not only the right insulin; it is also his blood pressure and cholesterol meds, which are now depleted.

As far as Camille is concerned, she has been a family friend for several years. That is all Ben has to do, to Tell Camille he has promised William and Fred safe passage to Tent City. His daughter, Jessica, would really go ballistic. Enough is enough. He just wants to tell William that today is the day that Officer Ryan will show up.

This morning, Jessica was on a different page. She knew that Joshua would be writing another letter. Jessica knew she had to respond to him. Joshua has indicated to her that he wanted to confront her father. First, this frightened her. She did not want any more problems. Her mind is reaching a fever pitch. Something has to give. Listening to Camille did send some flags up. In the end, she knew that Joshua was the right fit for her. She is trying to grasp the obligations of being responsible for daily bills. Her whole life, dad and mom paid for all her expenses. On the other hand, Jessica has been responsible. School did come first, and on weekends and nights, she did help her mom. How is that not being responsible?

If she did hook up with Joshua, she did not want it to be liability.

The power grid will be back in a few months. *All right,* she thought, *I can take this a little slower.* As long as it is between Joshua and her, her dad cannot interfere. If he did, she would run off again. To do that, though, would put even more stress on Joshua. With Joshua's letter in her hand, she read it so many times that she could recite it from memory. Looking at her bedroom mirror, she said, "Well, girl, time to grow up, time to write her own letter." She kissed his letter and grabbed a paper and pen to begin.

> *Dear Joshua, my love. I have read your letter countless times. So many times that I have it to memory. Life here is almost unbearable. I am trying to be cordial toward my dad, but it is hard. He seems sad, but it will not change his point of view. I think of you, Joshua, constantly, to be with you, to touch you. Even to smell your own body odor. It is my hope that soon, I can spend some time with you. My father can only do so much to stop me. I know you are trying to reach out to me about obligations. I want this to be a team effort. I will help in any way I can. I really want to make you happy, Joshua. I love you so much. I am willing to take our time. I will go to nursing school, I will contribute, just give me a chance. My whole life, I have studied and I have helped my mom cook and clean. My father will not be in our way, as long as you stand with me. My father needs to know. He can only delay, not stop our union. Love you, Jessica*

Jessica read her letter several times. It is hard to be calm and calculated when one's emotions are like an overloaded, circuit board. She sprinkled a little perfume on it. A smile came to her face, progress, it was a taste of progress. Now she had to figure out how to place it under the rock near William's house. Jessica put the letter in the plastic bag. It was early morning; time to go outside for some breakfast. Peace, that is what Jessica feels right now. Her dad was not there, thank God. Others, including Mr. Henderson's son, were there. Time to circulate.

It was different, neither Randy nor Sarah were here. Must have been a late night for them. It is way too early for the drunk. Camille was already up. I guess sleeping on the sofa can do that for you. Jessica decided after breakfast to take a bath herself. These sponge baths are getting old. She will wait for Randy to get up. If she tries to dump hot water on herself, her dad will interfere. At least the drizzle has cooled the air.

After a while, Mr. Henderson and the union man showed up. They both volunteered to heat some water from the well. It is a pain to take a bath outside, but it does work. Jessica smiled and said she would like to go first. Today something was different. Her dad and William were not there. Something must be happening.

After the water was heated, the union man poured a few buckets into the tub. He also put a few buckets of hot water near the tub. With the tarp closed tightly, Jessica stripped of her clothes. Gingerly, she put her toe into the warm water. Ah, just like baby bear, the water was not too hot nor cool. A touch of heaven. Maybe next time, she can light up a few incense candles. With a towel and small mirror next to her, she melted into a blissful escape, an escape from all the hardships caused from the EMP blast.

It was several minutes of soaking before an inner alarm went off. Raising her arms to wash herself, she noticed how thin she had become. Quickly she picked up the mirror. One hand held the mirror and the other touched her Face. "S——! I have to start eating. I look pale. I cannot let Joshua see me this way. Why didn't anyone tell me? Jessica lay the mirror down. She flung her arms over the side of the tub. With a deep breath, she just lay there for several minutes.

Time to stop being an insecure teenager. She made a vow to take care of herself. Growing up is so hard to do. Wouldn't it be a lot easier just to be Peter Pan? You can just fly around for a couple of centuries. No need to worry about school loans, down-payments, rushing to appointments. Just endless flying; just make sure your stupid hat doesn't come off.

As she lay in the hot tub, images of the divorcee and Camille came into her swarming head. "I know I have to stop eating like a rabbit. I just don't want to blow up. After all, she needs to please Joshua. She doesn't want Joshua to take an interest in other women. Ah, stop already! I am becoming an insecure teenager again. My mother is secure, and dad still loves her."

Jessica stepped out of the tub. The water was getting cooler and she didn't want to look like a prune. She put on her jeans. *Time to get a fresh pair of jeans.* Walking out of the tub area, she thanked the union man for his help and headed for her bedroom. There, she exchanged clothes. Jessica just made sure that the two letters stayed with her.

As she walked outside, the drizzle continued. It seemed like it was near noontime. Finally, Randy and Sarah showed up. Off in the distance, Ben and William's family also showed up. Camille too was there. She seemed deep in thought. Looking at William's face, he too seemed to be on a mission. It was not a normal day at the Randal residence.

Alice, Randy, Mr. Henderson, and most who were there did not sense anything different. It was Jessica who could sense a change. Something is going down. With the fire pit roaring, Alice and the divorcee started to cook. Several of the collaborative members were already looking to eat. It was past noon, and now even the drunk stumbled in. Hopefully, he still had a liver to function with. Jessica saw the drunk and immediately grabbed his arm. "Today we both have to turn over a new leaf," Jessica said to the drunk.

They both went to the fire pit and had a plate in their hands. When your stomach shrinks, the hunger pangs also seem to go away. Jessica and the drunk were not hungry. She knew, for their health, they both had to eat. The drunk had mixed feelings. He was not hungry; he also didn't like being taken away from his bottle. Like a baby sucking on a nipple, the drunk needed that constant high.

The only saving grace was that he liked Jessica. She was the only one who really cared about him. Besides, she was a young and pretty girl. Even though she lost a lot of weight, the drunk saw her through blurry eyes. *I guess it is better than rose-colored glasses.*

They both sat down together. Jessica was going to force both the drunk and herself to finish the whole plate. Every time the drunk wanted to wash his food down with an alcoholic drink, Jessica would banter him to drink water first. First time was hard. I am sure if she did this, once a day, both of their bodies would have positive effects.

After they finished, Jessica took the plates and had them washed. When she turned around, the drunk was already hitting the bottle. In reality, Jessica was only causing, a delay in the game. *Oh well,* she thought, *better than doing nothing.* As the drizzle came down a little harder, Jessica sought cover under one of the tarps. Mr. Henderson and his sons put up several tarps. His construction company had worked for many high-end customers. He knew enough to put the tarps on his customers' lawns.

Soon after Jessica sat down, Officer Ryan drove up in his antique motorcycle. He had his state police rain gear on. With the engine stopped, Officer Ryan, extended the kickstand out. Ben came to greet him. It was always a welcoming sight to see a police officer with his side arm. Although he was not on duty, Officer Ryan's uniform gave notice that this route was protected. They both went over to the fire pit. Officer Ryan was looking forward to a good home-cooked meal.

After they exchanged salutations and small talk, Officer Ryan turned to Ben.

"My wife has indicated to me that you were interested in getting William and Fred to Tent City," Officer Ryan commented as he kept enjoying his meal.

"Yes, Fred has many health issues—high blood pressure, cholesterol, and diabetes. He only has some old insulin. William feels he is a ticking time bomb. There is no way of knowing without some blood work," Ben remarked as William was looking on from afar.

"Hmmm. I see," Officer Ryan uttered as he continued eating.

"Then there is Camille," Ben said with a little sigh.

"What's her story?" Officer Ryan asked.

"Her nephew was killed, very sad. She wants to go to Tent City near the Mississippi River. There she can travel to Houston to give her sister the news," Ben said with a little deliberation. Ben sounded like a lieutenant to Carlo Gambino, the famous NYC mafia boss.

Officer Ryan put down his empty plate of food. He looked at Ben.

"Your wife is a damn good cook, thank you. Just don't tell Ann she has a license to carry and she is a good shot," Officer Ryan said with a little laugh.

"Do me a favor, Ben. Let me talk first with William alone. When I am done, I will talk to Camille," Officer Ryan commented as he picked at his teeth.

I guess the best way to a man's heart is through his stomach.

Ben nodded to Officer Ryan. He looked at William and put up his index finger. It was his way of saying he will be there in one minute. Ben went right over to Camille. He explained to her that Officer Ryan wanted to talk to William for a few minutes. She really had no say in the matter. When Camille came over to Ben's house, it was without any prior notification. It was the first time Ben even knew, that Camille was interested in going to a tent city. Ben has the upmost respect for Camille. She has parented her daughter Vivian very well.

Camille understood, she has come this far. She will wait. Ben then went to William and told him that Officer Ryan will speak to him alone.

All this undercurrent was picked up by both Alice and Jessica. After all, when there is a cold war going on, one notices every move your adversary makes.

Alice could not take the suspense any longer. She walked up to Jessica.

"Are you seeing what I am seeing?" Alice asked her daughter, Jessica.

"Yes ma, something is up! But what?" Jessica said.

"I am not sure. But in a while, I will go over and talk to Camille. This breakdown of communications with your dad has a big downside.

With dusk settling in, and most eyes on Officer Ryan, Jessica had a wild idea.

Timing is everything. She was definitely curious, but she had a more pressing task. She needed to put her letter under the rock near William's house.

As soon as Officer Ryan talked to William, he then talked to Camille. Camille was a survivor. It is better to show respect to police officers. It is a hard lesson that many did not get in the projects. Camille has seen too much. She only has the best interests of her daughter at heart.

Officer Ryan talked to William for a good twenty minutes. He has a good idea of William's predicament. There is only so much he can do. The EMP Strike has sent the East Coast into one massive journey, to a time before modern technology. Many elderly, disabled, families' dreams are all affected by this act of evil. As a Christian, Officer Ryan is just plugging along, stoically, hoping for something close to a miracle, a return to normalcy.

It was Camille's turn. With a poker face, William returned to his wife and Fred. Many eyes were on Officer Ryan. Most in the collaborative did not know the real purpose of his visit today. Camille was given a sign from Ben. With Ben's right hand extended out, he waved for Camille to come over to Officer Ryan. She had a good bath, fresh clothes, and had collected her thoughts.

Camille has had a hard life. She had brought up four daughters as a single parent. The men in her life have given her little support. Even her own family has not been there for her. Some have even been in trouble with the law. Yes, she has received housing and financial assistance from the government. To her credit, three of her daughters are on their own. They are doing well; she wants Vivian to break the chain. To have a daughter with a good job, a degree from a known and respected college. This would allow Vivian to travel, to meet interesting and successful people. If I may be so bold, it would allow her to experience the American dream: a house, a marriage, and be a soccer mom.

Tell me how cool would that be. Of course, with divorce rates near 50 percent, it still would be a fifty-fifty shot.

Camille will give it a hard shot. She is from a large and extended family and is close to her sister in Houston. Her sister's son stayed behind. With a third -degree black belt, he decided to open up his own karate dojo. Like his father, he followed his own path. He attended the Baptist church and tried hard to save as many as he can from a life of crime and drugs.

What real sadness. No newspapers to list his death. Not even a proper funeral service. The armory did give them a body bag. Without a funeral home, the body could not be prepared for a proper funeral. It was the church that he attended that allow them to bury him. With a few connections, a wooden casket was built. The grave was marked. Camille does have both anger and guilt.

Her nephew acted so fast; she did not have a chance to draw her gun, to protect him. Her nephew always stood up to evil and violence.

Camille will not beg Officer Ryan, but she will let him know she can protect herself as well as any man. *I am sure Officer Ryan will get the picture. Officer Ryan knows his own wife can hold her own as well as any man.* He is sure that Camille is of the same stock.

After Camille finished talking to Officer Ryan, he was ready to have a drink and unwind with Ben. His wife, Ann, had several relatives, out west. Officer Ryan and Ann knew it would take several more months before the grid was online.

There was one other pressing problem. The government was getting sketchy intel on what the situation was near some of the eastern cities. The commander of the state police barracks thought it would be great if Ann could give a presentation. She could let them know of what supplies are needed. She could also inform them of the various collaboratives that are functioning well.

Officer Ryan deeply loves his wife, but they both know duty comes first. There is a major tent City southwest of Evansville Indiana, near Shawnee National Forest. There they have a military command post. The commander of the post knows Ann would lay out the best strategy for stabilizing the various hotspots.

Such a road trip would be extremely dangerous. On the upside, it would be a great tool for needed surveillance. It is a standard practice that any trip out of a safe zone requires at least two people. The state police is running on a skeleton crew; to spare another officer would create more stress. Officer Ryan is a professional; he will go over the details with Ann. Now he must clear his mind and just talk to Ben and other members of the collaborative.

Camille was happy with herself. She has always believed in divine intervention. In her mind, the good Lord will show her the correct path. Camille went to sit down. On her way back, she asked the drunk for another shot. One shouldn't use alcohol as a crutch, but screw it—it's been a tense day. Alice saw Camille sitting by herself. She had to know what was going on. Curiosity killed the cat, but Alice needed to know what Ben's (her husband) connection is to all of this. Sad, isn't it? You're sleeping next to your better half, and you have to ask an outsider what is going on. It is like hiring a detective to see who is cheating on whom.

What they really need is a priest with a bullhorn. He could stand on a podium and announce, "All right, folks! Time for a group confession. Those of you who confess, will be saved. The rest of you, just exit the collaborative." Problem solved.

Alice slowly meandered to where Camille was sitting.

"Hello, Camille, mind if I join you?" Alice said in a friendly tone.

"No. By all means, join me," Camille said as she took a sip of her alcoholic drink.

"It has been tense for everybody lately" Alice said in a probing manner.

"I know. You're right, we are all very tense," Camille said with a sigh.

"Is there something I can help you with?" Alice commented in a bold way.

"I think it's in God's hands. Besides, you seem to be in in a pickle yourself," Camille uttered with compassion.

"You and Officer Ryan seemed to be in a very serious conversation," Alice said with a probing attitude.

Camille just turned and looked at Alice. "I guess you are not communicating much with Ben," Camille answered in a quid pro quo retort.

"No, you are right. There is a family feud because of Jessica and Ben. Ben really should have given Joshua a chance to talk. He just went off on both Jessica and Joshua. He never knew what really happened; he just divided the whole family. Jessica might have died on that trip, all because of his stubborn ego. It's not fair. He should've talked to me first. Jessica is also my daughter," Alice commented with a tinge of anger.

"I am very sorry. Family should mean everything. To be fair, Ben has a lot on his shoulders. He is trying to help me right now; I know he has a good heart," Camille said using a tone of compassion.

"I know he does. My daughter Jessica's well-being is also my concern," Alice replied with sadness.

"Listen, Alice, I can see you want to know what is going on, right?" Camille said very directly.

Alice took a deep breath. She felt ashamed of being insensitive to Camille. First, she just let out a sigh. She then took the palm of her right hand, put it over her left hand, which was on her left knee cap. Alice bowed her head for a moment just to collect herself. Inside she knew she had to keep her dignity.

Just as soon as she bowed her head, she decided, "Enough prodding." Alice then looked at Camille and started to get up.

"You're right, Camille. It is none of my business. Sorry for being so nosy," Alice stated as she started to get up.

Camille lightly grabbed Alice's pants with her left hand. Her right hand covered Camille's face. She started to cry uncontrollably. Camille let go with her left hand and used both hands to cover her face. Alice was stunned. She stood there while cradling her arms, as if she were holding a baby. The moment was extremely tense for both of them.

Alice just stood there with a tear in her eye. After a few moments, Camille just had her right hand on her face. She raised her left hand and pointed a finger at Alice. It was a gesture to give Camille another moment.

"They shot my nephew! Do you understand? My nephew was a good boy. He didn't deserve to die. His whole life was devoted to helping others. His mom (one of Camille's three sisters) moved out west. She had a hard life. The man she was married to was extremely abusive to her. He did not give any financial or emotional support. She did a good job raising her son (Camille's nephew). She feared for her life and moved out west. I owe it to her to tell her in person. I asked your husband, Ben, if I could talk to Officer Ryan. Your husband is trying to help me. I know there is going to be a road trip to another tent city. I have pleaded with Officer Ryan to let me be part of that road trip," Camille stated as she wiped the tears with the back of her hand.

Alice just knelt down and wrapped her arms around Camille. With tears running down both their faces, they just hugged each other for a few tender moments. It was a release from all their pent-up anxieties. Life after the EMP blast has been hard for many of the survivors.

* * *

Jessica was totally consumed by her own quest. There is blind obedience.

What about blind rationale? Jessica's thought process was the result of a doomsday scenario. The EMP blast has stripped away many hopes and dreams. She was not seeing that her own mother's emotions were in an upheaval. She knew her father was upset, but she felt it is was a quid pro quo. What about Randy, Joshua's father? Do not forget the morale of the collaborative.

In Jessica's mind, she sees her mother and father having their nest and their marriage. What about brother Randy? Hmmm, she sees Randy as happy within himself. He has a love for auto mechanics and his real baby "Red Antique Buick."

After all, the price and value only go up. She now knows that Sarah is very interested in Randy. It takes two to tango. Really, if Randy wants to settle down, everything is presented to him on a platter. What about Jessica? Her dreams, desires? She does not have a beautiful red car, but she sees Joshua coming in riding a white horse to save her from the abyss.

You're at a picnic. There is a day of activities planned for your group. A lot of time and money was needed to entertain the masses for the day. Suddenly, off in the distance there is an ominous black cloud. It will be here soon. What to do? You let go of many activities, but you do the important ones. This is how the EMP blast has affected Jessica's mental state. Joshua was to happen several years down the road for her. The impending storm just caused her life to fast forward, say a good five to ten years. She is determined not to be cheated from her own desires and needs.

Jessica noticed that her dad is talking to Officer Ryan. Her mom and Camille seem to be in a real intense moment. The window of opportunity has opened up. Time to act. Her stomach was knotting up.

Like a moth to a flame, Jessica sprang into action. Slowly she headed to the front door of her home.

"How are you, Jessica? Nice to see you again," the union man's wife commented. She did notice how much weight Jessica has lost. She decided not to mention it.

"I am fine. I just need to go inside and put on a sweatshirt and lie down a while. Nice to see you," Jessica said to the union man's wife.

Jessica gave the union man's wife a slight smile. It does not pay to be to rude to anyone. Jessica is on a mission; there has been enough drama.

Opening up the front door, she quickly went to the kitchen. There was enough light from the fire pit shining through the windows. Going through the silverware drawer, Jessica found a Bic lighter. It will be her temporary flashlight.

Going to her closet, she found her dark blue hoodie sweatshirt. Perfect! Like *The Girl from U.N.C.L.E.,* she set into motion. The hood would cover her hair. She has had enough experience with Joshua, dressing like a man so that she will not bring attention to herself.

It's not nice to fool the gods, so Jessica asked for a blessing. Usually one goes out the same door as one comes in. Tonight she is going out the back door.

There is a window of forty minutes where she will not be missed. Like a thief in the night, she made her escape. Quickly going on the other side of the road, Jessica headed toward William's house. Walking quickly is better than running.

Most everyone is at the fire pit having a good time. If anyone stayed back, someone running would raise concerns. The neighbors really watch out for any strangers.

Jessica's little heart is pounding fast. Faster and faster, she walked. The fast walk turned into a small panic run. *Thud!* She fell face first as she tripped on a few branches. With her arms and hands sprawled out, she just laid still.

Collecting herself, she carefully felt her face. No cuts or scratches. Her hands did draw some blood. Damn! A moment of silence, no dogs barking—whew! Jessica slowly got up and felt her side pocket. The plastic bag with the letter is still in place.

"Dear Lord, just stay with me in my time of need" was just a little prayer Jessica quietly mumbled as she continued her quest. She has put some distance from the fire pit. It now was becoming almost pitch-black. Stepping on the road at this point made more sense. Jessica could see the outline of William's house on the left. Now is the time to use the Bic lighter. She clicked it several times before it lit. Walking toward the big rock, there was a pair of strange eyes, staring right at Jessica. Her heart pounded faster. Like a deer in headlights, she stopped.

"Meow," it was a Ferrell cat. It just scurried off. *Crap, I need to get this done and go home,* Jessica though to herself. She pulled the plastic bag out of her pocket (it had the letter to Joshua inside). Superstitiously, she glanced around. Taking no chances, she knelt down, kissed the plastic bag, and put it under the rock. Hopefully Romeo and Juliet didn't go through any of this. Still, Jessica hopes her ending will be a better one.

Looking skyward, Jessica thanked the good Lord. It is a lot to go through, but it is also a team effort. What Joshua has to go through is a lot worse. He has to peddle his bike for several hours in a hostile environment. Even though the grid is down, communication is still important. Old Abe walked many miles through cold and snow to return his borrowed book. The whole adventure really builds character. I don't think either Joshua or Jessica will use this adventure on their resume.

As "The Girl from U.N.C.L.E." stealthily returns to whence she came from; it was mission accomplished. Coming back within the window of opportunity, she returned to the fire pit. She could have used the back door, but what if she was caught? See, if it was Randy, he could have said I was going to relieve himself outside. Jessica, being a woman . . . well, you know what I mean.

The drunk! Like calling a mulligan, Jessica went right to him. As soon as she reached him, she was safe. He, of course, offered her a drink. She took a very small glass and asked him to get her a plate of food. She did not want anyone to see her hands. In the morning, when Jessica is rested and can see properly, she will attend to it. With the small amount of alcohol, she did pour a little on her hands. This was a painful way to disinfect her hand. The drunk would go berserk, but he is happily getting her a plate of food. *Damn, did I think fast?* Jessica thought.

It was a fruitful night for many—Officer Ryan, Camille, and Jessica. Perhaps the man upstairs has moved the pieces of the Jumanji board. Maybe karma has finally arrived. When the drunk came back with Jessica's food, she smiled. With what is left of the night, Jessica is determined to pay attention to the drunk. After all, it will please the gods.

An EMP Causality: Part IV
Time for a Road Trip

DELIBERATIONS HAVE BEEN MADE. THE jury is now in recess. Slamming down his gavel, the judge declares, "Ladies and gentleman, time for last call." Camille has made her pitch with Officer Ryan. She is determined to find a way to travel out west where her sister lives. To Camille, family is important. She knows it has to be her. She must be the one to let her sister know that her son has died. Vivian (her daughter) will be fine with her other sister. Ben's son, Randy, has also been checking in with Vivian.

Camille has just poured out her heart to Alice. They both seem to have collected themselves. Alice has decided to mingle with the other members of the collaborative. Before Alice starts to mingle, she glances the surroundings.

She is checking on Jessica. It's kind of a "trust but verify" thing, a motherly trait. *Ah! She is with the drunk, Jessica will be fine.*

Camille could now took a deep sigh. It has been an emotional ride for her. During these troubled times, Camille sees herself as the matriarch of the clan. She takes the drink that the drunk has given her. Now she notices Ben talking to Mr. Henderson. She decides to join them. To stay only with either Alice or Vivian would ultimately cause a rift. Camille has decided to be neutral in this family feud. After all, in the past, she had to live without any man helping her.

As she approaches Ben and Mr. Henderson, Randy came up to her for a simple greeting. In Randy's mind, he wants peace with Camille and Vivian. There has been enough turbulence. His sister Jessica needs a few good friends for support. As quickly as Randy said his salutations, he immediately went back to Sarah and her mom. Slowly but surely, Randy is bonding with Sarah. Hopefully, it will not always remain platonic. If it does, either Randy's mom or Sarah's mom will have to hang up some mistletoe. They then can nudge Randy to walk under it with Sarah. That has to work.

Camille asked Ben and Mr. Henderson if she could join them. They both smiled and said, "Of course." The three of them made small talk for a good forty minutes. Mr. Henderson slapped his knees and said he is turning in. The fire is comforting, but he is having a hard time keeping his eyes open.

After Mr. Henderson left, Camille was alone with Ben. She looked at him.

"Ben, thank you for setting up the meeting for me with Officer Ryan," Camille stated with a genuine smile.

"You're more than welcome, Camille. I also had a conversation with Officer Ryan's wife (Ann). To be fair with you, Ann is thinking of going on the trip herself. William also explained to Officer Ryan that he needs to get Fred some medical help. The local hospitals are completely inundated with too many clients and not enough staff. It would be in Fred's best interest to go to a tent city.

"Oh no! That is going to be a problem," Camille said with alarm.

"Huh? What are you talking about Camille?" Ben asked.

It's a well-known fact that all road trips require a driver and one security guard or shooter," Camille replied anxiously.

"What are you getting at, Camille?" Ben asked in a perturbed tone.

"When is Officer Ryan going on his next assignment?" Camille asked.

"Late tomorrow morning, he will be gone for two days," Ben said tepidly.

"Will his wife Ann be at home?" Camille asked.

"Probably, so what?" Ben said with a touch of anger.

"What do you mean so what? You know Ann is a female and I am a female. They need a guard shooter to accompany them, right?" Camille said boldly.

"Your point?" Ben asked.

"Please, Ben! If Fred and William go, the air base will ask that a male guard shooter go with them. They know nothing about me. I know Ann can handle herself as much as any man. They respect and trust Ann. I need to talk with her. I have lived my whole life protecting my daughter. I carry a gun and I am not afraid to use it," Camille said with authority.

"Aye gads! I never thought of it that way. You have a valid point," Ben stated. "Look, you just sleep on my sofa tonight. We can take you by ca—" Ben was interrupted by Camille.

"No, she (Ann) needs to see me either bike or walk to her house. I have to show that I am my own person, then I can gain a little respect. I will have a talk with her, woman to woman. It is the only way," Camille said.

"I hear you. We have an extra bike. I will see to it that you can use it," Ben said with a touch of humility. At this point, Ben put his hand out. He did not want to hug Camille. He knew both Jessica and Alice were watching.

He is in enough dodo. Camille graciously shook hands with Ben. Being street-smart, Camille knew exactly why he put his hand out.

Both physically and emotionally drained, Camille said good night to Ben. As Camille was heading for the front door, Ben said, "Wait a minute." He wanted to light a few candles. Everyone needs to use the bathroom. Ben went into the kitchen and opened up a drawer. He was looking for the Bic lighter. After several minutes, Ben said to himself, "This is strange. The lighter was here last night." He then struggled to find a few candles in the dark. Camille was puzzled. Finally Ben found the candles and went to the fire pit. He lit several candles and bought them back into the house. At this point, Camille smiled.

How considerate Ben is. He carefully put the lit candles in the living room and hallway.

While this was going on, Jessica slapped her forehead. She felt the lighter in her front pocket. She forgot to put it back. Using it for a flashlight? Ingenious.

Not returning it? Really not cool. Jessica turned around and looked at the drunk while raising her empty glass. Both of them smiled. The drunk poured some more alcohol until Jessica waved her hands. It was a signal that that was her limit.

Soon like dropping flies, everyone reached their limit for the night. It was an eventful night. The governor has issued a reprieve. Everyone (including all collaborative members) lightened up for this night. The family drama/feud has taken a toll. Tonight there was less tension. Perhaps all can sleep well; the Jumanji board has definitely made a series of moves.

On the following morning, Randy woke first. Remaining neutral in this ongoing war has its perks. Not only can he smile at everyone; his shoulders are not burdened down. Cheerfully, he used the bathroom and extinguished the candles. As Randy was exiting the house, he noticed Camille sleeping on the sofa. Randy was going to say morning to her. She looked at him and put the cover back over her head. It was her way of saying, "Just go and let me sleep."

Closing the front door, Randy had to smile. All the family drama is locked up inside the house. Outside, he is free at last. A glorious morning. At times being alone with Mother Nature can be therapeutic. Last night, sitting next to Sarah and her mother was special. With a glowing fire, food, drink, and the company of two beautiful women, life doesn't get any better.

Funny how everyone tells Randy, "Just step away from your car, just do it." It's a slow withdrawal. He will always have a bond with his car, but maybe—just maybe—he now understand it's time to cut the umbilical cord.

Looking around, Randy saw the same fires and heard an occasional crack of a 9mm. Burnt embers were still pretty hot, throwing some small pieces of wood got the fire pit going. Time for coffee and breakfast. With the aroma of brewed coffee, the masses started to stir. Some of the combatants inside his house started to come out. First it was Ben, next Alice. The union man and his family came with some food to cook. It has become a morning ritual. For a better term, we can just call it "the Gathering."

Ben, unshaven this morning, needed some eggs and coffee. Randy cheerfully obliged his father. It was a strange truce. Both Ben and Alice said, "Good morning" to each other. Sad that it could not be "Good morning, dear." "Good Morning, Alice." No, it is just "Good morning." Like being at a summit with two archrivals.

"Randy, did you see where the lighter went?" Ben asked in bewilderment.

"It is in the top drawer in the kitchen," Randy replied.

"I didn't find it last night when I wanted to light the candles," Ben stated.

"It's there, Dad. I even saw it this morning," Randy said with conviction.

"Hmmm, I must be losing it. Okay, thanks," Ben said in a soft tone.

Jessica returned it before she went to sleep. She did not want to get up yet. She wanted Camille to exit the house first. She knew that Camille's presence would make her feel a little uncomfortable. She noticed Camille with Ben last night. There is enough tensions without adding anymore. She did not know Camille was discussing a personal problem and not the family feud.

Finally, Camille decided it's time. After using the bathroom, she exited the house. Jessica knows soon Joshua will drop off another letter any day now. Totally obsessed, it is the only thing that keeps Jessica from losing it. Electricity will be coming in several months, but it does not matter; life is not worth living without Joshua. Without family or a professional therapist to talk with, it becomes a minefield. Finally Mr. Henderson showed up for the Gathering. Camille smiled.

After he sat down with his coffee, Camille approached him.

"Morning, Mr. Henderson," Camille said with a big-ass smile.

"Morning," Mr. Henderson said cautiously. He knew something is up.

"After breakfast, would you mind heating me up some hot water for a bath?" Camille asked with a nice feminine charm.

Mr. Henderson just smiled. He raised his coffee to her.

"Anything for a charming lady like you," Mr. Henderson said with cheer.

Camille really wanted to impress Ann. If she could be tidy and clean in these conditions, perhaps Ann would be impressed.

It is a typical morning at the Randals' collaborative. Mr. Henderson is heating water for Camille. A few of the other women have also indicated they would like the same treatment. This morning business is good for Mr. Henderson. Ah! Off in the distance, talking to someone else, is Mrs. Henderson. She has her arms crossed, and she is looking at her husband. Mr. Henderson picked up a bucket of water and just shook his head. They have a good marriage. With two strapping sons and a good business, she wants to make sure it stays that way. Truth be told, most men like looking at a beautiful women. Mr. Henderson also enjoys it, but he is very happy with his business, sons, and a caring wife. "Look! But don't touch" is what he lives by. Besides, in the construction business, it's mostly men and beers anyway.

In the meantime, his two sons were lugging around the generator to various houses. Keeping food from spoiling is important to everyone. Camille, finishing her bath, is now trying the best she can to dry her hair. Like a multitude of females, Camille is obsessed with her hair. She even owns a few wigs. Many of our early colonist had wigs. There was even a wig party. I wonder if they all had to wear wigs. There are men who make a big fuss about their hair. Yet most just want a quick haircut when the hair starts to itch the back of their necks.

Officer Ryan just has his hair buzzed off at the prison. They have a generator and many who are willing to be barbers.

It was a very productive morning. Randy and Ben started to chop wood. Finally, Jessica came out of the house. Instinctively, Alice has decided not to come up to her. She did not want Ben to feel overwhelmed in this ongoing feud. Alice feels and hopes a resolution is forthcoming.

Right after the sun dial showed twelve noon, Camille sought out Ben. It was time for Camille to have a meeting with Ann (Officer Ryan's wife). Ben was really building up a sweat chopping wood. He saw Camille approaching him. He paused and wiped his forehead. With a quick mind, Ben called out for Randy.

"What's up, Dad?" Randy said to Ben.

"Would you mind getting the spare bike for Camille?" Ben asked politely.

"I don't mind, but I don't mind driving her either," Randy replied.

"No! It is better that she just uses the bike this morning. Camille is only going to Officer Ryan's house. She wants to do it by herself," Ben stated in a clear tone.

"All right, Dad! No problem," Randy said as he exited the barn.

Soon Randy bought the bike over to Camille. She thanked Randy and walked with the bike. As she neared Ben, Camille thanked him for his support.

Time for a good ride. It really is very safe, and the exercise will be good for her. Riding by William's house, Fred was up and about. Seems Fred never sleeps. Food is important to everyone, but in Fred's mind the birds must be fed. This morning Camille did not wish to talk to Fred. She said hello and kept on trucking.

When Camille reached Officer Ryan's house, Ann was outside with a push lawn mower. Officer Ryan now has access to a push lawn mower, courtesy of the prison. After he uses it, he always returns it to the prison.

A little out of shape, Camille is huffing and puffing. Ann saw her and stopped the lawn mower. Camille took in one deep breath and let it out. She did not want Ann to think she is out of shape. With Camille standing by the bike, Ann walked up to her.

"Morning. Strange to see you this morning. Are you exercising?" Ann asked.

"No, actually, I came by to have a talk with you," Camille stated.

"Ham, *okay!* What's up?" Ann said.

"I had a talk with your husband at Ben's place last night," Camille said.

"And . . ." Ann said in a curious voice. She did not know what to expect.

"My nephew was shot and killed," Camille said.

"I heard," Ann stated

"I need to tell my sister. Problem is, she lives out west. It is her only son. She has to hear it from me," Camille said with a little emotion.

"I am sorry. What has that got to do with me?" Ann said with a confusing tone.

"Everything. You are going on the road trip to a tent city out west," Camille mentioned.

"Yes, but we are just trying to secure a Humvee now. The Canadians have delivered a few old Humvees left over from the Iraq War. They flew them in last week to the air base. My husband is trying to authorize a trip as we speak," Ann said slowly but deliberately. Still, not knowing what is in Camille's mind, Ann was waiting with puzzlement.

"Look, Ann! I have respect for you and your husband. You have a good marriage. You're both police officers and you both respect each other," Camille spurted out.

"Thanks for the compliment, but I still do not understand," Ann stated.

"Very simple. We both know the air base will require a shooter guard to accompany you. They think only a man is qualified. I know they respect you.

If William and Fred accompany, you they will think only a man can keep you safe," Camille said very trustfully.

At this point, Ann started to stroke her chin. Her whole life had been geared to survive in a man's world. She lived with brothers who tormented her and had to keep up with the other officers.

"Do you want to come in the house for a few minutes?" Ann asked as she noticed that Camille was also armed. It gave Ann a reason to smile.

Camille put the stick stand out. She then followed Ann into the house. For over an hour, they talked and bonded. Ann had to get a feel for what kind of a person Camille is. They both exchanged stories about their youth and growing up. In the end, Ann understood where Camille was coming from. Ann also got the feeling Camille understood the mindset of some of these thugs. Not only did she think that, but also that Camille can handle herself well in a crisis.

Ann and Camille walked outside. Camille got her bike as Ann looked on.

"I will talk to both my husband and the air base. They are extremely understaffed. I will get back to you, Camille. Nice talking to you," Ann said.

At this point, they both just shook hands. Neither one wanted to hug since it was really their first meeting. Camille, being satisfied, started to bike back.

Relieved by her efforts, she felt a burden has left her. This time Camille saw Fred was still outside. She pulled her bike up to William's house. She did not want to neglect Fred this time. After talking for ten minutes, she continued on to the Randal residence.

Once she reached there, she met up with Ben and went over the conversation she had with Ann. Ben was happy for her. He also recommended that she stay there for a few days. Officer Ryan should be back in two days.

Everything was set in motion.

The next few days were a diplomatic nightmare. Alice would talk to her daughter, but not for long talks. She did not want to piss her husband off.

Camille tried to be an equal visitor. Now she understand why the drunk is the go-to guy during this troubling period. Randy found a win-win situation for himself. He spent most of his time around Sarah. This way he truly can say, "I know nothing."

A few days went by and the Jumanji board kept moving. It was time for Jessica to check under the rock. She gave it one more day. She knew Joshua must have left her a letter under the rock. For Joshua, it was a different challenge. As long as he did not use the jeep, his father did not care what he did. He knew Ben would not allow his daughter out of his sight.

What clever means can Jessica use to go to William's house? She cannot use Sarah anymore. What about the drunk? Nah, he will not even be up until noon. Even if he did, he would stumble the whole way. After pondering for several agonizing minutes, a light went off. Voila! A few loaves of bread were becoming moldy. She got the moldy loaves and went to her mom.

"Ma, I am going to visit Fred for a while. He will be happy to use this for his birds," Jessica announced with confidence.

"Ham, I don't know—"Alice was interrupted.

"I will be back soon. Don't worry," Jessica commented.

In Alice's mind, she was worried. She was worried a lot. There is no way she would let Jessica out of her sight. As Jessica walked to William's house, Alice followed but outside of Jessica's sight. Alice went as far as the union man's house. From there she can easily see William's house. It really became a cat-and-mouse game.

For close to forty minutes, Jessica spent time with Fred. She nudged him to go for a short walk. There, with a slight of hand, she was able to secure Joshua's letter. With her heart pounding fast, she slowly and carefully put the letter in her front pocket. After walking Fred back, she became excited and anxious. Inside was the letter, the answers to her existence. Inquisitive minds want to know.

Alice now felt embarrassed. She had to scurry back without Jessica noticing.

This "trust but verify" thing is getting old. Ben, in the meantime, was concerned about what was going on. Even when Alice was walking back fast, he was in bewilderment. He looked at Randy, but Randy was preoccupied with Sarah. Ben just let it play out.

As soon as Jessica came back, she quickly went into the house and entered her Room. She did not run; she knew if she did that, her mom would follow her. Locking her bedroom door with sweaty hands, she took out the plastic bag with the letter in it. First, she just put it next to her heart. After a short pause, she opened the plastic bag. Jessica pulled the letter out and began to read it:

Dear Jessica, I have read your last letter. This whole adventure seems so unreal. I am an adult, you are almost an adult, yet we are being controlled by others. Somehow life is not always fair. My father and I still do not communicate very well. Strange how my mom is still talking about you. I don't think she is getting the sensitivity from dad. The bike trip is long and dangerous. I have been tormented for the last several days. When I sleep at night, I see your smile and can feel your tenderness. During these times, I really miss not being with you. Jessica, something has to happen—time for me to be a man. Like you, I have no one to talk to or confide with. I must confront your father.

> *If nothing else, I will feel good about it; not just for me but also for you. It's not fair that your father is punishing you. He did not even let us explain.*
>
> *This way we can both show honor to him and ourselves. I think of you all the time. There will be a path. Just be strong . . .*

—Love Joshua

Love Joshua. That is all Jessica saw. Perceptive reading. Yes, she read the whole letter. But *Love Joshua* is what she is fixated on. She was on a cloud, being overjoyed, yet she had no one to share her joy with. She wanted to leave her room to express her happiness. Express to whom? Holy crap! Is it her and Joshua against the world? In Jessica's eye, this is the way she sees it.

In Joshua's eye, it is a different world. Once he confronts Jessica's dad, it's over. He knows he has his mom's blessing. His dad? Well, Joshua was on his own before the EMP. After electricity has been installed, he will go on his own again. His dad knew it.

Jessica just laid on her back. She has meaning, direction, and hope. It will take a while for her to come off her high. After a good half hour, she decided to come outside. Trying not to smile too much, she decided to ask Mr. Henderson to set her up for a bath. Might as well feel and smell like a woman. From this point on, confidence was building up inside of Jessica. What Jessica did not know is that both Alice and Ben also wanted closure.

* * *

Camille was outside talking to the union man's wife when she heard Officer Ryan approach. It was a moment of truth. One could hear his antique motorcycle from a long distance. The mufflers did not stifle the sound very well. Officer Ryan drove to within fifty feet of the fire pit. Everyone is happy when he shows up. Not only does he represent a sense of security, but he also keeps everyone abreast of what is happening.

As soon as he stopped the engine, he pulled out the kickstand. Taking off his Helmet, he noticed who was at the Randal residence. First he went over to talk to Ben. In a way, this made Camille nervous. If it was bad news, I guess he would inform Ben first. Camille was trying to compose herself. She has had to deal with a lot of negativity lately. She had her hoodie sweatshirt on. It was warm, but she was getting annoyed with all the bugs.

Today Officer Ryan was in his civilian clothes. Maybe his wife was called in to do a shift. The state police have been trying to alternate them. This way, someone would always be at their house. It keeps the neighborhood safe; plus, the Ryans have too many important documents and firearms.

After several minutes, Ben waved for both William and Camille to come over. Camille had knots in her stomach. William would make a good poker player. He always tried to keep his emotions in check. It took a few minutes for both them to walk over. When they arrived, Officer Ryan looked each into their eyes.

"I have talked with both of you. Both of you have valid reasons to go on this road trip. I have had a hard talk with Ann. She is one talented policewoman. She needs to brief the authorities as to what is going on here. I have all the confidence in her actions. Beyond that, she is also my wife, and I love her very much. I know the dangers that she is going to face.

It is the illegal biker gangs that concern me the most," Officer Ryan said as he paused.

For the next few moments, Officer Ryan had to compose himself. He put his right hand over his face. I guess the pain was more than he could bear. With his shirt sleeve, he wiped a tear from his eye.

"My wife and I had a serious talk. She knows that William and Fred have a serious medical condition. This definitely warrants a trip," Officer Ryan said slowly. He then turned and looked at Camille.

"Our arguments were about you. I told her I understand why you want to go. You have to understand that my wife's health and well-being are important to me," Officer Ryan commented and then paused.

At this point, Camille felt rejected. She knows she is up to the task.

What can she do? She really left no stone unturned. Her left hand was on her mouth.

"My wife is a stubborn woman. I guess it's her early childhood. Whatever you said to her made an impression," Officer Ryan commented as he was still looking at Camille." She insisted that you can match any man when it comes to protecting a love one. Get your things in order. She will be by in three days.

I must warn you, this will be a difficult and dangerous trip," Officer Ryan warned as he turned his head away. He didn't even say goodbye.

He paused and put his left hand on his face. After a moment of composing himself again, he started up his antique motorcycle. Without looking at anyone, he took his two fingers and waved them a few inches. It was his way of saying goodbye and "I will catch you later."

What a roller coaster moment! Camille could feel her heart pounding. Total shock! She is going on a road trip. Now she was given orders not only to guard her own life, but that of Ann's. She never thought of it this way. She realizes that Officer Ryan is right. Camille is taking the place of a man. Perhaps a much younger man who is in top shape. Camille now knows she must protect Ann at all cost.

William, Ben, and Camille did not talk. It really was what you call a "Kodak moment." It will define them in more ways than we can count. Instinctively, the three of them mingled with other people. There will be a lot of time for them to commiserate.

Camille sought out Randy. She wanted to go home for the night. It is important that she see her daughter and gets to spend the night with her. Randy agreed and asked Sarah if she wanted to go for the ride. At least Sarah's mom is happy.

Something is in the air. Alice and Jessica felt it. They both saw Camille's face. Alice knew she got her wish. Alice could only wish her the best. Jessica really didn't know what was going on. She only knew that a road trip of importance is happening. It has been a stressful day for everyone; not only for the Randal family, but for the whole collaborative.

Jessica really wanted to share her good news, but with whom? If Jessica was to enter womanhood, she needs to be responsible. She remembered the old saying "Loose lips sinks ships." No matter whom she told, it might come back to haunt her. Besides, she knew soon Joshua would have his confrontation.

Even though it is an unwelcoming event, it must be done.

Back at Daniel's house, Joshua has made up his mind. Today was the day that he must make peace with himself and Jessica. If nothing else, Jessica's honor must be restored. That night Joshua did not sleep very well. It is a long bike ride. To do the bike ride with a 9mm gun in his pants seemed unnatural.

Joshua is not afraid. He has already done it twice. The road has become a safe passage. Early in the mornings, at least twice a week, Daniel or another collaborative member made the trip. Most of the thugs stay clear. There are too many other vulnerable victims for them to attack.

It was early in the morning when Joshua got up. While his dad was still asleep, he used the bathroom to wash up and shave. Looking in the mirror in the early morning light, he muttered, "Time to cowboy up." He almost reached for the aftershave lotion to make a good impression for his encounter with Ben. But a little voice in his head told him, *This isn't what Clint Eastwood would do.* So Joshua dropped the aftershave idea and continued to prep for the trip. Checking his 9mm, Joshua made sure there was a round in the chamber.

Every split second would count in a firefight.

Looking in the refrigerator, he noticed his mom made a few sandwiches.

His mom heard Joshua walk by. Joshua walked up to his mom and kissed her on her forehead. Softly, Joshua said, "I am going for a bike ride. I will be back early afternoon."

His mom slightly squinted. She saw the 9mm in his pants. "Be careful, son! And by the way, if you see Jessica, say hello to her for me." She then rolled over and went back to sleep.

Joshua shook his head side to side. He raised his hands slightly and held his palms up. To himself, he muttered, "How in the world does she know?"

Stepping outside, he noticed a few of the collaborative members by the fire. They brewed some morning coffee. At first, Joshua was just going to ignore them. But if he did that, it might cause a problem for later, so Joshua went over and joined them for a few minutes. He explained he needed to go for a bike ride for a few hours. It helped him physically and mentally. Usually Joshua wore sneakers for a bike ride. In these dangerous time, he thought boots would be a better idea. He also had a sweatshirt but tied it around his waist. This hid his 9mm from the other collaborative members.

"Well, guys, see you in a few hours. I want to bike before it gets too hot," Joshua remarked as he headed out. In Joshua's mind, he had covered his bases.

With a water bottle, sandwich, and his 9mm, Joshua was all set. Today he does not have to hide from Officer Ryan. Hopefully, he will never have to hide from him again.

Joshua did not peddle hard. He wanted to make sure he will not be winded or sweaty. As the morning wore on, the sun started to really beat down. Every once in a while, someone would come out of their house. Most of the people have seen Joshua before. Besides, he is not dressed like the typical thug. With unruly hair, baggy pants, and potted faces, they always travel in packs, like wolves do. Joshua had spoken to the local residents a few times. To them, it was refreshing to see that Joshua is not afraid.

It was a long and hard ride. As he approached Officer Randal's house, he noticed Officer Ryan's wife peeking through the windows. Joshua kept peddling as he approached William's house. Outside, William was sitting on the steps.

Fred is chasing the squirrels away. William is in shock and did nothing. It was as if a gunslinger just entered Dodge. "Time to close the shutters on them windows."

Peddling for a few more minutes, Joshua could see the fire pit and several members for their usual gathering. Everyone stopped what they were doing.

Jessica was still inside the house, but soon Alice ran into the house. She wanted Jessica to come outside.

Joshua dismounted his bike and started to walk to the fire pit. He saw Ben. It was time, mano a mano. Ben was stymied as everyone else. Ben was about to say something to Joshua before he got any closer. Something inside of Ben told him to compose himself. He noticed his wife with their daughter, Jessica.

Alice had her arms around Jessica. It was not to protect her; it was to prevent Jessica from running to Joshua.

Joshua looked Ben in the eye as he put the kickstand out of his bike. Slowly, Joshua walked toward Ben. You could hear a pin drop. Only the noise of a faraway cracking of a 9mm could be heard. Ben noticed a bulge under Josh's sweatshirt. He knew it was a gun. *Too late, f——— it. I'd rather my family see me die like a man.* Joshua stopped fifteen feet away. Ben thought it was his move.

He had no idea what was going to happen.

"Mr. Randal, sir. I just need five minutes of your time. You never let either your daughter or I talk," Joshua said very deliberately. "Your daughter did nothing wrong. You have no right to be mad at her. It is me that you need to take out your anger on." Joshua, at this point, glanced around quickly and saw Jessica. It gave him even more courage to go on. "No one would accompany me to go on a short trip. I did not know your daughter was underage. For that I take full responsibility. We got into a bad firefight. People died," Joshua stated as Jessica interrupted.

"He saved my life, Dad. Damn, do you understand? He protected me with his own life! What's wrong with you? Jessica yelled in a loud voice. Alice still held onto her daughter tightly. The whole collaborative stayed silent.

"I will not lie to you. I do love your daughter and she loves me. You can only stop us for so long. Soon she will be legal, and several months down the road, electricity will be coming back.

Ben was totally speechless. It was as if he were the villain. He was a father, husband, and the founder of the collaborative. Ben fell to his knees and started to cry. In his mind, he has lost. He had lost the respect of his daughter, his wife, and the members of his collaborative.

Immediately, Sarah's mother (the divorcee who lives in the next house) ran to Ben.

"Everyone here respects you, Ben. Everyone," she said as she held Ben's head.

Joshua stopped talking.

It was a pivotal moment. Somehow the divorcee hit the right chord. Alice still held on to her daughter. Somehow, she knew it had to all play out.

On his knees, Ben had one hand held by the divorcee. With his other, he wiped away his tears. Ben stood up. He had to regain his composure, his manhood. Everyone stood silent. Joshua himself was in shock. He had no desire to bring Mr. Randal down. Basically, he accomplished what he needed to do.

"Okay, Joshua, I got it. I have made some mistakes. My own wife says I am pigheaded. I think it took courage for you to come here. For that I commend you.

Jessica is still my daughter. As long as she is under our roof, she will follow our rules. I also cannot tell a lie. I do have anger and hurt at what you did. Now, at least I know what happened. Jessica is a bright g—woman (He caught himself; he now knows she is a woman, but will always be Daddy's little girl). She needs her high school diploma and really should go on to a higher education," Ben concluded.

Not knowing what to do next, Ben made one more announcement. "You can stay for a short visit and have something to eat with my daughter. After that, Randy will take you home."

The family feud is officially over. Alice let go of Jessica and put both hands on her face. She is extremely proud of both Joshua and her husband. Jessica did run to Joshua; she really cried as she hugged him. For Joshua he felt he had a new family and is heading in the right direction. At first, Alice also wanted to run toward Ben, but there are still deep emotional scars that need to be healed. The emotional roller-coaster ride has taken a toll.

As Ben turned around there was the drunk with two drinks. Ben smiled and stated, "You're like the oversized St. Bernard dog always carrying a whiskey barrel." Ben patted him on the shoulders. "You're a good man."

With that remark, the drunk's ego shot up all the way to the moon.

Ben took his drink and slowly walked over to the Randy, Sarah, and her mother (the divorcee next door). Ben was going to say something to her, but she made a gesture. She put her two fingers on her lips. It was her way of saying "Silence is golden." Ben did a slight nod. She was a wise woman.

Joshua also used common sense. Now that there is less stress in the collaborative, he really felt that a short visit would be in order. He and Jessica talked for about an hour. Jessica was now trying to put a little weight back on. Both of them sat and held hands the whole time. Sometimes Jessica would squeeze hard. Joshua did not want to hurt her, so he just smiled each time she squeezed his hand.

Joshua got up and said it was time to leave. Jessica hugged him and for once, Alice had a smile. Ben just watched without emotion. Recovery will take a long time. It was time to leave. Jessica wanted to go for the ride. But Joshua intervened, "Baby steps. We need to take baby steps."

Jessica smiled and said, "You and you're damn logic!" Joshua's heart was filled with happiness.

As Joshua left, he said to Jessica, "I will bike down in two weeks." This will give them both time and also a little stability in their relationship.

Joshua put his bike in the back trunk of Randy's Buick. Sarah sat in the shotgun position and Joshua sat in back. Joshua asked Randy to drop him off a few hundred yards from his house. He still had to deal with his own father.

Randy smiled. Enough drama for one day.

On the way back, Randy felt it would be easier to go directly to Camille's apartment complex. Tomorrow is the day that Ann (Officer Ryan's wife) is going to stop by to pick up Camille and William. Going to Vivian and Camille's apartment complex is always a challenge. There are several apartment complexes near them. It makes it easy pickings for the gangs and thugs, like shooting fish in a barrel. With all those people going to the armory, many of them fell prey to these lowlifes.

It was a new experience for Sarah. She had a pair of her best designer jeans on. Before she left for the ride, Sarah struggled with which top to wear. Even her own mom got into the act. The mother went through her dresser for the perfect top. Sarah has a nice figure, but she does not want her daughter to be too revealing. "Ah, perfect!" she said of a red pull turtleneck sweater. Her mother insisted on a dab of perfume. Just a slight amount.

Finally the mother stopped fussing with her daughter. Poor Randy, doesn't even know he is being set up. Maybe it's a good thing. If it was left up to him, he would be aging along with his Buick. Difference is, the Buick becomes more valuable. His value (unless he becomes rich) declines. Looking at Randy's big smile, I do not think he is complaining.

Some date. Sarah is sitting shotgun with a rifle in her lap and Randy has a gun on the dashboard. The red Buick is a tempting, shiny object. The only saving grace is that he has been to her complex several times. Most of the times, Randy was accompanied by his father or Mr. Henderson. The thugs are cowards.

They are not going to engage in a firefight, too many other easier victims.

Each time Randy drives to the apartment complex, it seems to get worse. Very few of the stalled cars have their windows intact. I understand breaking into a car for supplies. Why do they have to be vindictive and break windows for the thrill of it?

Coming into the crashed gate, Randy sees more debris in front of him. There always seems to be a foul odor that permeates the air. It is a mixture of rotting garbage, ash, and possibly decaying animals.

Sarah is turning every which way looking for something. Randy handed her his handkerchief. It was still clean and folded. He just knew that Sarah would find the area and smell offensive. Little did Sarah know that Randy would use his handkerchiefs to check his oil level. It is a small secret that Randy will keep to himself.

Pulling into the complex always gets the attention of the existing tenants. Hearing the engine, Camille grabs her 9mm and runs outside. She knew in an instant why Randy came. This is going to take several minutes. Camille had her bag packed. It is going to be a tearful departure. Vivian and her sister knew Camille is going on a dangerous journey.

It took a good twenty minutes for everyone to say goodbye.

Vivian was given countless instructions on how to use a 9mm.

Randy promised he would be by at least once a week. Now that Jessica is home, Vivian will also be invited to sleep over at the Randals' house. It would be like escaping to a safe house.

Tears were in everyone's eye. Going off on a journey that is full of danger is one thing; going without the use of cell phones is quite another challenge. Randy did say to Vivian that once her mother reaches safety, the state police barracks will be notified. They have communication that was protected by a Faraday cage. Camille got into Randy's Buick. She sat in the back seat with a duffel bag. As Randy drove off, Camille turned around, wiping the tears with one hand and waving with the other. Randy and Sarah respected the moment and just kept quiet.

The drive would take a good half hour. Young thugs were spotted a couple times. Randy instructed Sarah to put the barrel of the gun out the window. With the death of her nephew, Camille had more anger than fear. She gave her daughter the use of her 9mm. In a way, it emboldened her to make this trip. Camille is delighted she is paired off with Ann. It will be "Thelma and Louise, Part 2."

Each time Randy saw two or more young males, he would slow down. Three people with at least two firearms is a little intimidating. Randy now was entering the safe zone. Anything beyond Atty. Schiller's house is almost like being in the green zone.

Dropping off one passenger and picking up another one gave a hint to Randy. Perhaps he was qualified to be an Uber driver. Ah, no cell phone, no use of credit cards. Scratch that idea. Still, the red Buick is one of the very few cars running. It is still a very classic ride that only gets better with time.

At the moment, there is peace at the Randal residence. Everyone can be themselves. It is still going to take a long time for Jessica, Alice, and Ben to bond again. Emotional scars take longer to heal than physical scars. Many times they never heal.

Sarah exited the car first. Next, it was Camille. She grabbed her duffel bag and headed for the Randal house. She is getting used to sleeping on the sofa. Unlike at her apartment complex, Camille always sleeps soundly at the Randel's. There are dogs, a fire pit, and many collaborative members with guns. At her apartment, Camille is the posse.

First things first: a hot meal and a hot bath. God, what a life. After chowing down, Camille spotted Mr. Henderson and walked toward him. Mr. Henderson was just sitting, enjoying the sunshine. Seeing Camille approaching him, he bowed his head. And, with a slight smile, he muttered, "Guess break time is over." Like a club med groupie, Camille was determined to pamper herself.

After her hot bath, Camille decided to get dressed and mingle. Dusk is starting to cover the landscape. The day has been evolving. There may not be any electrical light switches that work, but there have been emotional switches which were triggered.

Both Jessica and Alice made small gestures toward Ben. If one could step away from the fray, it was obvious that Ben was isolated the most.

Alice and Jessica still had a quasi-relationship. Jessica had Joshua and Vivian (if she chose to). What about Ben?

We all have breaking points. As strong as Ben is, he could not stop the onslaught of an emotional tidal wave. Seeing him break perhaps made the others understand his viewpoint. Jessica is now going to go on with her life. Hopefully, it will be a long and healthy marriage with Joshua. Time will tell.

She is young and can spring back no matter what is thrown at her. It is Ben's self-esteem that needs repairing. Alice is a strong Christian women.

In the end, she carried on with her motherly instincts.

Alice and Jessica feel they must help in that repairing. This is done with a few kind, gentle gestures: washing a few of his clothes, bringing a plate of his favorite food, making a positive compliment. Small and genuine—that's the key. The old saying "Time heals all wounds." We will see.

Our society has programed us to think, that it is okay for a women to cry. For a man to cry is a sign of weakness, yet any man who attends the funeral of a loved one (i.e., wife, mother, spouse, etc.) will most likely also break down. For me, I cry every time the postman comes. More bills!

The die has been cast. Camille headed off to the sofa at the Randal's house. A night to sleep well, resting her body and soul. It will be like charting a new course. How to pivot through the obstacles that an EMP strike has laid waste to? Still within Camille's inner self, she feels both anger and excitement: anger toward the thugs who killed her nephew; excitement that she will be traveling with another strong woman.

The venue at William's household is different. William's wife will be left alone. She has told William countless times she is uneasy about the trip.

Maybe she had a premonition, or she just does not want to be left alone.

William wanted to spend his last night at the fire pit. His wife said no. Like a condemned person's last wish, she deserved happiness.

William did have a talk with Randy. Now, Randy and Sarah will make it a point to look after his wife. Randy has also come up with the idea of letting Vivian sleep over. It would really be a win-win situation. If nothing else, misery likes its own company." Despite the many thoughts in her mind, it was time for some shut-eye. For most in the collaborative, it will be a normal night's sleep." For others, maybe not so normal.

In the morning, the sun shone brightly. Already, there is humidity in the air. Hard to sleep without a fan or air-conditioner. Waking up in a sweat is extremely uncomfortable. *I wonder how the pro tennis players can battle in ninety-degree weather with high humidity. At least they do not have to worry about their diet as much as the spectators in the stands.*

Camille is up early. After a little coffee and breakfast, she went to get a bucket of water. She wishes to sponge herself down. As she grabs a bucket of water, she notices the rabbits. They have plenty to eat. Everywhere you look, there is tall grass. The rabbits are accustomed to feasting near collaborative members. As long as one does not get too close, they chomp away and occasionally look up.

Behind the tarp, Camille sponged herself. She could hear other members starting to arrive. It is a very important and exciting morning. To hear Ben and Jessica exchange pleasantries gave Camille and others a smile. After wiping herself dry, she got dressed. There were a few dirty clothes she wishes to hand wash. They should dry quickly in this heat.

Slowly, more members came for their morning gathering. It became a bon voyage sendoff. It was mid-morning before William and family arrived.

What a contrast of emotions. Fred is joyous that he is going on a trip; he sees it as a vacation. William, well, he always has a poker face. It is his wife who has a sad and hapless look. Carrying Fred's bag with two hands, she has tears running down her face. She looks like little orphan Annie on her way to a homeless shelter. It must be painful for William. This is real a causality of the EMP strike. Many millions have suffered. Thousands have died. The elderly, homeless, handicapped, many who were dependent on the government. It certainly wasn't the best of times. But, for many, it was the worst of times.

This road trip gives hope for survival. Ann really feels she will make a difference. With a wealth of information, she will give the big government power player's valuable insight. Countless people are dying each day; the government needs to be bought up to speed. It is Ann's opinion that the common folks can act as an auxiliary. The two collaborative are proof of that.

Just supply the jeeps, firearms, food, and medicines at the local level to ordinary folks. They have a better feel and understanding of the people's needs. In the large apartment complexes, for example, the elderly, disabled, and sickly can be helped more efficiently in groups. There are local nurses and medically trained people who are capable of triage. The glass is always half-empty and half-full. The collaborative provide safe zones, a buffer from evil. Many towns have volunteer firemen. Even Arthur Fiedler of "the Boston Pops" was an honorary captain of the Boston Fire Department.

During World War II, the French resistance consisted of ordinary people who wreaked havoc on the Nazi regime. Just have key state police and military personnel deputize or appoint certain volunteers. Ann feels strongly that it will work. Taking Camille, Fred, and William with her makes the trip even more vital.

It was late morning and everyone is antsy. They are all waiting for

Ann (Officer Ryan's wife) to show up in a Humvee. Maybe one of the young kids can climb a tree. Up there with binoculars, the young kid can give out a signal. One if by ocean, two if by—oh, scratch that. How about one if driving slow and two if driving moderately?

Finally, when all seems lost, a new and strange sound is heard. Off in the distance, the sound is getting louder and louder. Nearing William's house, this new and strange vehicle is approaching. It is a Humvee in standard desert camouflage. A vintage Canadian vehicle used in the Iraq War. It is a lot larger than a jeep and looks fearsome.

Now, if the collaborative had a band, they would really welcome this new arrival. Trouble is, Daniel is at the other collaborative with his accordion. Smiles were on everyone's faces, except that of William's wife. Too bad Vivian is not here. She could give her some support. Ann drove up near the fire pit. She was wearing a pair of army fatigues. Along both sides of the Humvee were two large words: MILITARY PATROL. The air base is really trying to give Ann every advantage for her to be successful.

Ann tried to get a Humvee with a turret gun on the top. The brass at the air base has decided it is too much of a risk factor. One, they were afraid of collateral damage to innocent civilians; two, if Ann were to lose the Humvee to the wrong people, it would cause a great backlash.

Still the Humvee that Ann has is large. It sits four people comfortably. With a large and extended trunk, there is room for sleeping bags, tents, duffel bags, food, water, ammunition, etc. With a grate in the front and large tires, it is well-equipped to handle many crisis. At the air base, she had to go to the quartermaster's barracks. She was given several supplies. Eventually, the base commander gave her four firearms and three rifles. One of the rifles even had a scope on it. It was a daunting task that took Ann several hours.

She explained she is taking two adult males and one female. It gave the base commander a little sigh of relief. She did not tell them that Fred is challenged.

Even her husband bit his tongue on that one. Sometimes, silence is golden. Ann had a whole checklist of supplies that were packed. Tire kit, tire inflator, oil, toilet paper, jumper cables, first-aid kit, shampoo, soap, towels, flares, laundry soap, small toolbox, lighters, flashlights, medicine box, and ammo. The air base has been through this many times. Sometimes, going by the numbers works.

William and Camille loaded their duffel bags. William has one for Fred. His pants are cleaned but wrinkled. Around William's waist is a long sleeve shirt. The day is extremely warm. Having a tall but slender body, William is always paranoid about cold weather. One wonders why he remains in the cold climate of the northeast.

Camille is the polar opposite. She is always conscious about her looks. In her younger years, she carried a lot less weight. She was a stunning-looking woman. Perhaps the closest resemblance would be the woman in the animated film *Who Framed Roger Rabbit?* an hourglass shape. As years went by, children, stress, and gravity had an effect on her. She is still happy with herself and remains upbeat. Camille always wears a cross on her neck. To her, it is the beauty of one's soul that is important. If only the rest of us would look at life that way.

There is no expensive bottle of champagne to break on the Humvee, to launch their journey. Only good wishes and a tearful separation between William and his wife. As William climbed into the back of the Humvee, his wife really broke down. This sight tore William apart.

Even though he had a stoic personality, he loves and respects his wife.

Camille is riding shotgun. She turned to William and said, "God will be with you. He will keep you safe." The palm of her hand was behind her cross. She brought it to her mouth and kissed it in a sign of reverence.

As these last few emotional minutes expired, William remained silent. For one of the first times in his life, a tear ran down the side of his face. There was some real evil in his early years. The experience relegated him to a protective shell. Yes, he has seen a therapist and a physiologist.

William has an extremely high IQ. Every time he saw a professional, he knew what they were going to ask and how they were going to treat him. He decided to find answers within himself. He reads self-awareness books, and the book *Journey of Souls* by Dr. Michael Newton.

The closest thing to peace for William was, first, his marriage to his wife, and then taking care of Fred. William is a kind and sensitive person. Fred is living with a walking time bomb. He really needs a doctor to monitor his blood pressure and diabetes. It is a gamble. If anything did happen to Fred, William's fragile state of mind might be his undoing.

Ann started up the Humvee; everyone is waving, except William's wife. As they pulled out of the yard, the divorcee came up to stand by her, putting her arms around and rubbing her shoulders. I am sure the first few days will be very dramatic and painful.

Randy and Sarah watched William's wife with great sadness. Randy turned to Sarah and commented, "I think I will give her two days, then I am going to see if Vivian can stay with her. It will really be comforting to both of them." Sarah, with her arms folded, nodded in agreement.

The journey is afoot. Ann passes her own house. Her husband, Officer Ryan, is working at the prison again. They have been really short-staffed. The state police really need him for other pressing duties. They also sent a request for support to the air base and National Guard. Everyone is short-staffed. Getting supplies and protecting government installations is sucking up all their personnel.

Officer Ryan made a request of Ann to stop by the prison on her trip. The prison is in the middle of the state. The easiest and most direct route is traveling west on the Mass Pike. When the EMP strike went off, most were traveling east on the Mass Pike toward Boston. The route she is taking is often traveled by government officials with an armed escort. The gangs know it well and stay clear.

Since she does not have access to a GPS, Ann installed an old-fashioned compass on the dashboard of the Humvee. She had her Dozier and a US map in the front seat. After an hour's drive, they were going west on the Mass Pike.

Like a baby in a candy store, William, Fred, and Camille were in awe. The destruction of the EMP blast was in full view. Thousands of cars littered the Mass Pike. Military bulldozers and tanks had pushed them aside.

Definitely beyond the scope of Triple AAA. There were a few pedestrians walking and some others on bikes. The cars and trucks that were pushed had been damaged by the bulldozers. Many of the pedestrians were still looking for items that could be useful. Some were hoping for a ride, or help from the government.

As Ann was driving down the Mass Pike, Camille, William, and Fred noticed the sad looks on the faces of nearby pedestrians. If there was not a sign on the side of the Humvee, I am sure some of the onlookers would have pestered Ann for help. Overhead, they heard the noise of a large cargo plane. It was on its decent, about to land at the air base. There were no other commercial planes in the air. It was eerily reminiscent of 9/11, when President Bush ordered all airplanes to be grounded.

Ann had been on the Mass Pike for forty minutes; her exit was coming up. Her husband had taken this ride several times since the EMP blast. The only saving grace was the perks he now received. He gets his clothes cleaned and pressed, haircut done, home-cooked meals prepared, and the use of a push lawn mower. It is a strange atmosphere. All the prisoners are aware of the EMP blast; most are happy to be taken care of.

The Humvee entered into the main gate. As a guard pushed the gate open, Ann showed her license. The guard was expecting Officer Ryan's wife to show up. Ann was instructed to wait. It would be a good ten-minute wait. Officer Ryan showed up with a few goodies. A few of his friends were army reservists and donated their fatigue jackets. Might as well look the part. He also had a meatloaf casserole and a couple of other side dishes.

Ann turned to Camille and William and asked them if they needed to use a bathroom. It took only a few seconds; everyone thought it would be wise to use one. They entered the main office. The prison had generators for backup. What a strange and familiar effect. It was warm, and there was a fan going! Camille stood right in front and felt the breeze. It felt like heaven.

She turned to Ann and said, "No wonder your husband wants to work this detail."

After they used the bathroom, they all went back to the Humvee. It is getting on to early afternoon. Ann wanted to put in several miles before nightfall. She and her husband hugged and kissed (no salutes). Starting up the Humvee, Officer Ryan waved goodbye to the whole crew. Fred is impressed. He always had respect for police and firemen. They had given him a real fireman's hat and a few badges.

The prison was now out of sight. It is official—all four have separated from their families and friends. Like a Lewis and Clarke expedition, it was time to head off to the unknown. Traveling the Mass Pike is the easy part. The military and local authorities took great efforts to open up a path. Instead of plowing snow, they were plowing vehicles. It was like the great blizzard of 1978, when Governor Dukakis received federal help by flying in bulldozers from Ft. Benning, Georgia, to plow the snow away.

Watching out for debris and possible gangs, Ann drove cautiously. Game plan is to take an exit that is marked for New York City. Officer Ryan also gave Ann a digital camera. The air base has been receiving supplies from Canada and the western US. Taking pictures for the government will add value to this trip. Like Hurricane Katrina, there will be valuable lessons to be learned. If and when Ann feels that a picture should be taken, she or Camille will take it.

In the back seat, Fred was wearing his army khaki shorts. He had a short-sleeve shirt with a Pinkerton badge pinned on. Today, he was wearing his cowboy boots. Fred dresses to be happy. William has to pick his battles. Fred always puts his dirty clothes in the hamper; he enjoys being clean. He also had his headset on. It ran on triple A batteries. With several packages of batteries at his command, Fred is good to go. Ninety degrees outside and Fred is listening to "Jingle Bells."

Mid-afternoon. Ann finally reaches the exit for NYC (New York City). There were not as many vehicles on the road. When the EMP went off, it was early in the morning; most commuters were on the way to work. Leaving Boston the traffic was a lot lighter. Still, it is a shame to see some high-priced beauties bulldozed to the side.

While driving, they did encounter some light traffic. It usually was military (US and Canadian), a few bicycles, antique cars, and old motorcycles. They could not stop for the people walking. Ann cannot save the world. The pedestrians walking were looking for food and supplies. Almost all of them had a knife or stick for protection. It was not only the thugs they were wary of, but also packs of dogs set free by their owners.

It had been over an hour since they took the exit to NYC. Fred started to nag William. He is used to a regiment, and now he is hungry. Three squares a day. Just like the military (or prison life), William, being sensitive to Ann, kept putting his two fingers to his mouth and saying, "Hush." It wasn't long before Ann looked in the rearview and noticed what was going on. They had been driving several hours. It was time for a pit stop.

Looking for a good strategic place to stop, Ann noticed a large eighteen-wheeler on the side of the road. From that vantage point, she could see a long distance both behind and in front of her.

"All right, folks, time for a break," Ann announced as she pulled near the eighteen-wheeler.

"Look, guys, you two can take a bathroom break behind the eighteen-wheeler. Just let me know if you need toilet paper," Ann said as she got out a gas can and a hose. It was time to fuel up. Neither William nor Fred needed toilet paper, but they really had to pee.

Behind the eighteen-wheeler, Fred dropped his pants to pee. It is the only way he knows how to pee. When William takes him into a restaurant, it can be embarrassing. Too see another man drop his pants at the urinal often raises red flags. Many people do not know or understand the habits of challenged people. They might mistake him for a pervert, which is really sad. Most of the time, William asks Fred to use a john and tells him to close the doors. It usually works.

Finishing their business, Ann turns to Camille. "You're next. Toilet paper is in the back. Take some water to wash your hands," Ann said as she continues to siphon more diesel.

After Ann finished with the fuel, she took her turn in back of the eighteen-wheeler. Being careful with where she walked, she did her business. We can call it "squatter rights." Coming back to the Humvee, Ann took out the food her husband (Officer Ryan) gave her. Fred likes to eat heavy, but Ann knew that it would not be a good idea. This should be the last bathroom break for a few hours.

All feasted on a nice home-cooked meal at the prison. The inmates had it good. During this EMP strike, prison life is not "hard time"; it actually is "good survival time."

Fred is looking for ketchup. He puts ketchup on everything. If it is a badly cooked meal, no worries. Ketchup makes everything taste good. As long as he doesn't put ketchup on his ice cream, everything will be all right.

"Sorry, Fred, no ketchup this time," Ann said in an apologetic tone.

"How about a piece of bread? So I can sop up the bottom of my plate," Fred pleaded.

Ann went into the back of the Humvee and took out one piece of bread. She did not want Fred to have a bowel movement until they camped, so she gave Fred the piece of bread.

It is time to get the show on the road. With necessities done, it is off to NYC. At least they wanted to go south before they veered westward.

William helped wash Fred's plate. William himself only ate a few cashew nuts. As he is cleaning the plate, Camille turned to Ann.

"That boy needs some meat on his frame," Camille said in a constructive way.

Ann did not reply to Camille's comment. As a policewoman, she has learned how to measure her words and actions. Police business has a lot of liabilities attached to it.

Fred put his headphones again. This time he is listening to "Deck the Halls." Maybe God is blessing him in a strange way. To keep him happy requires the simplest things in life. William is just meditating. The late afternoon sun is starting to drop in the sky. The real hot part of the day is over. It is becoming tolerable to Camille, Fred, and Ann. To William, it is time for his long-sleeve shirt.

They had driven for a little over an hour since lunchbreak. Something is in the air (like a Phil Collins song). They were accustomed to the constant fires and debris. The landscape is changing. They are coming closer to the epicenter of the blast. There is actually some small tree damage and blown-out windows.

The other change is a very large fire. Ann had a change in her facial countenance. It is now an expression of concern. She glanced at the sun. It's position shows her that it is now late afternoon.

The day has been long and eventful. Debris on the road seems to be increasing. During the trip, they have seen occasional pedestrians, military transports, and a rare antique vehicle. For the last few miles, Ann was not seeing any kind of life. There is not even a stray dog. While the others in the Humvee are unaware, Ann has a keen instinct to her surroundings. Up ahead there is a large sign sitting on a tripod. Their travel slowed. It seems the bulldozers had given up on this stretch of the road.

NO FURTHER ACCESS, ALL VEHICLES MUST TAKE NEXT EXIT, the sign read.

By the army core of engineers, Ann just stopped the Humvee and put her hands on the steering wheel.

"Well, guys, I guess we are going into the suburbs," Ann said cautiously.

Deep inside her, she knew something is very amiss. Did the government just run out of assets? Or was the damage near the epicenter too overwhelming? There is an old saying, "Curiosity killed the cat." In her mind, she wanted to drive toward this new forbidden zone. Camille had Ann's camera and took a few pictures. Wouldn't it be nice to have a few pictures?

Pictures of the forbidden zone. It would give the trip even more valuable information.

As they exited the highway, Ann looked at her compass. It is now pointing in a more westerly direction. It is the direction that they must travel to get to the tent city near the Mississippi River. The forbidden zone is southeast.

It is coming up to late afternoon. There is still a good three hours till dusk. Up ahead there is a fork in the road. The right fork took a westerly direction; the left a more southerly direction.

Ann had to take the left turn. Camille, well, she is used to danger. She had a 9mm gun and a camera. She totally trusted Ann. Way up ahead there seems to be another roadblock. Ann just stopped the Humvee.

"Camille, in the glove compartment is a set of binoculars. Will you please hand them too me?" Ann said politely.

"Thanks," Ann stated as Camille handed her the binoculars.

Off in the distance is a roadblock. There is an army jeep with two soldiers shouldering their rifles. What to do? She does have an official document signed by the commander at the air base. She looked in the rearview mirror. William has a very tense look on his face. She turned the rearview mirror just so slightly. Fred had his headphones on, singing off key. Ann smiled and turned the Humvee around. Her mission is to reach Tent City safely. Somehow she sees Fred in the same category as children and animals. They are the innocent and must be protected. After all, she is a policewomen. "To serve and protect."

Déjà vu! Back to the same fork. This time Ann turns right. William, well his face is less tense. The large fire seems to be getting closer. Driving for several minutes, the houses seem to be spaced further apart. Soon she saw a clearing.

In the middle of it was a small pond. I was getting late. At best there is only an hour and half of sunlight left.

Ann pulled off the road and drove slowly. The grass seems to be over a foot tall. Stopping near the pond, Ann got out of the Humvee.

"We are going to set up camp," Ann said with a little authority.

William had to poke Fred to get his attention. Fred got out of the Humvee. He walked a couple of feet and started to drop his pants. He thought this was a bathroom break.

"Not yet, Fred. We are sleeping here tonight. Just wait a couple of minutes," William said in a gentle voice.

William helped take out the two tents. They had about one hour of sunlight left. Camille grabbed the small shovel and dug a hole for a quick fire pit. Fred enjoyed looking for small pieces of wood. Time to heat up supper. Even though there were still leftovers of the meatloaf, Ann wanted to add a few different can goods to the mix.

William is pretty handy. He decided to put up both tents. William and Fred would sleep in one. The other will be for Ann and Camille. Tonight will be William's first time to sleep with a firearm next to him. The Humvee is off the road and there doesn't seem to be anyone around.

Not one to take any chances, Ann is setting up several trip wires. She puts posts in the ground and strings a wire across them. The fire might attract a thug or hoodlum. Seeing a military vehicle usually sends out warning signals to most of them.

William turned to Fred and told him it's okay to use the bathroom. Fred walked a good fifty feet from the Humvee to pee. Camille and Ann are now used to Fred's habits and accepted them gracefully.

Lastly, William had to dig two small holes on each side of the Humvee. One hole is for William and Fred, the other for Ann and Camille. They were all very concerned with the environment. Camille asked Ann if it's okay to take a few pictures. Receiving Ann's blessing, Camille took a few of the group.

William is a little chilly, but the others enjoyed the cooler evening. The fire kept the mosquitoes away. The last thing they had to worry about is ticks.

No sense surviving this dangerous trip then come down with Lyme disease. Sitting around the fire and enjoying each other's company relieved tensions. Before Fred ate, William dipped a syringe with a little alcohol. He then drew some insulin from a vial that he had. Fred doesn't even react to receiving the shot.

Off in the distance, everyone could see the large fire. Since the EMP blast, there have been multiple fires, but not of this magnitude. It is in the direction they are traveling. Tonight everyone is going to go to sleep early. Tomorrow promises to have many challenges.

EMP Causality: Part V
Danger

Sleeping out of their green zone is just not cricket. All night Ann and the others experienced the same sounds, the same smells. The occasional bang—*Bang!*—of a 9mm gun is followed by the smell of burnt ash. Before the EMP blast, this would be a rare occurrence. It probably would make the local news. Now, the news stations on the East Coast are kaput.

Everyone except Fred tossed and turned. Ann gave a flashlight for William and Fred. Even though they are camping, when nature calls, it's hard to find that hole in the ground without light. The only exception might be William. He eats so little. It stands to reason, if very little is going in one end, very little is coming out the other. All right, I got it. I'm moving along now, folks.

The only one who really needs sleep is Ann. Camille and William have offered to drive. Camille explained to Ann that she has driven from Boston to Orlando on multiple occasions. Twice she drove straight through without any sleep. Ann is definitely considering it. Her only hesitation is they are driving a military vehicle. Although she has the base commander's blessing, she is still a Massachusetts police officer. What authority gives Camille and William permission to drive a military vehicle?

One thought I had is that Ann could deputize them. Like the movie *Blazing Saddles.* Then again, the misfits said, "We don't need any stinking badges." Ann is a pragmatic leader. She has a natural instinct to do the right thing. When and if the time is right, she will let Camille drive.

Coming out of his tent, William slapped a mosquito at his check. He went to the pond to sponge himself. After brushing his teeth and washing up, he grabbed a few dirty clothes to wash. The weather is warm. Mostly likely it will be another muggy day. William really wanted to contribute. He is determined to start a morning fire before Ann gets up.

Ann did not sleep well. Driving into the abyss is stressful enough. Having the safety of three others is a lot on her shoulders. She heard the flames of the morning fire and knew it was William's contribution. Perhaps for the first time since she started this road trip, she is relaxed.

Ann curled up in a fetal position. With a smile on her face, she decided to sleep for another hour or two.

Camille stretched her arms and saw Ann. She quietly exited the tent. Before she did, she took the camera and took a few shots. This way she can show it to her husband (Officer Ryan). See, she really was sleeping by herself. In reality, they have a great marriage. Why would either of them cheat? They both have guns. Now that's what I call "trust and verify," or how about "Go ahead, make my day and cheat"?

"Good morning, William" Camille said with a roll of toilet paper in her hand.

"Morning, Camille. I took it on myself to cook a little breakfast for everyone," William replied. He found a skillet in the back of the Humvee.

"Ah William, I need to use the spot that you dug for Ann and me," Camille said while shaking the roll of toilet paper over her head.

"No worries! I see nothing," William said.

At this point, Fred is smelling food and started to exit the tent. William put his two fingers on his lips. He quietly told Fred to wait a few minutes. Fred almost always listens to William. He is stuck to William's hip. Fred knows he is his lifeline. He has always been a good advocate for Fred. In Fred's mind, he sees William as his protector and provider.

"All set," Camille yelled out as she headed for the pond. She too wanted to wash out her dirty clothes.

At this point, William told Fred to come out. Fred said that he needed to use the bathroom. William got him some toilet paper. He also gave a heads-up to Camille. Fred sees the use of a bathroom in a different light. Privacy is not as important to him as others. It is not a bad thing; It's just one of his own natural habits.

Camille took her washed clothes and hung them on a nearby branch. By the time they leave, her clothes should be dried.

Fred loves to mimic his friends. So he walks down to the pond to sponge-bathe himself. He deeply wants to be accepted by the people who surround him. In his eyes, he feels he is normal. Perhaps that is why he is happier than most of us. No bills, no appointments to drive to (although very few are driving now). No meals to cook or laundry to wash. Though he did enjoy putting the clothes in the washing machine and later in the dryer.

Camille comes over to William, deciding to help with breakfast. It also gives her time to bond with William. Camille is street-wise and finds William intriguing. William is a good listener. When he speaks, he chooses his words carefully. The best way I can describe it is, you are at a party and you meet a high-price lawyer. Whatever subject you engage in, the lawyer is listening attentively.

He really is not enjoying himself; instead, he is analyzing and finding holes to everything you say. Now imagine you come back several months later and you go to another party. Stressful week! You have a few cocktails to unwind. Wouldn't you know, it's the same lawyer? With a slight buzz on, you engage in a conversation with the lawyer. This time he interrupts you and says, "That is not what you said last time!" He walks away, making you feel like a fool.

William is not spiteful. He would just listen and store everything you tell him. Scary, isn't it? He missed his calling; he should have been a detective. Can you imagine how many cases he would solve? Then again, I should have been a professional tennis player. Hard to start at middle age with a potbelly.

The morning is going smoothly so far. Ann has gotten a few hours of beauty sleep. (To her husband, she is always beautiful.) The sound of a crackling fire—and the sight of her new friends—makes for a nice start.

"Morning, troops," Ann said.

"Morning," both Camille and William replied.

"Got to use the hole," Ann said with a roll paper in her hand.

"Got it," Camille said as she raised her hand in acknowledgment. She was facing the fire, which means her back was to Ann.

William also raised his hand in acknowledgment. Camille and Fred started to enjoy breakfast. William is breaking a few pieces of bread apart and slowly digesting them. With the amount that Fred consumes, he makes up for the two of them. As they were enjoying each other's company, William looks up.

He sees several youngsters on bicycles. They were staring at the Humvee and the movements of William, Fred, and Camille. Ann is out of sight, since the hole is behind the Humvee.

"Ann," William said in a deliberate but moderate tone.

"What?" Ann replied with a loud and perturbed voice.

"There are Chileans (slang for children) on the road," William responded as he continued with his cooking.

"Thanks, I will be there is a few minutes," Ann responded.

It took a good ten minutes, but Ann arrived at their little fire pit. She saw the children on the road. All told, there must have been at least six bikes. The ages seemed to vary between eight and fourteen years of age. To invite them down to eat might cause a stampede. Besides, they only packed food for just the four of them.

Determined to enjoy their morning breakfast, they sat there for a good fifteen minutes. Just as Camille stood up, one of the children took off on his bike. Surely he is going to inform somebody of the military presence. Hopefully, it will be their parents and not a biker gang. Maybe in LA, biker gangs use children for runners, but not in the suburbs of the East Coast.

"Time to pull up stakes," Ann said in a measured tone. She carefully checked that her pistol is still holstered. She did not want to pull it out. She knew it would scare their new onlookers. Both in the military and police academy, they were taught to clean and take care of their firearms. Usually Ann does that right after breakfast. Today she used a little discretion. Eventually, when they stop for another break, she will clean her weapons.

They all pull together as a team. William filled in the two holes. He also dismantled the little fire pit. Camille and Fred worked on taking the tents down. Everything needed to be folded and systematically loaded in the back of the Humvee. Remember that old info commercial, "Like it never happened"? This is their game plan.

On the road, the children with their bikes just observed. Soon the lone biker returned with several adults. There was also another kid. He is just walking his bike. Seems like the back tire is low. The middle-aged adults look like a motley crew. The men were unshaven, and their hair looked like they had been in an electrical storm. The women seemed like they were having a bad hair day. They had wrinkled clothes, the type found in the bottom of a Salvation Army clothes bin. If they only had a couple of pitchforks, they could pose for a picture for an old farmer's almanac, 1930s style.

Ann started up the Humvee. They have left the area clean. Pulling up toward the road, Ann told Camille to lay her gun on her lap. The adults and children just seem to be hapless victims of the EMP strike. These are desperate times with desperate people. With the engine running, Ann decided to exit the vehicle.

"Hello, what's up?" Ann asked.

"Are you sent from the military to help us?" the spokesman asked.

"Just a forward scouting expedition; we are gathering information," Ann said in a calculated manner.

"See that fire? That is a whole apartment complex burning to the ground. Hundreds of families are homeless. Where are they going to sleep? Eat? How are they going to live?" the spokesman said with anger.

"I don't know," Ann said with a sad look on her face.

"Those damn young thugs. They need to be shot. We can't even go to the armory. They intercept us and take everything. Young girls are raped. A few have been killed," the spokesman said with a tear.

"What about the commander at the armory?" Ann asked.

"The major? He is a piece of army bureaucratic crap! We told him what is going on. He stated they are understaffed and he had to follow orders," the spokesman said in disgust.

Ann shook her head. She got up and walked around for a few minutes. Her mission is to see everyone delivered safely to a westward tent city. She glanced at the motley bystanders. Next she looked at William and Camille. Ann put her finger up to the bystanders to signal *Give me just one moment.* She then walked back to the Humvee. Arriving at the door with Camille, Ann put the palms of her hand on the door.

"Look, guys, my mission is to see all of you safely to a tent city. I really think I need to talk to this major. Something is very wrong. "People are dying," Ann said in a slow and worried tone.

Camille seemed to understand. William, on the other hand, had a real worried look on his face. Ann did not want to ask or debate with William or Camille. She had to look at the big picture. Yes, Fred's life is important. At the same time, the lives of hundreds might be saved. Bottom line: It is for the good of the many than just for the one. There is an old saying: "It's lonely being at the top." When the buck stops and your left to make the decision, you fall or rise with the outcome. When a pro team has a bad season, they fire the coach. The same goes for the CEO of a company. If profits are way down, often it is bye-bye!

Ann walked backed. She carefully and slowly gazed at the whole motley crew. They in turn had their eyes and hopes on Ann. Not only were they badly dressed, but there was a ghastly appearance to their body frames. After a few seconds of silence, she turned to the spokesman.

"Let's go. You can come with us. I need to talk to this major. The rest of you, I want you to sign your name on this piece of paper. I am going to see that you get some supplies," Ann said with authority.

The spokesman climbed in the back with William and Fred. It is a tight fit, but the ride is hopefully short. William found his body odor a little offensive. Better that he just kept quiet. The spokesman showed Ann the directions.

Hopefully, if all goes well, they should be there in twenty-five minutes. Driving along, Ann noticed that the large fire seemed to be turning into a real whirlwind of black smoke. It is not a good omen.

Taking many turns and watching out for debris, everyone in the Humvee heard screams. Sounded like a young girl and an older woman. Ann at this point drove a little slower and alerted all inside to be quiet. Making the turn, Ann and Camille put their guns on their lap. William put a rifle across his lap, with the barrel pointing to the outside window. The spokesman and Fred both seemed to have a worried look on their faces.

Coming into a clearing, Ann saw a group of civilians. They were coming back from the armory. The food and supplies were spilled all over the ground. Two thugs with guns were violating the young girl. Not only is the mother screaming, but she is holding onto her son. Her son wanted to protect his sister, but her mother is afraid he will be shot. The screaming helped stifle the sounds of the Humvee.

"That's the same two thugs who raped and killed a young girl last week. It is why we are afraid to go the armory," the spokesman cried out.

Ann stopped the Humvee fifty feet before the group. Besides the mother, daughter, and son, there were four others. There is an elderly man, a middle-aged woman, and two teenage boys. Instinctively, Ann and Camille opened their door and walked out with their guns. William opened the rear door and exited with his rifle. He then went in front of the Humvee and kneeled. He raised his rifle and pointed it toward the two thugs. He is determined to give cover to Ann and Camille.

Ann has taught Camille to use two hands on her gun. It is more accurate when firing. The elderly man and two teenaged boys noticed them coming. One of the thugs saw the elderly man and two teenage boys turn their head. He knew something is awry. He immediately saw Camille and Ann coming with their guns.

He also noticed the Humvee and William pointing his rifle at them. The thug is a coward. With just two women, he might have a chance in a firefight. With William kneeling with his rifle pointing at them, the thugs would both be dead.

The thug alerted his friend. He said, "Let's get out of here." The other thug looked up and was shocked. It is the army Humvee and William with the rifle that really frightened him. They started to run.

Bang! Ann shot her gun over their heads.

"Stop or we will shoot," Ann yelled out loudly. Ann then turned sideward; Camille, mimicking her, did the same. This gave the thugs less of a body mass to shoot at. Ann then moved in closer. Camille and William stood their ground. Both thugs wore baggy pants just like all the other gangbangers.

"Drop your guns and put your hands on the top of your head," Ann stated as she walked sideward, closer to the thugs.

At this point, Camille who is a good twenty feet behind Ann decided to also walk a little closer. After she finished, William followed their lead and did the same. Both of the thugs were acting erratically. Their twitching and body signs showed indecision. Ann seized the moment.

"Simple! You both need to drop your guns or you're both dead," Ann yelled in a commanding tone.

The younger thug threw his gun on the ground and put both his hands on his head. Camille then walked a little to her right. This gave the remaining thug a zero chance to survive a firefight. Looking at William and the Humvee told him the three of them are professionals.

"Okay, you win." The remaining thug threw his gun on the ground. He then put his hands on his head.

"Step back five feet," Ann commanded sharply.

Ann then walked up and kicked the two guns to the side. Still looking at them, she picked up both guns. At this point, the molested daughter ran to her mother. There, both her mother and brother hugged and cried.

"Now both of you drop your pants," Ann stated while she put the guns under her belt.

"What? No!" yelled the older thug.

Bang! "Just do what the lady says," Camille yelled as smoke came out of her gun.

Ann, with her gun still pointing at the two thugs, turned and looked at Camille. When the gun went off, Ann momentarily crouched her head. She muttered to Camille, "What the f——?"

Camille just stared at the thugs. The younger thug dropped his pants. He obviously peed in his pants. The older one decided it was a losing battle and complied with Ann's wishes.

"Step back another five feet," Ann commanded. At this point, the thugs were totally humiliated." Camille! Would you mind checking their pockets?"

With a sour look, Camille obeyed. She did not want to go through the younger one's pants. Ann threw her police gloves to Camille. She found extra clips of ammo and several narcotics.

Ann walked over to the distraught mother of the molested daughter.

"Have you ever fired a gun before?" Ann asked.

"Heavens no! Why?" the distraught mother retorted.

Ann took one of the guns that was under her belt. She handed it to her.

"Here, hold it with two hands. Always aim for the middle of their body.

Take a deep breath and exhale. As you exhale, pull the trigger. You go that?" Ann asked.

"I think so," the distraught mother replied.

"Repeat what I just said," Ann stated with a commanding voice.

The distraught mother took a deep breath and repeated exactly what Ann had said. With the situation under control, Ann told the two thugs to pick up their pants and never came this way again. Being a Massachusetts police officer, she has no authority to arrest anyone out of her state. The thugs thought that Ann and Camille were in the army. The distraught mother and the others thanked them profusely.

Time to continue on. Ann, William, and Camille climbed back into the Humvee. Once in the Humvee, Ann turned around and looked at Fred.

"You okay, Fred?" Ann asked with sympathy.

"Yes, I'm okay. Why didn't you arrest the bad guys?" Fred asked.

"Do you watch a lot of TV, Fred?" Ann asked.

"I did, until William turned off our electricity," Fred answered.

William just shook his head. Ann and Camille just smiled. They continued with their trip to the armory. The rest of the trip was uneventful. Finally they were in the sight of the armory. It was an army Humvee, so she decided to drive as close as she could. Ann stopped about fifty feet from the armory. It is a beehive of activity. There were two large army trucks that were being unloaded. Several miles away, the black smoke gave everyone a somber disposition. It seemed like they were behind enemy lines, and that the war was just ahead of them.

Ann noticed the portable bathrooms. She asked William to take Fred there. Next, Ann suggested to the spokesman that he get in line. Camille stayed with the Humvee, at least until someone else came back. She then grabbed her dossier and headed to whoever is in charge.

Sitting at a desk near the front door is a sergeant with a clipboard, a middle-aged man with a stout body frame. He is definitely a lifer in the army. The saying goes, "There is the right way, the wrong way, and then there is the army way." The sergeant looked like he did everything by the book. Perhaps it is good for discipline and morale. In a way, Ann can relate to him. She and her husband have followed the rule book when it comes to law enforcement. But, after the EMP strike, she and her husband knew it was time to adapt in order to survive. It is the reason why Ann wanted to talk to the major. Time to adapt in this difficult circumstance.

"Sergeant, I would like an audience with the major," Ann asked without showing any fear.

"Do you have an appointment with him?" the sergeant asked.

"No, I haven't, but I have traveled a long way. I am on orders from the air base in Massachusetts.

"Your name?" the sergeant asked.

"Officer Ryan," Ann replied. She did not want to say anything more to the sergeant; it would have compromised her meeting.

The sergeant looked at her. He saw no bars on her fatigue jacket. Her pants were not military. He seemed confused. The Humvee is definitely military and Camille also had a military jacket on.

"You wait here, and I will see if the major will talk to you," the sergeant instructed as he went inside.

After five minutes, the sergeant finally came out. He walked down the steps. Looking at Ann, he stated, "The major will see you. You have five minutes of his time. Leave your gun with me."

"Thanks," Ann replied as she pulled out the gun she had holstered. The other gun she got from the thug was with Camille. She walked up the stairs and knocked on the door.

"Come in," the major replied. He was sitting at the desk signing papers. The major is looking over the manifesto that was handed to him. It has a list of the supplies that were on the two trucks. Usually, a lieutenant or captain would have taken this assignment. But the military had to use what assets or personnel they had in the area. The major lives nearby and was home on leave when the EMP blast went off.

Ann walked right up to his desk. He lifted his eyes and noticed she is not military. Being straight by the book, he put his pen down and locked the palm of his hands behind his head.

"What can I do for you . . . Officer Ryan? Is that what you go by?" the major stated.

"Yes, I am Officer Ryan. I am a policewoman assigned to a Massachusetts police barracks. We have a good working relationship with the air base. I have been asked to be a liaison for the air base. I am traveling to the tent city west of here," Ann stated.

"Fine, what's that got to do with me?" the major asked.

"The supplies are not reaching the people who really need help. The thugs and gangs are intimating, stealing, and accosting the survivors," Ann stated firmly.

"We are on orders to distribute supplies from the armory. We are short-staffed. It is sad, but there is nothing I can do about it," the major replied.

"Yes, there is something you can do about it. You can set up a civilian auxiliary. Just supply them with transportation and a few weapons. They can help and everyone is happy," Ann said cheerfully.

"Are you nuts? Supply the civilians with jeeps and guns? I don't think so," the major said in a loud and definite tone.

"Look, major, people are dying. We just saved a young girl from being raped.

We have already set up two collaboratives in Massachusetts. It works," Ann stated as she put her dossier on the table.

"You're wasting my time. I have no orders from command," the major retorted. He refused to even look at her dossier. "Besides, I am not taking any orders from a civilian policewoman. Your time is up," the major said in his arrogant and condescending tone.

Ann put her two hands on her dossier. She was ready to leave and turned to the major. "I am just going to have a few pictures of your armory and of me.

The commander of the air base had a digital camera flown in from central headquarters. He wanted to make sure I document everything. In four days, I have a meeting with someone who has two stars. I think you call it a two-star general. I will inform him of your attitude. He will be impressed that you did not look at the dossier. He will also be impressed that you did not want to take advice from a "civilian policewoman."

The major was speechless. Ann just looked up at the major. As she touched the door handle, she turned to the major.

"Don't worry about it, major. People are dying each day. I am sure the two-star general will give you a new assignment. Maybe an outpost for NORAD in northern Canada. Or maybe Cape Horn in South Africa. It should be like a Club Med vacation," Ann said with a grin as she exited the armory.

Ann picked up her gun and walked quickly to the Humvee. She approached Camille.

"How did it go?" Camille asked.

"Quick! Grab the rifle with the scope. Bring the camera with you. Camille, I want you to shoulder the rifle. Next, I want you to take pictures of me and the armory. I will explain later. Please, do it right now."

Camille exited the Humvee. She and Camille walked a good thirty feet.

Ann did not want the major to see Fred. She feels it will raise too many questions. Camille took the rifle. It had straps, so she shouldered it as Ann instructed her. Camille started to take pictures.

Inside the armory, the major is signing papers. A corporal is assisting the major. After a few seconds, the major stopped.

"Corporal, what is that Officer Ryan doing?" The major asked.

The corporal walked over to the window. With his two fingers, he parted the blinds, then turned around to the major.

"She is having someone take pictures of her. Another female with a scope rifle is also wearing a fatigue jacket. There are two men sitting in the back seat," the corporal stated in a descriptive manner.

The major snapped his pen in two.

"Damn! Just wait here, corporal," the major stated as he headed for the door.

Camille and Ann just finished and were turning around.

"Officer Ryan, hold on! I think I have been a little rash. Why don't you bring that dossier inside so we can talk," the major commented.

Ann did not want to humiliate the major. She turned to Camille and asked her to wait in the Humvee. They went inside and Ann laid out a feasible solution. Now the hapless victims and the military can coordinate a solution. Ann also told the Major that she has already given out two firearms. One to the distraught woman and one to the spokesman that accompanied them. It was a good meeting. The major took care of the spokesman. He had one of his men transport him back with supplies.

As Ann is meeting with the major, William got into the pharmacy line. He brought all of Fred's medical records on the trip. When the major and Ann exited the armory, Ann went over to William. The sergeant was a little more receptive.

William did get a few vials of insulin, a few syringes, and a small number of blood pressure pills. It was more than enough to take care of Fred until they reached Tent City.

Ann started up the Humvee; they were glad to leave. The spokesman not only walked away with supplies; he also had a 9mm to protect him. Checking in the rearview mirror, Fred seems to be in a good state of mind. William is also happy he received the insulin and blood pressure pills for Fred.

Westward bound, that is what the needle on the compass is showing.

Ahead they turned onto the major road that leaves the armory. The road has been cleared by the military. Countless vehicles were pushed aside. They were all mashed against the guardrails. Broken windows and mangled steel is all that is left of a once thriving highway. A real EPA nightmare.

Straight ahead is the massive fire that they have been fearing. With black smoke and ashes falling on the road, it seemed to act as an evil gatekeeper, an unwritten sign to stay away. What choice does Ann have? Behind her leads to NYC. The military seems to be blocking most roads. To the left or right, Ann would be heading back into the realm of the thugs. One encounter for today is enough. When you play Russian roulette, sooner or later the real bullet winds up in the chamber.

Like approaching a Mount St. Helens eruption, everyone could not only see the flames, but also feel the intensity of the heat. Carefully, Ann drove with her lights and wiper blades going. William put a handkerchief over his nose. Ann quickly got a bottle of water. She poured a little on everyone's head just to stay cool. The main gate to the apartment complex seems to be obliterated. The sign melted away. As they were passing the apartment complex, one sign was still intact. It read: STUCK IN TRAFFIC? IF YOU LIVED HERE, YOU WOULD BE HOME. Hopefully, they had fire insurance.

Free at last. Ann wanted to put several miles between her and the fire. The only vehicles they noticed were military. Some civilians were trying their luck with the mangled vehicles. Using a crowbar and a weapon, it seemed like a game of treasure-hunting. I guess when there is no HBO on your TV, you need to resort to a new hobby.

The Humvee is cloaked in ash from the fire. Without windshield wiper fluid, they would be totally blind. The breeze from driving does help, but Ann knows their morale is starting to drop. The sun is near its high point of the day, and the humidity is increasing. Everyone's nerves are being tested.

They are not battle-hardened tested troops. Both Camille and Fred are starting to sweat. It is not a good sign. Ann saw a large eighteen-wheeler on the side of the road. Time to make a pit stop. Pulling up next to the truck, the Humvee came to a full stop. William went into the back and grabbed a towel for Camille and Fred. Fred let William know he had to pee. He was instructed to go behind the Humvee. Ann started to siphon off some diesel fuel. With Ash everywhere, it seemed they came from the frontlines of the battlefield.

"Look, guys, I know you're hot and irritated. Take a few sips of water. I will be looking for a pond or reservoir," Ann stated, so they would have a little hope.

It was a short break. Now Camille had a towel in her left hand and binoculars in her right. Riding shotgun, Camille is on the lookout for any decent-size pond or reservoir. After a half-hour of driving, William noticed how uncomfortable Fred was; Like a little kid asking "Are we there yet?" William turned the question to Camille, "Any Luck?"

Camille put her left index finger up. Driving a few hundred yards further, Camille kept her finger up.

"Up ahead I see a large pond on the right," Camille said cheerfully.

Everyone's frown is now turned upside down. Camille pointed to Ann where to go. It was off the road a good quarter mile. Ann looked for a way to exit the highway. Eventually, she saw a break with the side guardrail. It looked as if the army bulldozers took part in the railing out.

Down a slight embankment, Ann traversed onto the connecting road. Camille directed Ann; there were only a few turns. Soon they saw signs that directed them to the large pond. It turned out to be a public beach for the local residents. A smile is on everyone's face. An actual sandy public beach. Time for a little pampering. Right now everyone is ready to take off their clothes and redeem their spirits. What happens at this pond, stays at the pond. Period!

As the Humvee started to pull in, they soon found out they were not alone. There were at least eight to ten others: a few senior citizens, a middle-aged woman, a young girl in a bikini sunbathing. Most notable is two teenage boys fishing with an older man. The older man is a little above average in height, weighing close to 220 pounds. His rough hands were typical of a middle-class working man. Next to him was a .22 rifle.

Startled, everyone seemed a little stunned to see any kind of moving vehicle. A military vehicle pulling in near them really is unexpected. The girl in the bikini raised her head and sat up. The older man lifted his .22 rifle. The military vehicle had a sign that read MILITARY PATROL. What caught everyone's eye was that it was covered in ash. The older man pointed to the two boys to just stay there. Were the occupant's friend or foe? Maybe it was the spoils of war? Many thugs and gangs could have overpowered this hapless military vehicle.

It is a moment of trepidation for the older man. His .22 rifle is cradled by his two hands. The side window is covered with ash, and it is hard to see who the occupants were. Everyone at the beach is a little tense. Slowly, the driver's door opens. A female slowly raises her head. It is Ann. To the occupants at the beach, this is a slight surprise. Ann walks in front of the Humvee. She has her army fatigue jacket and a pistol that is holstered.

Soon the front passenger door is opened. Out steps Camille and another female. At this point, it is a little shock and awe. Camille also had a gun, but she had it in her belt. It seems Ann choreographed the occupant's movements. She did ask Fred and William to remain seated. William did put a rifle on his lap. With the window slightly cracked, he viewed all the action. William is determined to protect Fred at all times.

Slowly with her dossier, Ann walked toward the man with the .22 rifle. At this point, no one at the beach seemed nervous or threatened. Ann looked haggard. With her face covered with some of the ash, and her body odor reflecting the humidity of the day, she came within fifteen feet of the older man. Every few seconds, the man did glance at Camille since she is carrying a pistol.

"How are you? My name is Ann. We are on a mission to a tent city, which is west of here," Ann said slowly.

"Are you in the military?" asked the older man.

"No, I am a Massachusetts state trooper. I have been commissioned by the air base in Massachusetts. I am carrying an older man with his provider. He needs medical help. We have been through a lot today. Really, we need to cool off and get out of these grimy clothes," Ann said as she handed the older dossier.

Camille is instructed not to make any sudden movements. Ann just stood still. The older man slowly thumbed through the pages of the dossier. He saw a picture of Ann in her police uniform. There is an official seal from the commander of the air base. The older man is impressed and started to relax.

"Bring your friends over," the older man said as he waved his hands for them to come.

With two females in charge, they didn't fit the profile of thugs or a gang. Besides that, they were older, and Camille had a full figure. William and Fred also exited the Humvee. William did carry his rifle with him. Fred is with him—a man in his seventies; this in itself made the beach goers at ease.

"We need to wash ourselves and our clothes," Ann quipped. "We have laundry soap with us."

"I have a water pump. My father had an old cast-iron water pump in his barn. I installed it here so the neighbors can have fresh water. You have to prime it and start pushing the handle up and down nonstop. It's over there," the older man said as he pointed. "Why don't you take turns? You can wash your selves and your clothes. It is located behind the tall grass, which gives a tad bit of privacy."

Ann let William and Fred go first. She and Camille walked over to the pond just to put water on their face and neck. They talked with the older man. He is a truck driver. His rig is one of the causalities that the army bulldozed. A total loss.

It took a good twenty minutes for William and Fred to finish. It is now Camille's turn. William and Fred looked clean and refreshed. They also washed and wrung out their clothes.

Fred, Ann, and Camille decided to swim in their underwear. William just sat with his rifle. He is just too timid to let anyone see him in his underwear. The two teenage boys giggled. Camille, being too heavy, gave the boys a free show. The young girl in the bikini just waved her hand at the two boys. She told them to grow up. The two boys looked at the girl in the bikini and continued to giggle. The older man just smiled. It is a good distraction from the dismal effects of the EMP blast.

It is near mid-afternoon. Overhead there seem to be thunder clouds forming. William started a little fire so they all grabbed some grub. The two teenage boys donated a few fish they caught. It is their way of paying a pittance for bad behavior. The older man and his wife joined them for a light lunch. Camille got her camera now that she is clothed. Someday, when she finally goes home, she will have a lot of stories to tell her daughter Vivian.

It is a quick lunch. Raindrops were starting. Everyone said their goodbyes. Ann shook the older man's hand and wished him well. The skies let loose a deluge of water. It is a signal from the man upstairs. "Time to pack up the rodeo and move on." With the rain, even the Humvee got its wash. The beachgoers ran for cover. Most hid under a tree. A few just ran down the road, heading home.

Ann started the Humvee. With the windshield wipers going, they can see again. As they left the beach area, they deposited the remains of the ash on the sand. Everyone's spirits have been lifted. with their bodies cleaned and their bellies full, everyone felt human again. Even William had a smile on his face. The lighting seemed like a flare gun in the middle of a battle. The intensity of the rain limited the speeds of the Humvee. They had no deadline, but after four days, I am sure Ann's state police barracks will be in distress. They are hoping to receive a call from command central at Tent City.

Today is their second day, and it's time to put a few miles away.

Heavy rain was impeding their journey to Tent City. As the old English saying goes, "It's raining cats and dogs." Ye old folklore explains that during heavy rains, the cats and dogs would slip off the roofs of thatched roofs. Other, less pleasant versions state that the dead animals would surface with rising waters in the bad sections of the cities.

There is a lot of English culture and tradition in the Boston area. It is also found in much of the original thirteen-colony states. Taking a train ride from London to Cliffs in Dover, one can see familiar names: like New Boston, Scituate, Gloucester, even Dover. When the outcasts settled in New England, they brought their language, religions, family values, cookery—they brought everything except their form of governance. The early settlers developed a new form of government. One for and by the people. They were farmers and workers. For a few months each year, they would go to the local state capital to enact laws.

Their main goal was to have a small and less obtrusive government but an army to protect them. King George had a large army. They were spread out throughout the world; the strong conquering the weak. There was a pecking order, a systematic way of governing. The first shots were fired at Concord and Lexington, Massachusetts. The patriots were outnumbered 77 to 250.

The British won most of the battles. It was their old ways of fighting that became their undoing. The patriots hid behind trees. The British with their red coats marching in formation became easy targets. The patriots were free to fight their own way, to govern their own way. It is a concept that King George could not handle. England's budget was draining too fast.

Even the Great Wall of China ran into financial problems. A large military can protect a society, but at the same time it can be its downfall. Just ask Napoleon. My bad, you can't! He's dead. Napoleon marched his army too far and too fast. Not enough money or supplies. He met his Waterloo.

Fast forward to today. We possess a large government, massive law enforcement, powerful military, and too many politicians. In effect, we have made a full circle to becoming what King George was. People are depended on government from cradle to death. The long arm of the law—from amber alerts to the top "most wanted"—is extremely powerful.

The EMP strike was a major calamity knocking out much of our electricity-dependent infrastructure. Still, there are other possible calamities. How about a major earthquake along the San Andreas Fault? A biological attack? A category -five hurricane? The list goes on, and the government can only do so much to respond. They are sending supplies to armories along the East Coast. But, with depleted assets and strained resources, it is a game of endless mistakes.

Ann and the folks at the air base operate as members of the civilian law enforcement and military arms of government. They may be doing their best, trying to rise from the phoenix, trying to help people survive and flourish again.

The government, operating inside its own large bubble, has forgotten the greatest resource of all: the free will and spirit of its own citizens—a spirit that helped with many inventions: electricity, phone, TVs, combustion engines; even our own creations: Hollywood, music, tennis, baseball, football, fashions, etc.

Ann's mission is to deliver this valuable dossier to central headquarters, now located nearer the Mississippi River. Fred, William, and Camille are on this road trip for other reasons. All of them understand the dangers. With the Humvee, adequate supplies, and weapons, the group feels confident. Camille is taking pictures with a digital camera: one from central headquarters is flown in on a military cargo flight.

Just as quick as the summer rain storm started, it ended. Like a divine cleansing, the water has washed the dust off the roads and the vehicles that littered the roads. Ann has missed the entrance point where she exited. She is relying on a compass. It was the same instrument our early ships and pioneers used. She knew sooner or later there would be an entrance to a major road or highway.

As soon as the rained stopped, Camille and William opened a window. The breeze felt heavenly. Fred is in his glory. He is a passenger in an army vehicle, wearing army khaki pants. It is too warm to put his army fatigue jacket on.

He is wearing a white undershirt. With his headphones, he continued to listen to Christmas carols. The only thing bothersome is his singing. I don't think there are enough lessons for him to sing on key. At least there are no dogs howling.

Finally, a sign up ahead that shows an entrance to a major highway! The compass is still pointing in a westward direction. All systems are a go. There has been lost time at the armory and the pond. Why the rush? If it takes a day or two more, it is still worth it. The terrain is different and the license plates are mostly from Pennsylvania. Somehow they have missed being near Philly or Lancaster, Pennsylvania. Lancaster is where many of the Amish live. Miles of eloquent farmland tilled by a group who don't use electricity. To them, the EMP strike isn't even a blip on their radar screen. Their only problem is to watch out for outsiders. Desperate people will do desperate actions to obtain food and water.

It has been close to an hour on this Pennsylvania highway. Up ahead there is a tandem of army bulldozers and street sweepers. What a shame. The crunching noise of some very expensive vehicles has gone silent. Humans go from dust to dust. All these vehicles go from metal to metal. I don't think there are enough barrages to send them all to Japan. When electricity is finally turned on, the long lines won't be at the gas pumps; they will be at car dealerships. They'll have massive HELP WANTED signs. Qualifications? You must be able to breathe, walk, and put an *x* on the appropriate form.

Last part of the day has been uneventful. Pennsylvania is one long state. Looking at the sun tells Ann it is somewhere between 5 and 6 p.m. "Time to look for a good spot to pitch a tent. A safe place that is not near any city dwelling. Hmm! Hotel six leaves the light on for you all night. Too bad they were also affected by the blast. Their business is also kaput. I wonder if any of the gangs take up residence there? Maybe they did an upgrade and went for a Ramada Inn or Hilton. Without any pay, I don't think the door person will greet them."

Finally, Ann sees a clearing with a slight incline. Perfect! It seemed like a staging area for the army bulldozers and sweepers. The guardrail has been demolished for a good hundred feet. Ann drove in. There is only one way in and one way out. Sitting a good hundred feet from the road, the Humvee doesn't stand out. Still a couple of hours until nightfall; it does not make any sense to drive any further today. No one wants to get hemorrhoids. There are no pharmacies to pick up a doughnut-hole seat or some preparation H.

Before the mosquitoes and other little critters emerge, William started to unpack the tents. Ann put up the outside perimeter trip wires. It will alert them if any foe—two-legged or four-legged—is almost upon them. Camille decides to help with a light supper. Tonight's special? K rations out of a can! What? No candlelight or dinner with soft music? This roughing it with nature is getting old. In Camille's mind, she is one with any Chinese buffet. Looking at the bright side, they are all on a crash diet. Where are you, Dr. Oz?

Fred! Don't forget about Fred. He also wants to contribute. He grabs the little shovel.

"Where do I start digging the his-and-her holes?" Fred asks with a smile.

William smiled. He puts a little marker for each hole. Fred gets on it. Both Camille and Ann found Fred to be a blessing. They have learned a lot about him, and it puts a good perspective on their own lives. William always seems to be calm. If he ever explodes, it should be a doozy.

The divine master has drawn the curtain on this day. It is now almost pitch-black. The moon is shining very little light. Each of the four have their bellies somewhat full and bladders emptied. With no livestock farms around, they can start counting stalled vehicles instead of sheep. Tomorrow, Ann wishes to start early. She figures they are almost at the end of Pennsylvania. Hopefully, they can traverse through Ohio and into Indiana. Fred has been given his insulin shot.

Camille, Ann, and William are getting used to sleeping with a firearm next to them. Good night!

* * *

Randy and Sarah had been quiet for the last hour. It has been two days since Ann left. William, Fred, and Camille are missed. The daily gatherings at the collaborative are not the same. It seems so eerie; no one even mentions their names. It's a superstition, like don't walk under a ladder. Exit the same door that you came in. There have been thousands who died due do to the EMP blast. Ben has worked so very hard to shield his neighbors from harm. At least his mind is off his daughter Jessica.

"I think we should check in on William's wife. She has not been out of her home since last night" Randy said, with a worried look on his face.

"I know! I know!" Sarah said in a despondent tone. "She is not used to being alone. I guess I have a little more respect for the drunk. He has been living without his wife for years. The pain he is in, it's almost unbearable."

"Look, why don't we go over there and bring a plate of food?" Randy quipped. "It's been hot and muggy. How can she stay cooped up in that house?"

Strange. Randy and Sarah are doing things together. They are acting like a married couple—a real marriage that works. Maybe they should move in with each other, but where? The barn? There's no bed or a bathroom. Hmmm! How about Randy's Buick? One would have to sleep in the front seat and the other in the back seat. On second thought, Randy would freak out if Sarah got the Buick dirty. They would have a fight. Sarah would storm out of the Buick and move in next door to her mother. Now, there would be another family feud (Sarah and Randy). Scratch this little episode! Let the courtship continue as is.

Sarah went over to the fire pit. She asked Alice for a plate of food. Sarah grabbed a little water and went over to Randy. Both of them headed over to William's wife's house. After knocking on the door for several minutes, Randy opened the door. He yelled out her name for several minutes; no answer. Finally, they approached her bedroom. She is curled up in a fetal position. In the clutch of her hand, she has a picture of the three of them. It was taken over a year ago. Fred, William, and his wife went to the White Mountains in New Hampshire.

Randy and Sarah just looked at each other. William's wife is staring into the abyss. Her body is here, but the mind is in a trance. Her body is wet with perspiration. From the strong odor, it is obvious she desperately needs a bath.

"Wake up! Come on, wake up! William is not giving up on you!" Sarah said in a loud voice. "William and Fred need you! He is doing this for all of you. When he comes home, he needs his wife. Come on, you need to eat. Do it for William," Sarah panicked.

Hearing the word *William* several times triggered her. It is the key word that took her out of her trance. She must have laid on the bed for most of the day completely paralyzed. It is extremely warm; the only sound is that of a fly buzzing around her head. Like someone trying to save a drowning victim, Sarah did not give up. She saw her eyes and face move every time she mentioned the word *William*.

With the plate of food in hand, Randy just stood there. Just like the first critical moments, when a patient enters the ER via an ambulance, the team assembles. It is the ER doctor who takes charge. Even though

Randy is nervous, he is extremely impressed with Sarah. Sarah is acting quickly and with all her wits. She grabs the shoulders of William's wife.

"You need to sit up. William is going to be fine. He needs you to be strong. Come on, time to eat," Sarah said as she now sees that she is responding. "Come on, you can do it"

With her trance broken, William's wife carefully looked at Sarah. Then she glanced at Randy and the plate of food. She realized her body is dirty and wet.

She felt embarrassed.

"Please eat! We are your friends. William wanted us to look after you. Henderson is preparing a bath for you," Sarah remarked as she looked at Randy. She nodded her head. It is a signal to Randy to go outside and locate Mr. Henderson.

William's wife sat up. Sarah started to feed her like an elderly patient who needs help. After a few bites, William's wife took the fork from Sarah. She started to eat on her own, at a slow pace.

"I really look bad, my clothes . . . I feel—" William's wife said as she was interrupted.

"Shush!" Sarah said as she put her two fingers on her lips. "Keep eating. Mr. Henderson is preparing a nice hot bath for you. You need some fresh clothes. You're a beautiful woman. Let's keep it that way. A man wants to come back to his own home and his beautiful wife," Sarah remarked in a soft feminine voice.

It took several minutes for William's wife to eat her plate of food. Her mind is still drifting. It is almost like shock therapy. Many times our own minds play tricks with us. There is an old Christian saying: "God never gives us more than we can handle."

Slowly, Sarah guided William's wife to get up. Together they went through her dresser draw. Finding clean clothes and underwear, both Sarah and William's wife went outside. Randy and Mr. Henderson were hastily heating up the water. Randy carried the water to the tub. Mr. Henderson just kept heating a new pail of water. Good team effort. Sarah did walk her to the tub, all set for a tiptoe into paradise. William's wife did indicate she wanted to undress in private. She only wants her husband to see her in the birthday suit.

Sarah smiled. She definitely could relate to that. Closing the curtains, she gave William's wife all the time she needed. As she exited the hot tub area, Randy approached her. There is a good three hours of sunlight left. Randy is going to Vivian's house. He informed Sarah that he will take Steven (Mr. Henderson's son) with him. Randy is going to do a full-court press to pressure Vivian to stay with William's wife. Randy told Sarah to just tell William's wife that she will be staying with her. When they finally get word from the state police, Officer Ryan will go to Ben first. It is in Vivian's best interest to be nearby when Officer Ryan comes by.

Therapy, everyone needs therapy during these trials and tribulations. Vivian's mom, Camille, is on the journey. Ben is slowly trying to heal with the fallout with his daughter Jessica. Then there is Steven. He has been turned down by Jessica and Sarah. They say, the third time is always the charm. For Steven, without transportation or the internet, pickings are slim. Very slim.

Steven is just happy to get out of the area. Besides, he always has a laugh with Vivian. They can both jest Randy because of his obsession with his Buick.

It's like fishing; you get a bite from a large fish. If you pull too tight, you'll lose the fish. If you give it too much slack, you'll lose the fish. It has to be handled like a pro to catch the big fish. Steven and Vivian only go so far. They always end up with a compliment for Randy. It keeps his ego up.

this second day since the departure at the collaborative has been tense. Emotions have reached the breaking point.

Watching out for each other is really the true definition of a collaborative.

Many emotional wounds have been exposed. Randy and Sarah are attempting to apply the Band-Aids to soothe the hurt. When the two of them arrive at Vivian's apartment complex, Vivian had a big smile. Like William's wife, this is hard on Vivian. She truly feels the warmth and love of her aunt (Camille's sister), who is staying at her apartment. There is something that Steven and Randy bring to the table. Vivian cannot put her finger on it, but it is there. Maybe because they both have a good family structure? Even though there was a feud between Ben and Jessica. Maybe because Steven and Randy are hard workers with good morals? Or maybe just maybe they are two men who have not tried to BS and use her.

It did not take a lot of persuading to have Vivian join them. Vivian let her aunt keep the 9mm gun. Her Aunt told Vivian she will be fine. As long as one person in the complex has a gun, the thugs will stay away. Instead of spraying cockroach spray, they use a gun. Got to keep the vermin out. As night fell on the collaborative, it seems the emotional fires have been brought under control.

Thunderstorms that have traveled through Pennsylvania, New York, Connecticut are now in Massachusetts.

Vivian is with William's wife. Funny how two people who are afflicted by the same wounds can comfort each other. The heavy rains and lighting are God's way of talking to them. It is telling them the storm is just as bad for Ann's occupants as it is for Vivian and Camille. Sooner or later, the storm will end. They need to be strong.

* * *

"To serve and protect." It is no longer Ann's professional code; it is personal for her. She swore to her husband and Ben that everyone will arrive safely to "Tent City. Even though Ann is very capable, she is also blessed with her passengers. Camille has lived her life in some dangerous projects. She can read evil and carries a gun. What more do you need? What about William? As the old saying goes, "Be leery of the quiet ones, they are the most dangerous. They are constantly assimilating information."

The compass on the Humvee is pointing west. The early morning treasure hunters were at it again. Every once in a while, Ann saw a stray dog. Some countries find dog meat a delicacy. In our western culture, most of us find that repulsive. Yet early settlers ate rattlesnake and, during desperate times, horse meat. Primitive man hunted and ate mostly animals. This really brings me to the concept of vegetarians. I believe they do it not just for health, but they believe the whole process is barbaric. What if the animals were on top of the food chain? Really, to each our own.

* * *

When I first saw the movie *Planet of the Apes*, I was amazed at Hollywood's subliminal messages. I think they were letting us know that mankind had become too uncivilized. Crime, drugs, homicides, corruption, gambling, nuclear war—the list is never-ending. Now the apes are in control. It is obvious they are immensely stronger, faster, and can jump. Who says apes can't jump? I saw very little of what they ate. I don't think they ate humans. That would destroy the purity of Hollywood's morality theme. The apes were civilized.

Charlton Heston starred in the original *Planet of the Apes*. With his wit and determination, he tried to reason with the apes. My two main takeaways: first, both Heston and Hollywood had to show the Statue of Liberty destroyed—it is the symbol of a free mankind; second, Charlton was determined to show off his chest. It's his way of saying, "Look at me, aren't I sexy." Now he can demand the big bucks and have a whole cackle of female groupies swooning over him.

Now we fast-forward to today. There are females serving in combat roles, even a female who was a temporary NFL coach. So now it is proper to have a female take the lead role in the remake of *Planet of the Apes.*

So for argument's sake, they release the film first on Redbox. Just stay with me, folks. The man of the house is coming home from a tough week at work. They are a typical middle-class family: husband, wife, one boy, and one girl. You know, the dwindling middle class: overworked and overtaxed.

He tells his wife he will pick up a movie. He checks Redbox. "Hmmm. My dad watched the original. It is harmless. Everyone will be happy. Planet of the Apes *remake,* thought the caring husband.

He comes home, both he and his wife unwind. The little boy asks if he and his sister can start the movie? With a smile, the dad says,

153

"Why not?" They start the movie. The wife is preparing supper, and the husband is taking off his suit. Next, he is thumbing through the bills.

After twenty minutes, the little girl screams, "Mommy! Mommy!

The wife runs in to see what is wrong. There on the TV, the lead female actress, a Linda Carter–wannabe has her top off. She's doing the same thing as Charlton Heston. The little boy is in awe; he still watches. The little girl runs to Mommy. She holds on tight and buries her head into her mommy's waist.

Just then the dad runs in. *"How could you?"* the wife screams. The little boy keeps watching. The husband is speechless and is totally stunned.

The wife says, "Come on, children. We'll watch something in the master bedroom."

"No, I want to stay with daddy," the little boy said.

At this point, the wife unplugs the TV, grabs the little boy, and drags him unwillingly to the master bedroom. She slams the door hard. *Damn,* thought the husband. *Doesn't the accused at least have a say?*

After a few moments of being a deer in the headlights, the husband looks around. He grabs his laptop. Like Inspector Clouseau, in *The Pink Panther,* he quietly tiptoes to dark parts of the house, a place where even housemaids won't venture into. There the husband opens his laptop. With much anticipation, he googles an interesting video. It's obvious he will be sleeping on the sofa tonight.

A B-rated flick: *Debbie Enters South Chicago.* With a pounding heart, he clicks on the video. He then reads, "Sorry, this video has been deleted because of massive gunfire."

"What?" screams the frustrated husband.

I guess the actors' guild ran out of Debbie's. The production manager is tearing out the last strands of hair on his bald head. "How can a guy make a living?" an angry production manager proclaims.

When a vampire looks in the mirror, he sees nothing. I wonder what the production manager would see.

With the decline of our morality and the rise of violence, Moses has been summoned from the vault. A little shaken, he brushes off the cobwebs and dust. Forty years roaming the desert without a McDonald's or Holiday Inn can affect your state of mind. He is instructed to climb Mt. Arafat. There he can do a quick overview of the world. He scours the world, his eyes become fixated on Hollywood. He is especially shocked at the section that produces those B-rated movies.

"What? Forty days and nights of rain and you still don't get the message?"

Moses stated with a loud roar.

With his statuesque body, he raises his right hand. His index finger releases a massive bolt of energy. He fires at the decadent Hollywood producers. A direct hit would send them to the lower bowels of the earth. Hopefully, there will be no collateral damage to the innocent. From halfway across the world, the bolt of energy barely misses and hits the Pacific Ocean. A thunderous explosion causes a seismic wave felt all the way to Antarctica.

This aroused the aliens living under the ice cap. Quickly, the aliens climbed up their frozen steps and sat in their makeshift bleacher. They immediately understood what Moses was doing. Soon they gave him a standing ovation. A second bolt is shot off; this one is even closer. Still, though, it landed just off shore, in the ocean. The aliens are ecstatic; they start doing the wave. They bought up their organic munchies.

The head alien texted Al Gore on his intergalactic cell phone. Al was in Antarctica last year. He received the Universe Peace Prize. A real prestigious award for his fine work. He was given a ceremonial key to a planet that the Aliens neutralized with extreme prejudice. Al also received the hottest beta release of the new 'Inter-apple' galactic cell phone. It is one of a Limited edition it runs on— a "Dura Anti Matter" power pack, guaranteed to last an eternity—at least until the Earth is vaporized by their expanding sun.

Al was so choked up with emotion, he offered the aliens some of his expensive caviar. The aliens said thanks, but no thanks; they were on a diet. They can't afford to add more weight to their large heads. Al understood and climbed into his large jet and left for home.

At home next to his large pool, Al is with his financial adviser. He didn't hear the four-tone text message from the aliens.

"You've done well for yourself, Al, with this gig. You have amassed millions in your account," the financial advisor said in a cheerful note.

"I know, I know. I still feel insecure. I need a few more million for my aging years," Al retorted.

"Hmmm. How about solar panels on this fine large house of yours?" the financial adviser replied.

Al just waves his hand at the idea. It's a no go.

"What about downsizing your jet? Or maybe fly economy class?" the financial advisor said.

"Are you kidding? My time and my privacy are important to me. Come on, I pay you mega bucks. Come up with something," Al replied with a little anger.

"I got it! Why not raise your speaking fees?" the financial advisor said with excitement.

"Bingo! You're the man. I know why I hired you. Would you like some of my expensive caviar?" Al said.

"No thanks, I am here for the mega bucks," the financial adviser proclaimed.

"I can relate to that!" Al answered as they ended their meeting.

Moses is loosening up. The third bolt should be the charm. The aliens were crossing their fingers. They see the earth as a ship without a rudder. They know Moses is going to right the ship.

Looking at his target, Moses releases his third bolt. This should be dead-on. Just before impact, there is a divine intervention. The bolt is disintegrated and falls harmless to the earth.

"Now, Moses, I wanted a report. You are trying to interfere with mankind's free will. You're a good man, just have a seat," said the higher power.

A disgruntled Moses sat down. The aliens went back under the ice cap, but not before they cleaned up their mess. Al told them to keep the environment clean. Sitting down, Moses looked at his carved-out stone with the Ten Commandments. Next, he glanced at the B-rated Hollywood producers.

Frustration has reached its limits. Moses picked up the large stone and started to chisel in an eleventh commandment: *Thou shall not partake in any B-rated Hollywood productions.*

Zap! A higher power took the large stone tablet from Moses. Quickly, the eleventh commandment is undone.

"Moses, thanks for your assistance. Time for you to go back to from whence you came."

Reluctantly, Moses climbed down Mt. Arafat, mumbling all the way. "I had this. Really, I did."

* * *

It's been several hours of driving for Ann. They are a number of miles into Ohio. After a lunchbreak, Ann stopped to refuel the Humvee. At the side of the road, they came upon another military vehicle. After a short break, its driver told Ann that the tent city is really southwest of here. After thanking him, she drove off looking for the next exit. The hot payment was amplifying an already warm day. Taking the next exit, she looked at her compass. Southwest, it is. At least when they stop, they can find a shady tree. The drawback, more cars littered the road. Ann is also on the lookout for debris. Too hot to try and change tires.

After driving the back roads, many people came out to greet the Humvee. It seems there is a real nasty biker gang terrorizing the neighborhood. Seeing the sign MILITARY PATROL, most people felt they are now saved. Camille and William had their rifles at the ready. In a way, they do look official, as long as they don't get out of the Humvee. Fred, with his khaki pants and Western cowboy boots, would burst their bubble. Maybe it could be a new kind of army—you know, from Flintstone Valley.

All we have to do is rename Camille to Wilma.

It really seemed like a decent suburb. If there was a way to cut the grass and remove the stalled cars, this neighborhood would be ready to go.

After driving on for a few minutes, they came upon two middle-aged men. One had a hunting rifle and the other a baseball bat.

"How are you doing?" Camille said as Ann stopped the Humvee.

"We are fine. Are you from the military?" the man with the hunting rifle asked.

"We are going to Tent City." I am to meet with a general at command headquarters. We are commissioned from an air base in Massachusetts. We just got off the highway," Ann said from the driver's seat.

"Well, ma'am, we really need help. The biker gangs are coming from the southwest part of the country. I guess they feel the pickings are easy around here," stated the man with the hunting rifle.

"You seem to be a doing a good job. I don't see any broken windows on the houses that we just passed," Camille answered.

"We're trying, but this gang is really vicious. They have already raped and killed several people," said the man with the hunting rifle.

"Thanks for the heads-up, I will let the authorities know. We have to push on,"

Ann said politely. They waved to the two men and headed forward.

Looking in the rearview mirror, Ann saw the concerned look on William's face. Nothing she can do. They all knew the trip had its element of danger.

Camille and William had their rifles at the ready. After a good twenty-minute drive, they were rounding a bend. Noises of motorcycles can be heard. Soon, it was screams of someone in pain. Ann saw a group of people several hundred yards ahead.

As they got closer, it was apparent that the screams were coming from a victim who was being tortured. The Humvee stopped just a hundred feet from the bikers. Ann and Camille exited the Humvee, each putting on bulletproof vest. With their rifles raised, Camille and Ann approached the bikers. Ann asked Camille to stay a good twenty feet apart. Ann wanted to make sure the bikers were in a crossfire.

It seems the leader was a man close to six feet tall. He weighed at least two hundred pounds. With bulging forearms, he had a pistol in one hand. In the other, he held a young man by his hair. As he pistol-whipped the young man, the screams sounded piercing.

Just as he was about to pistol-whip him again, the other bikers noticed Camille and Ann. There were six bikes: five men and three women. Two of the women rode piggyback with their boyfriends. One woman rode alone, and three men rode alone. Ann and Camille saw two bodies lying nearby: one of a young man who was lying in his own blood; the other of a young woman with her clothes ripped off her. Camille, being a mother of a young girl, is shocked and angered. Her whole life, Camille protected her daughter from these evil lowlifes.

"Put down your pistol and raise your hands," Ann shouted.

Hearing this, William grabbed his rifle and exited the Humvee. Logic told him he had to back them up. After Camille and Ann, William and Fred would be next. William made sure the safety is off. He stood behind the Humvee and rested the rifle along the hood. His eyes were on the tattooed man. Even though they were outnumbered eight to three (leaving Fred out of this), they still had three rifles drawn to only one gun (the tattooed man). As the old saying goes, "The bigger they are, the harder they fall."

The tattooed man mumbled, "Now I got to deal with these two dumb b——" as he turned to face Camille and Ann.

"Look! This is not your concern. Just walk away before you get hurt!" the tattoo man said in an arrogant manner.

Ann glanced at the two bodies, mostly at the poor young girl. One of the other bikers noticed Ann glancing. Slowly, he put his right hand on the stock of his gun. Camille noticed. Slowly, she shifted her eyes on this thug. During the whole time, William just trained his rifle on the tattooed man. No matter what, William is determined to protect Fred first, then hopefully his friends.

Ann sensed she had to force their hand now. Any delay and the others would also draw their weapons.

"Put your hands on your head now!" Ann screamed in a louder voice.

Just then, the biker who had his hand on his stock yelled, "F—— you" and drew his gun.

Bang! Camille shot him in the head. He fell quickly. The tattooed man instantly raised his gun and fired one shot wildly. It missed Ann by a few feet. A rush came over William, his heart beating very fast. He let go a series of volleys. All of them hit the tattooed man. Ann, regaining her composure, also fired one shot at the tattooed man. It was over in a matter of a few seconds.

The firing stopped. The other bikers did not want to challenge them. The tattooed man's girlfriend is in total shock. She cried loudly. She really thought her boyfriend was invincible. She stooped down and cried, "Baby! Wake up, please wake up!" With blood all over her hands, she stood up and yelled. "You damn b———"

She grabbed her boyfriend's bike and with the other six bikers took off. It was a temporary retreat. They only went a few hundred feet. Quickly, Ann and Camille went to the aid of the tortured man. With blood and tears running down the side of his face, he is in physical and emotional pain. Ann ran back to the Humvee and got the first-aid kit. She started to put alcohol on his open wounds.

As Ann is applying first-aid, the bikers stopped a couple hundred feet away. For all practical reasons, they were out of shooting range.

"What's your name?" Ann asked as she is blotting the side of his face.

"My name is Pedro. That's my sister on the ground. They raped and killed her. My friend tried to stop them. We had no weapons. They shot him several times," Pedro said as he is pointing to his friend, who is lying in his own blood.

"Why? My sister just had a small child. Our parents were in New York City.

They died when the EMP blast hit. The tattooed man's girlfriend kept egging him to rape her." Pedro started to cry.

"William, can you bring the shovel?" Ann asked while she attended to Pedro.

Camille collected the guns from the two dead bikers. She lay them on the ground near Ann and Pedro. Meantime, the bikers drove a little closer. They stopped behind a ridge a hundred and fifty feet away. William grabbed the rifle and the shovel. He dug a grave. Being anal, he made sure it was a perfect rectangle. The whole time, Tattoo's girlfriend is looking. It is an uneasy truce.

With the grave dug to perfection, he helped Pedro lower his sister in the grave. William put his hand on Pedro's shoulder. He also glanced at Fred and the biker's gang. He could feel tension in the air. As if being in the eye of the storm, William grabbed his rifle and headed for the Humvee. Bad vibes seemed to permeate everywhere.

Ann offered Pedro the shovel; she wanted to let him go first. Pedro dropped one shovel of dirt on his sister. As the dirt landed on his bloodied sister's corpse, Pedro broke down. Camille put both arms around Pedro; he is crying profusely. Ann decided to finish filling up the grave.

It took several minutes for Ann to finish shoveling. From a crouched position,

Pedro raised his hand. He indicated to Camille he is all right.

Both Camille and Ann were now at the grave. They both laid down their rifles so that they could do a prayer. Ann did glance at the bikers and at William. William felt torn. He is always a respectful person. He is a natural to give the eulogy. Seeing the bikers really made him feel uneasy. Why are they still around?

Are they looking to bury their friends, or are they looking for revenge?

The bikers were just sitting on their bikes. It seems the tattooed man's girlfriend has filled the vacuum of leadership. It is either that, or they were giving her respect because of her loss. She had a real evil stare. That saying "If looks could kill"—the tattooed man's girlfriend not only had the look; she had an itch to fulfill her rage.

With Ann and Camille standing in a reverend posture, it seemed they were in a vulnerable spot. The bikers were either being respectful, or they were still waiting for a better opportunity.

"Pedro, would you like to say a word or prayer for your sister?" Camille asked.

Pedro lifted his head and wiped tears from his eyes. His emotions were swirling with both anger and shock. He lifted himself. As he started to step toward his sister's grave, he noticed the bikers looking. He then looked at Ann and Camille. His sister's and his friend's killing were too much for him to digest. He lost his parents, friend, and now his sister. He needs time to grieve; he cannot handle burying his sister this quickly. It is simply is too much for him to process. The pistol-whippings he took were already enough to put him over the cliff. His rage reached a crescendo. He quickly turned around and picked up the gun lying on the ground.

Bang! Bang! He fired two shots in to the tattooed man's corpse. The floodgates of hell just opened up. Tattoo's girlfriend's face seemed to explode with anger. She started her bike and came for Pedro. Seeing Ann and Camille at the grave site, the rest of the bikers followed suit. Pedro is not afraid—has anger filled his heart? Seeing the bikers come for him only increased his anger. Pedro ran straight at Tattoo's girlfriend with the gun pointing at her.

William, leaning against the Humvee, picked up his rifle and chased after Pedro.

"Stop, Pedro! Stop! They're going to kill you!" William screamed.

A moment later, Pedro started to fire his gun. His aim is terrible. The bikers responded in kind. All guns from the bikers were fixated on Pedro. Many of the bullets found their mark. Pedro is fatally shot.

William stopped and knelt down. He had his bulletproof vest on. He instantly raised his rifle. Now, he is in no man's land. He cannot outrun the bikes. Both he and Ann already had their rifles in hand. They ran to help William. With her heart beating fast, Ann yelled out, "Not on my watch."

With Pedro down, the bikers focused on William. William did fire at the tattooed man's girlfriend. She is hit. Losing control of her bike, she hits the ground tumbling multiple of times. With adrenalin running through everyone's veins, this became a moment of life and death.

Camille and Ann were a good fifty feet behind William. They both took up firing positions. The rest of the bikers were concentrating on William. They fired. Several bullets missed, but one scrapped the side of his head. Being hit, William stopped firing. *Bang! Bang!* One bullet went through his shoulder, and two bullets hit him in the chest. The force threw him backward several feet. He was now on his back.

This all took place in only a few seconds. Ann and Camille started to shoot.

They both hit the man and woman riding together, falling to the ground as their bikes crashed. The other bikers came to a screeching halt. They were so fixated on William that they forgot about Camille and Ann. Instantly, they turned around, knowing that they had lost this skirmish.

As they started to turn and ride away, Ann gave chase. Camille did not understand why she was doing this. Ann stopped. With her scoped rifle, she shot both men, one at a time. Now only a lone female is left. A good hundred fifty feet away, Ann had her in her scope. With sweat running down her cheeks, she had her finger on the trigger.

Just then, the woman on the bike raised her arm and threw her gun away. Is it not a sign of capitulation? She desired to live. In the background, Camille is yelling at Ann. "Stop! Stop! It's over."

Ann took her finger off the trigger and bowed her head. She turned around and went to the aid of William. She looked at Camille.

"This is the second time they came after us. There would have been a third time. It had to end," Ann said with emotion.

"I know! That last girl knew she lost her friends. I doubt she will be in any more biker gangs," Camille stated with confidence.

William is lying on the ground in excruciating pain. Fred exited the Humvee yelling, "William! William!" Ann quickly got the first-aid kit. Camille took off the vest. William's chest had some mean black and blue marks.

Ann quickly attended his shoulder and the side of his head. Camille put pressure on the wound. Ann told Fred to get blankets. They are trying to prevent William from going into shock. Camille and Ann worked well together. They have done as much as they could. With blankets covering him, all three lifted William. They put him into the back seat of the Humvee.

Fred rode shotgun and Camille sat in the back seat. She had William's head on her lap.

"William, you're going to be all right. Don't fall asleep." If William was not shot, they would have stayed and buried Pedro and the bikers. But they were dead and nothing could bring them back. It is William's well-being that must take precedence.

Like a bad horror flick, the Humvee exited the scene. Behind is a trail of carnage that will be detailed in the archives of history. While Camille is trying to keep William calm, Ann keeps telling Fred that everything thing will be all right. It might be false bravado, but at least they are still alive.

EMP Causality: Part VI
The Last Leg

"FRED, THERE IS NO NEED to cry. We'll get William to a hospital. Like a puppy that lost his master, Fred feels totally insecure. Each time he turns around, William's shirt seems to be covered in more blood. Carnage and corpses littered the battlefield. One of the engines of a bike is still running, lying on its side, smoke and fumes still flowing from the carburetor. The landscape looks like an opening picture to a horror movie.

Ann's sweating palms are on the steering wheel. Her mind is in overdrive. Talk about multitasking. She is trying to reconstruct the same path they came in. She knows the man with the hunting rifle will help guide them to a hospital. Occasionally, she looks back at Camille to make sure she is helping William. Camille really seems to handle herself well in a crisis.

Then there is Fred. Ann has had a lot of experience with domestic violence. Usually, it's a husband and wife, or boyfriend and girlfriend. They are the most dangerous. Anyone of them in a moment of rage can take their frustrations out on a police officer. Fred is in uncharted waters with Ann. There is a lack of training in the police academy about the needs of the challenged. How does she handle his behavioral habits? What about his insulin shots? His medications? How will Fred respond to another authority figure? Many questions, few answers.

In a crisis, Ann acts like a trained professional. Calm, she must remain calm.

The EMP strike has thousands of stories. Some of the outcomes do not have happy endings. This is her moment in the spotlight. Eye, hand, and mental coordination must function like a well-oiled machine or quarterback in the last few minutes of a tight game. It brings out the best and the worst for most of us. They say we humans only use a small portion of our brains.

Ann is trying to use all she can muster.

William, the quiet one, has a photographic memory. (Do you think they have a digital camera implanted in their brains? —Just a thought) Ann is the driver. She is remembering each turn, heart pounding! It is now familiar terrain. Houses without broken windows; this is the spot. She starts beeping her horn.

Honk! Honk! "Damn! Enough already," said Camille as she covered her ears.

Ann stepped out of the Humvee. A few people came out of their homes. Just as she was ready to shout, she saw the two men running toward her. They were the same two men she talked to before. A pure judgment call, but she did not have a rifle in her hand. She did not want to seem threatening to the friendlies. The two men came right up to her. They saw William in the back seat. In an instant, they knew Ann and her crew met up with a biker gang.

"You meet up with the biker gang?" the man with the rifle said.

"Yes, we need to find a hospital ASAP," Ann responded.

"It looks like he lost some serious blood. There is a nurse a few houses up the street. Let her help him now. Then I will show you the way to the hospital," the man with the rifle said.

He and his friend ran, and Ann followed them. As one knocked on the neighbor's door, the other man ran to the back of the Humvee. They set up a triage spot right on her front lawn. Many of the neighbors now came out of their houses. They knew the Humvee is a friendly. With a clean sheet, they put William down gently. The nurse works the ER at a city hospital. She prefers living in a calm suburban neighborhood. Working the ER for a city hospital seems to befit her nicely. Getting paid for something you like to do makes life a little more rewarding.

Instead of a neighborhood block party, it is a neighborhood ER party. Several neighbors assisted. The nurse tore off William's shirt. She quickly attended to both wounds. With a sterile needle and thread, she stitched his open wound.

Some of the neighbors gave William a new undershirt and shirt. As the minutes passed, William seemed to be stabilized. One of the neighbors had an antibiotic medication that he recently got from the armory.

"Unreal! I appreciate your help," Ann said with a sigh of relief.

"No problem. There are still good people out there," the man with the rifle commented. "Give the nurse a few more minutes and I will take you to the hospital. It's not far from here. They are really short-staffed."

"One more favor. There are several bodies. Would you mind giving them a proper burial?" Ann asked with a little hesitation.

"We only have one rifle among us," the man with the rifle stated.

"No worries. I have collected several more," Ann said as she went to the Humvee. "Here are three more that should help protect your neighborhood."

"Thanks. I'll see what I can do," the man with the rifle commented.

With William and Fred in slightly better spirits, they loaded up. The neighborhood is happy that the biker gang is extinguished. The man with the rifle showed them how to get to the hospital. William still needed a doctor.

Fred needed to get an insulin shot. Riding inside the Humvee, the man with the rifle asked Ann to stop. From that point, Ann would be able to find the hospital herself. The man with the rifle bid adieu and walked back.

As they neared the hospital, there appeared to be a mob of people. Looks like Black Friday, the day after Thanksgiving. In front of the hospital is a heard of people and a barrier with a guard. A person with a clipboard is trying to do triage. Too many people. Ann drove her Humvee as close as possible. She decided to be a little aggressive. Beeping her horn, she carefully drove through the mass of bodies.

Coming up to the guard, she exited with her dossier. Trying to act important, she was looking for a leg-up for entrance.

"Ma'am! You'll have to take your turn. Just like the rest of the people," the guard said in a deep, authoritarian voice.

"Look, we have a shooting victim. We just took out a biker gang that has been threatening your neighborhood," Ann stated as she showed him the few guns that she still had.

"I will try and see what the nurse says," the guard stated.

"No! We put our lives up, and we need help or he will die. I am taking him in,"

Ann stated as she drove closer.

Camille got out of the Humvee and asked Fred to help. Gently, Ann, Camille, and Fred helped carry William inside the ER doors.

"Stop! What are you doing? We did not give permission. We have too many patients," an overworked and angry nurse yelled out.

"He risked his life to protect yours. He's lost a lot of blood. He needs help now!" an impatient Camille retorted.

"Nurse, it will be all right. Put him in the hallway. See what type of blood he is and put him on an IV," the doctor said. "Are you from the military?"

"We are commissioned from the air base in Massachusetts. We are on the way to central headquarters at Tent City," Ann answered.

The doctor just looked. He is totally swamped. The nurse also looks haggard. The only saving grace is that they get hot meals and a hot shower. In this post-EMP blast, that alone is considered a luxury.

Camille asked where the blankets were. William is shivering. Even though it's extremely hot, his loss of blood has an effect on his body temperature. Camille went down to housekeeping; there she procured two blankets. The hospital is overloaded with patients. Like an overbooked ship in a third-world country, it seemed impossible for all these patients to be attended too.

It's been a grueling and an emotional day for them. Camille took Fred down to the cafeteria. It gave Ann a needed break, a reprieve from all the responsibilities.

Ann desperately needed to emotionally unwind.

Many at the hospital were really looking for the basics: food, water, and a hot shower. What few shelters that are running cannot handle the load. Then there are the elderly and disabled. Like a magnet, the hospital seems to attract the multitudes that are within walking distance.

As the minutes turned to hours, the illusion of receiving timely care in the ER had greatly dissipated. Their road to Tent City seems to be paved with anguish and sorrow. When a nurse traverses down the hallway, she is greeted with an avalanche of pleas for help. Camille had bought up some apple sauce and cranberry juice for William. He is really shaking.

Seeing William shake is a new and disturbing sight for Fred. He has always seen William as a monolith in a world of dependency.

Even though Fred is challenged, he knows that William represents life itself.

In a complete breakdown, Fred wrapped his arms around William and started to cry. Soon he started to beg William, "Please don't die, please!"

Everyone in the hallway took notice. There might be some real cases that actually require immediate help. That being said, it does not take a medical genius to see that William's condition is starting to deteriorate. Camille had her hand over her mouth, and Ann was getting very upset. At this moment, a doctor ran out of the cubicle he was in. He immediately took stock of the situation.

In normal times, a doctor would start yelling, or at least speak in a loud voice. These are not normal times. The nurses are all at their breaking point. Most good doctors appreciate the assistance of a well-trained medical staff. The doctor immediately went into action. He drew a little blood from William, then gave him a sedative to calm him down.

With the help of Camille and Ann, the doctor got William onto a bed in a cubicle. The nurses, seeing what the doctor is doing, immediately sprang into action. They really respected the doctor and knew that as overburdened as they were, the doctor gave them a second wind.

The medication seemed to calm William down. Soon he is being given a blood transfusion. With the transfusion taking place, it almost seemed an angel descended down. The angel touches William's face and slowly his face begins to come to life. Camille, Ann, and even Fred could see the old William coming back to life. It is a very tense moment, but cries of joy can be heard.

This emotional roller-coaster has been really draining on everyone. Camille,

Ann, and Fred are all sitting down on the floor near William. The doctor had to attend to others and just left the cubicle. The waiting game continues, but it really doesn't matter; William is stabilized.

Sitting on the floor, Camille is reflecting on their harrowing experiences. Before they left on their trip, they heard stories of the biker gangs and thugs. When one hears about shootings, storms, and other acts of disasters, your mind plays tricks.

You feel sorry for the victims, but you know it doesn't involve you. Sometimes, reality really sucks when you are them.

It's a good thing that they are tired. When there is this massive downtime, social media comes to the rescue. Without any social media, the three of them are sleeping on the floor. Instead of waiting for a connecting flight, they are waiting for a room to open up.

It took a few hours, but progress was slowly forging ahead. A nurse entered the cubicle to wake them. They got their room and, like being a refugee camp, all four camped out. It was an exhausting night. At least there was air-conditioning and their own private bathroom. Life is good. Fred finally gets his insulin shot. The night is finally coming to a close.

Tomorrow is another day. No man left behind. They started with four, and whatever it takes, they will get to Tent City with four. The chemistry is good. Like family, everyone is concerned with the welfare of each other. Before she fell asleep, Camille took a few pictures with the digital camera. In the years to come, these pictures will be precious. As Camille was putting the camera away, she glanced at her three friends. All were asleep. Camille lifted the cross that was attached to her neck. She kissed it and said a prayer of thanks to the Almighty. She procured blankets and pillows for everyone. Tonight they have all been truly blessed.

* * *

Sarah has learned not only to knock on William's wife's door, but also to walk in if she doesn't answer. It's been three days since Ann and

William left for Tent City. There has been no word yet. This might be a good thing.

Most local authorities are trying to keep documentation for those who have perished. Last time William's wife had a meal at the fire pit, the union man had the survival radio on. The news was discouraging. In the south, the elderly have been affected by the summer heat. Those who live west of Pennsylvania are being invaded by biker gangs.

William is a very sensitive and passive human being. It bothered William's wife that he was accompanied by two females. Not for any infidelity, but for his own safety. In her mind, how can two females possibly protect her husband and Fred? If Ann's husband, Officer Ryan, was on the trip, her outlook would be entirely different. William's wife has no one to talk to, or share her fears with.

William's wife feels comfortable with Sarah and Randy. They are both sensitive and good listeners. Still, William's wife has no family or close friend to comfort her. Life is not always fair. In times of crisis, it is those who are defenseless who often suffer the most. During Hurricane Katrina, the elderly were left to drown or starve to death. Countless pets were set free to fend for themselves. Going from complete dependency to abandonment is a shock to a domestic pet, never mind an elderly person.

Under a little pressure, Sarah coerced William's wife to join the others at the fire pit. Sarah did ask the union man not to put on the survival radio. He understood. When you're the King of your household (as the union man is), one can be a little insensitive to the feelings and the needs of others. To be put in your place by a younger person, especially a young female, can make you come down to planet Earth.

At the fire pit, William's wife is joined by the other members of the collaborative. Immersed in her own sorrow, William's wife notices that Ben and his daughter actually exchange pleasantries. Maybe the polar cap is slowing melting. It does bring a temporary smile on her face. Constant worrying and stress is really damaging to your physical and mental state. Any kind of break from this anguish is much appreciated.

As they were eating and making small talk, Randy left for a mission. He has traveled to Vivian's complex. There he attempts to bring Vivian back with him. Vivian likes and respects Randy. When he got there, Vivian was surprised yet happy. Her situation is a little different than that of William's wife. She can confide in her aunt (Camille's sister).

Randy would make a good trial lawyer. He thinks fast and is very logical in his thought process. Vivian indicated she is comfortable with staying with her aunt during these delicate times. Randy said he understood. He understood Vivian and her aunt for their close family bond. Still, he expressed to Vivian that William's wife is not afforded this kind of support. Secondly, when word comes it will be Officer Ryan who is the messenger, he will first come to the collaborative. Thirdly, Randy told Vivian that her mother is a good Christian, and that William's wife needs help. They would both relate to each other well.

Randy's logic is undeniable. It is also with the efforts of Randy's dad (Ben) that got Camille (Vivian's mom) an audience with Officer Ryan.

"It's been three days since they left. I feel in the next day or two, we should get some kind of word. Randy is right; you need to keep William's wife company.

I know that is what your mom would want," Vivian's aunt commented. A little kindness and reverence might make things better around here.

"Give me a few minutes to pack a few things and say bye to my aunt," Vivian said politely.

Taking his cue, Randy went outside and waited. After fifteen minutes, Vivian and her aunt came outside. They both hugged and genuinely showed each other their support. Her aunt put her bags in the back seat.

Vivian always enjoys riding in Randy's nice polished Buick. Of course, the aunt kept the 9mm gun. It not only kept her safe, but the complex as well. It is better protection than a Keep Out sign. It is the only thing that these local thugs understood.

On the ride back, Vivian kept up a false front. She enjoys her freedom from her Mom. Vivian knows as a single parent her mom protected and fed her. To be brutally honest, Vivian is also extremely concerned. These local thugs with their 9mm guns are a threat. The biker gangs are a different class of evil. The local thugs were given birth because of the EMP blast. The blast created a vacuum of lawlessness. The local thugs filled this vacuum. The biker gangs are a different animal. They have been in existence for years. They have their own colors and their own codes. Life is cheap to them. Kill or be killed. It doesn't often get any simpler than that.

Living in the projects, Vivian understood this evil. She has become street-wise. Even though she enjoys her independence, she knows her mom has taught her well. Deep down, she really loves and respects her mom. To this end, she knows and can relate to William's wife.

Coming into the collaborative, the shiny Buick always brings a smile on everyone's face. It is not only their lifeline, but it is damn pleasing to see an automobile that can still run. Before the EMP blast, traffic was annoying. Being stuck in endless traffic jams was stressful. Now just hearing an engine is music to the depraved masses.

They drove up to the fire pit. As Vivian exited the Buick, everyone at the collaborative was happy to see her. The one who was especially excited to see her was Jessica. Vivian was and still is Jessica's best friend. Jessica really wanted to share her good fortunes with Vivian. Her boyfriend, Joshua, and her dad (Ben) have come to a tenuous understanding—a truce even!

Jessica is so thrilled that she offered to get Vivian's bags from Randy's car.

Randy, acting like King Solomon, interceded.

"Sis, not right now. Thank you! I will handle it," Randy said to Jessica, his sister.

Randy knew Vivian was here for William's wife and vice versa. He is also trying not to offend his own sister.

Sarah, Randy's girlfriend, witnessed this little friendly episode. She is impressed with Randy. Then there is Ben (I know, you already forgot about him). We don't want to isolate him again. This time, if he is isolated again, he might do something drastic, maybe like driving the shiny Buick off a cliff. Now where would the collaborative be without Ben or that shiny Buick? See! I got you!

Perhaps for the first time, Vivian and Jessica were not on the same page. Vivian is extremely polite. She is happy for Jessica and happy with the turn of events. Jessica is now at peace with her dad. She feels her relationship with Joshua is going well. Vivian just listened. Jessica saw sadness on Vivian's face. She asked Vivian, "What's wrong?" For once, Vivian is not so eager to share her feelings. In Vivian's mind, she wished she had a dad in her life, especially one that had always been there for her.

Now Vivian is just concerned about her mom's safety. Vivian gave out a half a smile. Randy is right; William's wife and Vivian really need each other. At least, until this ordeal is over. Randy sat down next to Sarah. He wanted events to play out. He knew Vivian would be able to figure out a proper course of actions with his sister.

After a few hours, Randy and Sarah knew it was time. Sometimes in life, you need to give in to the natural flow of events. Trying to choreograph or control a time line will only backfire. With half a heart, Vivian showed minor interest in Jessica's little soap opera. She thought Joshua was a nice-looking man. When the lights come back on, Joshua will be back at making a sound living. Maybe the relationship will blossom into a fruitful and everlasting marriage. All Vivian cared about is that Jessica try other waters. Jessica thought differently. Now Vivian is moving on. If they do get married, Vivian and Jessica's relationship will definitely change.

It was near lunch when Sarah got to speak with William's wife. It was a little easier this time. She told William's wife that Vivian is here. After all, Vivian's mom (Camille) is with William on this dangerous journey.

Before a bonding, there has to be a courtship. Both Randy and Sarah understood this. Sarah told William's wife and Vivian that they should have lunch together. With great compassion, Sarah arranged a private sit-down for the two of them.

These are trying times for everyone. Jessica has been through a lot herself. She now understood what her brother was doing. Jessica felt a little stupid at first, but she did gain a little more respect for her brother. In fact everyone, in the collaborative understood what was happening.

The two of them talk for over an hour. Finally, with a tear in each of their eyes, they both stood up. Vivian approached Randy and asked if he would bring her bags over to William's wife's house. With Sarah watching and trying not to cry, Randy cheerfully obliged. Before Vivian went to William's wife's house, she showed a little class to Jessica. She went over to Jessica and told her that until they hear from Officer Ryan, she needed to stay with William's wife. Jessica did understand. After all, Jessica did do what is best for her.

At any rate, now there is no reason for Ben to drive of a cliff. With the assistance of Randy and Sarah, the home fires seem to be under control.

* * *

A soft constant humming noise of the generators can be heard. It gives the hospital life. Waking up this morning seems strange. A little bit of civilization is reintroduced into Ann and her friends. Camille has gone outside with Fred. They have gone to the Humvee to get a change of clothes. Outside already seems like an oven with hordes of people that never seem to go away.

The overflow of people keeps a constant stress load on the hospital staff. Every few days, the army sends in supplies. The masses of people sense this. The hospital represents relief and hope. There are signs that give directions to where the nearest armories are. In the fog of a disaster, it takes a while for the government forces to be organized.

How is it possible for the elderly and the disabled to get to the armory? The doctors are all at a breaking point. Finally they developed a shuttle service. A triage nurse can eliminate the majority of these people. Every few hours, a military bus transports many of these people to a local armory. Basic medications like blood pressure, cholesterol, diabetes, etc. can be given at the armory. The triage nurse handles a multitude of people without extensive tests.

It's sad, but there are several armed guards. Camille and Fred just grab the clothes and reenter the hospital. The needy seem endless. Camille feels grateful that they were able to receive help.

In the room, everyone is up. William is no longer shivering. A big smile is on his face. Fred hugs William until Camille told him to be careful. It is the beginning of the fourth day. Ann is a little concerned. She knows she has to get word back to the state police barracks.

It took a few hours, but the same doctor visited William. Everyone is grateful for the work the doctor has accomplished. They were all on the same page. The doctor indicated that William should stay three or four days to fully come back. The hospital desperately needs the room for other patients. Ann is anxious to continue their journey.

There is an air base a good three-hour drive away. It is where the hospital gets its supplies. The doctor has arranged that a bed be put into one of the army trucks. It will leave early afternoon.

The journey continues. In the Humvee, Ann is driving and Fred is riding shotgun. In one of the army trucks, William is in a hospital bed. He has the IV stand next to him. Sitting near him is Camille. She is his personnel attendant.

Family—that is how each of them see themselves. The biker gangs and thugs will not bother a convoy of army trucks. This is the first time that they are traveling in real safety.

Instead of a fast-moving ambulance, it is a slow-driving army tuck that is transporting a patient. "They arrive at the air base in just under four hours." There is a beehive of activity. As they drive through a checkpoint, Ann can hear the various cargo planes approaching the airstrips. The planes are not only from the military but from several other countries.

As the convoy stopped, an army ambulance truck arrives. It is there to transport William to a medical unit. Camille insists that she stay with William. This gives a little relief to Ann. She can now register with command post. Fred is blown away by all of the military personnel. He has always had an admiration for the police and military.

Ann and Fred arrive at command post. She carries an important dossier from the military at the air base in Massachusetts. She is given an audience with the commander. Fred is asked to wait in the lounge. Fred is happy. He has his headset with him. While listening to Christmas carols, he also has one of his puzzles with him. It really does not take much to keep him occupied.

Ann shows the dossier to the commander. She asks that a call be made to the air base in Massachusetts. She wants the commander there to contact Officer Ryan, to let them knows they are all safe and will contact them in a few days. The commander obliged. The commander seems a little short and overweight. On his desk is his family picture. His wife looks stunning—a tall blond with a haircut that makes her look Swedish.

What drives a beautiful woman to marry a man who is not very attractive? Could it be power, money, talent, or a combination of many things? Was Anna Nicole Smith a beautiful thirty-plus woman really in love with an eighty-year-old man? Or was it greed?

* * *

When I was young (I really was), my dad took me to a summer stock in Rhode Island. There I saw Sammy Davis Jr., one of the Rat Pack. To see him live was exciting. At my first glance, Sammy Davis appeared short and very thin. With a glass eye, I imagined him to be a cowboy, playing a bad man in a Mexican villa. He would have to shoot a few innocent people just to prove he is tough. You know, the Napoleon effect (short-man complex); instead, he sang "Candy Man."

During intermission, I witness several young women approaching the stage. They were throwing their contact info for Sammy Davis to see. A few also threw some off their undergarments on stage. Stunned, I asked my Dad what was going on. Basically, the answer I got was a need-to-know basis. I was too young to know.

Later in life, I went to the Bosch Belt, a resort in the Catskill Mountains, southeast of New York. I saw Buddy Hackett perform. He was funny in the movie *It's a Mad, Mad, Mad, Mad World*.

First his son (Sandy Hackett) sang a few tunes. His talent seems mediocre and the audience booed (tough crowd). His son said, "If you hire my dad, it's a package deal." More boos. In a sick way, I thought it was funny. After a few drinks, who cares?

Up front there are several young women sitting. Now looking at Buddy, to me he seemed round. With a squinted-eye look, he could be a human buoy, bobbing in the ocean. Buddy began his performance.

The jokes were about passing gas in elevators. From there the jokes seemed even raunchier. I did not see the humor. I would have rather had his son come back on. The audience loved it, especially his group of young females.

The show ended and quickly Buddy exited the stage. The back of the stage emptied to a hallway that led to several hotel rooms. Like a Macy's day sale, the young females chased after Buddy. I don't know what they would do if they caught him. If I was allowed to give Buddy advice, I would tell him to just stop. You're too out of shape to run. Just put your hands up (signaling the girls to stop) and say: "Look, girls, my twigs and berries are for show. They don't work anymore. You want my son? He is practicing his new song, 'All Night Long,' He's three doors down."

Fast forward to today, equal rights. Imagine Susan Boyle under the same circumstances. She became famous in spite of Simon. For argument's sake, let's say Susan has a following of several young bucks (you know, strapping young men). They throw their briefs or jockstraps on stage with their phone numbers. How would Susan react?

Not being a Vegas odds maker, I would guess it would be ninety nine to one that she would be horrified. She would either cancel further shows or maybe insist on chicken-wire fencing. It is the type of fencing they used in early barroom performances. If the audience disapproved, they threw beer bottles or food at the entertainers. Really, though, Susan may not have the typical Hollywood looks, but inside she is a beautiful person and definitely has talent.

* * *

It's only been a few days at the air base, but William seems strong enough to travel. It is a half-day ride to Tent City. The base commander is impressed with Ann's dossier and is sensitive to what they have been through. He arranges a military escort for them to finish their journey. The information in the dossier is vital to command central.

Reunited again, the four of them are in the Humvee. Even though it is still hot and humid, there is joy. The closer they get to Tent City, they notice a multitude of road signs and convoys on the road. They are now in a safe zone.

Bureaucracy finally seems to have gotten a foothold.

Excitement fills the air. Like driving across the desert and entering Vegas, they all see a massive city of tents. The tents are donations from corporations and countries from all over the world. Each tent has a sign on it that has its donor's name on it. Entering the main gate seemed like Disneyland. Several rows of people and trucks are all trying to enter the city. At each row, there is a security guard and an official with a clipboard. Checking for weapons and contraband always slows down progress. If you will, it resembles a TSA checkpoint. Driving her Humvee, Ann is given special treatment. Just the same, she had to relinquish her firearms. Her personnel gun will be issued back to her when she leaves Tent City.

After entering Tent City, they go to the main reception. It is the largest tent in Tent City. Processing took several hours. Ann's reasoning is simple: she had orders to go to command central. William and Fred needed medical attention. Camille is different; she needed to get transportation to see her sister.

They have all gone through pain to arrive. It is Camille whose journey is still not over. How do you tell your sister that her son was killed by a group of thugs?

They got a family tent so that the four of them could stay together. Electricity has been brought in from the outside. Ann had her meeting at central headquarters. They are impressed with her insights. The command headquarters released new directives. There are a few hundred armories serving the masses. They now have a plan with the aid of local citizens to help themselves. The collaborative model is a good model. It will save hundreds if not thousands of lives. It is to this end that Ann felt she had pioneered a new way to handle a massive crisis. Of course, she owes this brainchild to Ben.

After power is restored, the US military will have a new manual, a way for the common folks to help survive a major crisis. If Ann had her druthers, she would name it after Ben. That is not the army way. I am sure it will have its own name.

Tent City is the largest in modern history. It expands for miles. The government really is trying to restore the East Coast. To steal an old phrase with a twist, "To make things great again," they need to restore old jobs and the masses need to go back to their original homes. Tent City is a buffer zone. To allow resettling in the west would create a huge vacuum. Nature may abhor a vacuum in a constructive way, but we know that biker gangs and thugs will take advantage in less charitable ways.

Camille took out the digital camera. The four of them had multiple pictures taken of them. The camera does belong to the US government, but I am sure they will be allowed to keep the pictures. There are no sensitive areas that would whet the appetite of the Russians.

On the last day, the four of them stayed close together. Each of them will never forget their experiences. William and Fred needed two more days of medical care. With Ann's meeting completed, she decided to stay around until William and Fred get their releases. For Camille, it is a different story. She book a bus ride to her sister. She is going to stay with her for a week. The military will give her a flight at the end of her stay. When she does receive a flight back to the air base in Massachusetts, I am sure Officer Ryan will be there for a personal escort.

The commander of central headquarters gave Ann, William, and Fred a military escort to the air base. Before they entered the military vehicle, the commander gave Ann a citation. Then he looked at Fred and gave him a special military hat. Fred is totally overjoyed. As Fred put on his military hat, the commander gave Fred a salute. A military PR personnel took pictures. They will be forwarded to the air base in Massachusetts.

Aboard the military plane, Fred, Ann, and William reflected on their trip. They also had a moment of silence for all those who perished. On this flight, they bring hope for their friends. William, William's wife, and Fred will again be reunited. Officer Ryan and Ann will continue as police officers. What is more important is that they continue as husband and wife.

* * *

Officer Ryan drove his antique bike up to the fire pit. The sound of the motorbike was heard by everyone in the collaborative. It's kind of like a Paul Revere warning. Everyone rushes to the fire pit. Desperate for news, they huddle around Officer Ryan. Officer Ryan is almost never a show boater. Today, just this once, he looks for the drunk. Sarah and Vivian are holding on to each other as if a violent storm is upon them. He walks over to the drunk and asks for a shot of whiskey.

Officer Ryan holds up the glass and pivots his body so as to see everyone.

"Today God has truly given us all a blessing. I have gotten word that all four have arrived safely at Tent City. Fred, William, and my lovely wife Ann should be arriving in three days. Camille will be staying with her sister for a week. She has already received a flight pass on a military plane. It should be here in a week after the others arrive."

Although everyone is overjoyed with happiness, Officer Ryan interrupted the joyous occasions with one more statement:

"As a state police officer, I have witnessed a lot of hardships and sadness. I wish to give a special recognition to the countless innocent people who have lost their lives. Lastly, I give my heartfelt appreciation to Ben. It is he to whom we owe a debt for our survival."

It is this last statement from Officer Ryan that gave Ben his salvation. Both Alice and Jessica had to reflect on their own actions toward Ben. Truth always wins in the end. It is within the deep emotional wounds carried by Ben, Alice, and Jessica that the light of truth needs to shine.

Officer Ryan stayed to enjoy some food and a few drinks. The collaborative is honored to have him. Being a classy guy, Officer Ryan circulated and talked to everyone. I always admire a seasoned law enforcement agent; they not only have to act properly under a major situation, but they are trained to check their emotions. A heated exchange really resolves very little.

As far as the Randal family goes, all parties should share a little blame. To be brutally honest, the only way for wounds of this family to heal lies with Jessica. Yes, Ben could have handled himself with more sensitivity. Taking a step back, he only cares for a solid footing in his daughter's future. Jessica needs a little more growing in her life. Someday, if God blesses her, the light will go on if she has her own child.

There is always a back door (your computer geeks know this). Joshua, although infatuated with Jessica, is a little more level-headed. It is something Alice senses. Strange how females are more in touch with other people's vibes. I guess it goes all the way to the Neanderthal man. The man of the cave spent his time hunting big game. When he came with the dinner (probably many meals with one kill), he could pound his chest and savor the moment. Now the woman of the cave had to deal with a lot of emotions. What if one of the young-ins act up? What if one family member was ill? She also would have to worry that he isn't the food for a large animal. What happens if he fails to bring home the bacon (or bison)? What happens if he is too successful? Will another woman try to steal him away? So many emotions.

I think you get the picture. Many times men can be simple little creatures: food and sex. Somebody, please turn off the lights and stifle the narrator.

In time, it is Alice who must broker a solution. When the time is right, she will have a good talk with Jessica. Alice is shrewd. Like a good poker player, she will observe the courtship between Joshua and her daughter. She feels Joshua will rein in her daughter. At least he was man enough to face Ben. He also seems to have enough talents to be a good provider. Everything has to play out. We can only be hopeful.

Ann's trip is very fruitful. Central command sometimes needs someone from the outside to see things from a fresh prospective. Millions of people were affected by the EMP blast. The military is extremely strained. Not only are the threats from hostile adversaries causing a heightened alert, but now there are more domestic threats like biker gangs and thugs. On top of all these problems, the military needs to supply food, medicines, and supplies.

What Ann proposed makes sense. Orders were given out. All the armories were advised to use locals in helping with distribution and protection—not a vigilante group, but just protection.

In the following weeks, Vivian greeted her mother. That is one scar that can never go away (Camille's sister's son). Losing your only child to evil is the worst event any parent can go through. It did make the bond between Vivian and her mother even stronger. In time, Camille had extended an invitation for her sister to stay with her. But why not wait until there is electricity? I am sure they will.

Officer Ryan did bring back William and Fred to the collaborative. William's wife is so excited, she could not control herself (as long as it is not a puppy they would urinate everywhere). She ran to the Humvee. When William stepped out of the Humvee, she immediately put her arm out and hugged William. As she started to cry, William shouted out with pain.

"What's wrong?" William's wife exclaimed.

"I was in a bad firefight, and I was hit," William said as he opened up his shirt.

With her hand over her mouth, William's wife is speechless. I guess she needs to be bought up to speed. William knew he could not tell her until he arrived home. Now they are home, William, his wife, and Fred make three. It is three that makes this family complete.

Within a few months, news spreads fast. The power grid is being restored in Massachusetts. In the army, the saying is "As you were." It will never be the same, but perhaps it can even be better? If we don't learn from history, then we must repeat our mistakes.

To take a hot shower, make a phone call, turn on the TV, dishwasher, how about sitting down in a riding lawn mower? Driving in your car with the radio on. "That will be a hot coffee with a croissant." Simple pleasures that the Neanderthal never experienced.

As Ben was stroking the hot embers in the fire pit, he hears a military jet overhead. Maybe it's a symbolic gesture, or a reconnaissance flight. Taking pictures of the damage, whatever it is, it does show the government is starting to get a handle on everything. In a few days, the fire pit will go as the horse and buggy. At least when the fraternities have their annual bonfires, maybe they can honor the survivors. Nah! That is too much to wish for.

With a smile on his face, Ben knew the trials and tribulations have finally come to an end. He picked up the family Bible. He looked at trails of the passing jet. He gave thanks to the almighty—tomorrow is the begging of another journey.

An EMP Causality: Epilogue

There is excitement in the air. Fred is outside waiting for the state van to pick him up. It has been a little over a month since the electricity has been turned back on. Instead of a young couple seeing their child off for his first day of school, there are middle-aged caretakers seeing off their elderly client. William and his wife were all smiles. William is healing nicely from the wounds of the firefight. Fred can hardly wait see his girlfriend, Lou Ann.

Jessica is officially engaged to Joshua. They both agreed to wait until she is finished with college. Like bookends, both Joshua and Jessica's mom have been reining in Jessica. Both of them really want to give proper guidance to a young bride-to-be. The emotional scars between Jessica and her dad, Ben, have begun to heal.

Officer Randal and his wife, Ann, have been real heroes. Donations of police vehicles are coming from many allied countries. Law and order has finally come to Boston and the eastern US. The state police are now able to take over as the military is slowly withdrawing. It is with great pride that the commander of the state police award the first vehicles to Officer Ryan and his wife.

The union man has been called to a union hall meeting. Now that public transportation is established, most arrive for the meeting. There is an overwhelming amount of work to do. Although he is now distrustful of the government, he still remains a loyal Democrat. The only caveat: the union man will not allow any lawn signs or bumper stickers for any candidate.

It took a year, but Randy and Sarah are finally married. Truly, a marriage made in heaven. That Sunday afternoon, as Randy and Sarah left the hall, they went outside for their first ride as husband and wife. Please! No limousines, horse and carriage, or any other typical wedding protocols. It is Randy's classic Buick: red and buffed as it always is. Their chauffer? You guessed it, Officer Ryan. For the first time, Randy has to sit in the back seat. Feeling the clean seats, he looks out at all the well-wishers. On the back window of the Buick were two signs: JUST MARRIED and the other: THIS VEHICLE SURVIVED THE EMP BLAST. There was another sign along the side of the Buick: PLEASE DON'T TOUCH. Only kidding! But I am sure Randy would have liked this one.

Instead of dragging traditional beer cans, there were several empty plastic gallon water jugs. Officer Ryan, with a big smile, took the newly married couple to an unknown destination. Let's hope it's not an antique auto show. "Cheers! To a long and healthy marriage."

Camille is finally rising up. No longer living in an apartment complex, she has purchased her own piece of the American dream. She owns a home in the suburbs. She was given a large advance from a publicist. Camille is now doing a book tours on her new book, *A Journey into the Wastelands*.

As for the drunk, the EMP blast gave him a purpose. He was needed to lift the spirits of the collaborative. Now that the electricity is on, he walks to the abandoned fire pit. He raises his glass for the last time. He wishes everyone well. He is alone and the time has come. He had picked his wife's wedding dress from the dry cleaner. After writing a note and "last will," the drunk calls for an Uber driver. As the Uber driver arrives, he meets him and he leaves the front door of his house wide open. He knows his neighbors will enter to find out what is wrong.

As he enters the Uber driver's car, he brings his wife's wedding dress, a rose, a hundred dollar bill, and a bottle of champagne. It was the last day of October, Halloween, mid-afternoon. The expensive ride went on to the western part of Massachusetts, near the apple orchards. There he asked the Uber driver to let him off. It is near the spot where he proposed to his wife. The Uber driver looked confused. The drunk said, "It's all right." Although a tip was already calculated in the fare, the drunk gave him a crisp one-hundred-dollar bill. He just said thanks as the drunk walked into an open field.

It is near the spot where he asked his wife to marry him. The air is chilly on this late Halloween afternoon. The drunk stops and strips to his underwear. He carefully folded the wedding dress and put it on the ground. He popped open the bottle of champagne and took a few swigs. Next he took his wallet out and put it on his folded clothes. They say hypothermia is really a kind way to die; certainly kinder than many other ways. On this Halloween night, the drunk is giving himself a treat. He lies down with the wedding dress under his head. With a rose on his chest, he looks skyward and mutters, "Honey, I'm coming to you." He passes on with contentment and a smile on his face.

A notable mention: the lawyer at the end of the collaborative put up a sign. His office building in downtown Boston will take months to be ready. He has a sign on the edge of his lawn: IS IT TIME TO SUE? WALK-INS WELCOMED.

Ben and Alice are now empty-nesters. After a few visits with a marriage counselor, they have decided to make a change. Selling their suburban home, Ben and Alice bought a new condo near his work. He wants to be within biking distance. Many doctors enjoy biking to work, why not a microbiologist? When he gets his new car, it will be parked under a Faraday cage in the garage.

There you have it! Folks and accounting of our collaborative members. I hope you have enjoyed—what? You're talking to me? Really! Talking to me? I look to the left, then to the right. Hmmm. Nobody else is here. You want to know about Steven and Vivian? Is that right? Okay!

Steven and his brother have taken over their father's business. Mr. Henderson has decided to retire. The business is really going well; this will give Mr. Henderson a nice weekly check. In the 1800s, the saying was "Go west, young man. There is gold in them there hills." The rush was on, and dreams of getting rich permeated the air. Fast forward to post–EMP blast. There is a new saying: "Go east, young person (politically correct)! There is gold in the suburbs." Steven is working seven days a week. His younger brother is engaged. It is approaching Christmas.

He is too busy to join a dating service or to find a new love online. He has been turned down twice (Jessica and Sarah). Every once in a while, he would text Vivian to see how she is doing. He did not want to do it too much. After all, he is busy and does not want to lose her friendship. Although he is busy, it is the holidays and he does feel sad. With his mom and dad retiring and his brother engaged, It is a lonely time to go through the holidays.

Vivian is finally breaking the family tradition. Instead of living her life in the projects and living off of government help, she is in the big apple. Vivian is enrolled in a four-year degree program. With her mother's help (financially), she is taking a course in forensic studies. She is certain she will get a job with the FBI or NYPD. Vivian loves her independence. She is meeting new people from all over the world. Many different men have been courting her. There are potential lawyers, med students, and future Wall Street tycoons. Vivian is in cloud nine with all the attention she is receiving. Still, there is an emptiness inside her. Confused, she does not have a handle on it. What she knows is when she receives a text from Steven, her heart beats fast. She quickly looks for a private spot where she can read and respond to him. During these brief exchanges, she is another world—a world of fulfillment.

She is going home for the Christmas holidays. Her mom and sisters will be there. Her sisters are married or have their mates. Vivian must concentrate on school first, and love will come in time. As she travels on the train, she receives a text from Steven. "How are you doing? Will you be around during the holidays?

Would you be interested in getting together and going for a ride?"

Vivian is thrilled. Her schedule is tight. After many texts, they agreed to meet on a Sunday afternoon right after Christmas. Steven arrives at Camille's new house. He is impressed. Camille is happy to see him; it's been a while and Steven will always be a part of her memory during those troubling times. Camille lets her daughter know that Steven is here. It took a while; Vivian is not always a fast mover. At least she shows up on time to her classes.

After a few minutes, Vivian and Steven went outside. Steven has bought a new 350 4x4 pickup truck with a fitted Faraday grill over the hood. Steven was wearing expensive boots from Bob's store. Both of them wore informal clothes. After all, it is not a date, but just two good friends going for a ride, right? Many of Vivian's new girlfriends would be disappointed with a man in a pickup truck. Some of her new and rich girlfriends might even refuse. To Vivian, it was perfect.

Steven loaded up his transponder with enough funds to take a trip. It seems the politicians on Beacon Hill have put new tolls on most highways in Massachusetts. The politicians have a saying: "Never let a good crisis go to waste." Steven asked Vivian if they could take a ride to some of the seaport towns on the north shore. It is a two-hour drive. During the summer, Rockport and Marblehead are real tourist attractions to thousands of people.

For the first hour and a half, Vivian and Steven laughed. They talked about their experiences surviving the EMP blast. They especially laughed at the time they visited the junkyard. Vivian was so nervous she had to pee twice. Both of them forget their everyday lives and enjoyed the moment. During the last half hour, they were quiet. Vivian put her left hand on the car seat; Steven put his over hers. She responded by clinching his hand with a gentle squeeze. They were both in harmony.

They reached the seaport town. Even though it was chilly, both walked hand in hand. Neither one put their gloves on. Feeling the warmth of each other gave them both a glow that has been missing in their lives. Finally they reached a special tourist spot. Out in the bay is the famous Red Lobster Hut. Painters from all over the world try their hand to capture its ambiance.

Still, with no gloves on, Steven grabs a railing.

Vivian, still resisting to put her gloves on, glances at Steven. She sees a tall solidly build man. Not as tall as the Patriots' Rob Gronkowski (they call him "the Gronk") but pretty tall. He is the father and boyfriend image that has been missing her whole life. She knows his character is structured by high morals and that they have a solid family structure together. It is something she has pined for her whole life. Steven notices her glancing at him, but still stares at the Red Lobster Hut.

"Vivian," Steven spurted out.

"Yes Steven," Vivian answered as she blew on her hands to warm them.

"Do you ever hope to have children?" Steven said as he still looked forward.

Vivian is stunned. A tear flows from her eyes. She composes herself and wipes the tears from her face with the back of her hands. She slowly turns left toward Steven and faces him. With her two hands, she grabs Steven's right hand. Steven now turns and faces Vivian.

"Yes Steven, and to your next question, yes," Vivian said with joy. She knew Steven was a little gun-shy from being turned down twice before. She just wanted to help him a little. "But first, can we go to the restaurant."

"Of course! Is there anything wrong?" Steven said with a puzzled look.

"No, I just have to Pee," Vivian said with utmost happiness.

They held hands for a few moments longer. On this chilly New England night, two hearts beat as one: Karma."